Kimberly ran her hands do[wn]
the muscles benea[th]
W9-AVS-798

She dug her fingers into a hard ass, the kind that would put *Buns of Steel* to shame. Warm lips trailed down her neck, and she arched into them; in that instant, when the man above her filled her to her limit, she went liquid beneath him, giving herself up once again to his sensual assault.

Time stood still, and her only cognizant thought was how smooth his skin was, how it warmed beneath her fingertips, and how the muscles beneath it bunched in tension to hewn granite. Everything about him excited her, everything about him amazed her, and everything about him took her to a place she had never gone before.

In a slow, deep rhythm they moved as one, and Kimberly knew she would never again feel so alive, so beautiful, or so lit up as she did at that moment in this man's arms. And, like Cinderella, she would flee her Prince Charming long before the sun would make its appearance for the new day, to return to her reality which, up until a few hours ago, she thought wasn't half bad.

He sank his teeth into her neck. *"Precia,"* he whispered against her sultry skin, "come for me again."

And, not wanting to disappoint this man on any level, Kim did.

"An edgy, suspenseful romance with shamelessly intense passion. . . ." —Romance Junkies about *Skin*

"A blast of hot air; a fun female fantasy. . . ." —Fresh Fiction about *Good Girl Gone Bad*

Have Yourself a *Naughty* Little Santa

KARIN TABKE

POCKET STAR

New York   London   Toronto   Sydney

Pocket Star Books
A Division of Simon & Schuster, Inc.
1230 Avenue of the Americas
New York, NY 10020

This book is a work of fiction. Names, characters, places, and incidents either are products of the author's imagination or are used fictitiously. Any resemblance to actual events or locales or persons, living or dead, is entirely coincidental.

First Pocket Star Books paperback edition November 2008

POCKET STAR BOOKS and colophon are registered trademarks of Simon & Schuster, Inc.

For information about special discounts for bulk purchases, please contact Simon & Schuster Special Sales at 1-800-456-6798 or business@simonandschuster.com.

Cover design by Richard Yoo. Illustration by Frank Accornero.

Manufactured in the United States of America

10   9   8   7   6   5   4   3   2   1

ISBN: 978-1-4767-4481-0

To Kim. Merry Christmas.

Prologue

Silver Legacy Hotel and Casino, Reno, Nevada

Sometime between "I never should have had that last Cosmo" and "This is the best sex I've ever had!"

KIMBERLY RAN HER HANDS DOWN A SMOOTH, HARD BACK, the muscles beneath tightening. She dug her fingers into a hard ass, the kind that would put *Buns of Steel* to shame. Warm lips trailed down her neck, and she arched into them; in that instant, when the man above her filled her to her limit, she went liquid beneath him, giving herself up once again to his sensual assault.

Time stood still, and her only cognizant thought was how smooth his skin was, how it warmed beneath her fingertips, and how the muscles beneath it bunched in tension to hewn granite. Everything about him excited her, everything about him amazed her, and everything about him took her to a place she had never gone before.

In a slow, deep, rhythm they moved as one, and Kimberly knew she would never again feel so alive, so beautiful, or so lit up as she did at that moment in this man's arms. And, like Cinderella, she would flee her Prince Charming long before the sun would make its appearance for the new day, to return to her reality which, up until a few hours ago, she thought wasn't half bad.

He sunk his teeth into her neck. *"Precia,"* he whispered against her sultry skin, "come for me again."

And, not wanting to disappoint this man on any level, Kim did.

One

"Well, put chains on the damn tires!" Kim ordered the car rental guy over the phone.

"Sorry, lady, the advisory is clear. Stay off the roads. *Emergency vehicles only.*"

Shit! Nick would kill her if she wasn't in Evergreen by the end of the day. "Look, I have to be in Evergreen by this afternoon. How much do you want to make that happen?"

"Lady, 80 is closed. It'll be twenty-four hours before the plows will have it cleared, and that's *if* the snow stops right now. Taking 82 into Evergreen will be another two, maybe three, days. Nobody is going in there, and nobody is coming out."

She slammed down the phone and whipped back

the heavy curtains of the window, blanching as bright light pierced her corneas. A whiteout glared back at her. Snow! It was freakin' everywhere! The blizzard of the decade was not supposed to hit for another twenty-four hours. She only needed an hour to get to Evergreen. Like a petulant child, Kimberly threw herself in a tantrum on the rumpled bed in her hotel room. "I don't want to be here!" she shrieked. And despite the immaturity of the action, it felt really good. She didn't let loose often, but when she did, it always made her feel better.

She smiled and warmed. Like last night.

Just as quickly as it erupted, her smile waned. Guilt assailed her, although it shouldn't have. It wasn't like she was *officially* engaged or that her soon-to-be intended gave two shits who the hell she slept with. Frustration gripped her, and the fact that she felt anger at Nick right now bothered her on several levels. She didn't love him. He didn't love her. Their impending nuptials were a business merger, pure and simple.

So why was she pissed?

She relaxed and settled more comfortably back into the sheets. *Let's think this through, Kimberly. Just as you would an acquisition.*

Last night had been an anomaly. Plain and simple. Not only from the one-night stand angle but also from the pure carnal indulgence of the encounter. Her skin warmed. Yes, last night had been a stress release she hadn't realized she'd needed. And for that value alone, it had been worth it. A girl couldn't buy that kind of de-stressor. And knowing her physical health was directly tied to her mental well-being, Kim had no regrets.

She closed her eyes and relaxed back into the thick, downy pillows. A long breath escaped her and she pressed her hand to her chest, the rapid thud of her heart belying her casual dismissal of the gravity of her late-night tryst.

What if she ran into that hunky stud she'd twisted up the sheets with last night? If she couldn't get out of Reno, neither could he. She twirled a long blond strand of hair between her right index finger and thumb. Heat spattered across her cheeks. If she looked in the mirror right now, she would see that her neck and chest were red and splotchy. She hated that. It was a dead giveaway that she was nervous or embarrassed, or, well, anything other than the hard-ass persona she had worked a life-time to perfect. In her business, perception was every-thing. And despite her iron will to tamp it down, the heat continued to rise in her cheeks.

For crying out loud, it wasn't like she was a prude or anything, but, oh, good Lord, the things that man had done to her last night! And she didn't even know his name! She flung herself over and cradled her hands under her cheek. A slow, dreamy smile curved her lips.

His spicy, masculine scent still lingered in her hair, on her clothes, and on her skin. She closed her eyes and inhaled him deep into her lungs. God, last night had been incredible.

She hadn't wanted to shower. It would wash away the last trace of him, and she wanted the subtle reminder of him for just a little longer. Her body thrummed. She wanted more than a reminder. She wanted him again. Hell, maybe she should go back up to his room and while away the hours. . . .

Kim rolled over onto her back and squinted against the bright light of the snow streaming through her window. But she knew she wouldn't go upstairs. For a lot of reasons, the number one being he was the kind of guy who liked women too much. And she was the kind of woman who had been burned by his type one too many times.

Stupid, stupid, Kimberly. Always going for the men who gave women like her a token glance before they moved in on the supermodel type. Except this guy, last night. For reasons only known to him, he had paid no attention to the high-maintenance girls flitting around him like annoying gnats on a sweaty dog. Not that Kimberly didn't have high-maintenance fees—she did, but she just never felt she could compete with those exotic sex-kitten types. She was more, well, basic. "A handsome natural attractiveness," *Forbes* had said when she'd been interviewed last year. "Not the kind to distract in the boardroom, but a solid beauty who would withstand the ravages of time." Great; she felt like a Chevy.

As one of the three "Women of Steel" *Forbes* had featured, she'd found the article a letdown. In her eyes it had screamed that she couldn't do anything right in her personal life, but watch the hell out when it came to acquisitions. She was Land's Edge's number one gun for hire, and she always landed her mark. *Always.*

Kim smiled despite dredging up painful reminders of why she was still single. Again. It didn't matter really, because last night, basic had trumped sexpot, and she had had the night of her life. Thanks to vodka-fortified bravery, she had been all too willing to follow that hot Latin stud up to his room, and there she'd discovered firsthand what all of the fuss was about. He was big, he was sexy, and he'd been the most passionate lover she had ever had the pleasure of slipping between the sheets with.

He'd made her feel things she had never felt before, including a natural orgasm. *Multiple* natural orgasms. Boy, she'd really been missing out.

When their gazes had caught and locked across the smoky lounge, time had stopped for her. Even from a distance she'd been able to see straight into his dark, soulful eyes. She'd felt like something had knocked into her chest, and it had scared the crap out of her. She'd quickly looked away and prayed he would go away. He hadn't. He'd approached her in the crowded bar and said she looked like she'd needed some company. She might have a knack for picking losers, but she wasn't naive. She'd rolled her eyes and turned away from him, giving him the classic brush-off. He'd persisted. His low, husky laughter had done things to her insides she'd tried to ignore. When he'd sat that tall hunky body of his down beside her and bought her a drink, she'd known she would have jumped through hoops right then and there had he asked her to.

Kim's lips tightened. Because the cold, ugly truth was that he'd nailed exactly how she'd been feeling at that exact moment. Talk about timing! She *had* needed some company. She'd cocooned herself away for so long in her work that she hardly remembered what it was like to feel attracted to a man.

Figures, the minute she lets her Stay-the-Hell-away-from-Me sign down, one swoops in for the kill. For crying out loud, did she have a Hit-on-Me-I'm-Lonely sticker on her forehead? Kim looked up at the ceiling. She was thirty-eight, divorced—twice—and didn't even own a cat. She owned a swank condo in the Hollywood hills, which, even four years after she closed, didn't have furniture except a bed and the requisite office furnishings. Her life was lived out of a suitcase. And hell if she could remember the last time she'd let a guy see her naked.

She grinned. But she'd hit the jackpot last night.

It hadn't taken long for him to touch her hand and give her *that* look. And it had taken her brain only a fraction of a millisecond to stand up and follow him up to his room. She had no regrets, except maybe she would have liked to have stayed longer. She didn't even know his name, and it didn't matter. Guys like him didn't remember girls like her, and she would be the better for it.

Such was her emotionally unencumbered life. And that was exactly how she wanted to keep it. Emotionally unencumbered. Speaking of emotionally unencumbered, Kim reached across the bed, dug her cell phone out of her black Chanel bag, and hit a button.

"Gold," a deep male voice answered. She scowled at the voice. It wasn't like he didn't have caller ID and know it was her.

"Hello, Nick, it's Kimberly."

"What do you have?"

Her scowl deepened. How was that for *Hey, honey, how are you?* It bothered her that all of a sudden Nick's aloofness bugged her. Theirs was a purely platonic relationship, but one that they both agreed would be better served united. A merger. Neat and clean—just like an acquisition for them both. He didn't want kids, neither did she. He wanted to own the world, so did she, and they both knew that together, there would be no one or nothing that could stop them. They were, in Kim's mind, sharks of the highest order, and she didn't have a problem with that. She had long ago tired of getting her feelings hurt by picking the wrong men and diving headfirst into relationships that left her holding the bag. With Nick it was a corporate merger. She smiled. Yeah, she couldn't wait.

"Hello to you too."

"Kimberly, I've got a lot on my plate right now. Knock off the drama."

"Of course! I mean just because we're engaged, how silly of me to expect a smidge of emotion from you." She hated that she'd just said that. It showed weakness.

"We'll be *officially* engaged when Evergreen is in the palm of my hand."

"Yes, boss."

Nick sighed on the other end of the phone. She could see him now in his penthouse office in the Century Building in L.A. Standing at his window peering out over the smog-laden city, knowing he owned a nice chunk of it, and hungry to own it all. He'd come out of the welfare system in L.A. He'd scholarshipped to Stanford, where he'd earned degrees in business and law. He was the most driven man on the planet, and he had proposed a partnership in Land's Edge, as well as a merger in the bedroom, when she landed Evergreen.

"Kimberly, let's not argue."

And he was right. She knew the score. No emotion. Funny how things worked out.

After she'd worked for years as an acquisitions consultant for Nick, at the High Desert Resort and Casino closing party he'd said to her, out of the blue, "We're exactly alike, Miss Michaels." She'd agreed. It had been kind of sad to her when she'd realized that. He'd gone on to explain. "We both like money, power, and the thrill of the hunt." He'd raised his martini glass toward the celebrating group of Land's Edge employees. The High Desert Resort and Casino had been a monster to wrestle into submission. But after nearly a year of sweating blood over that one, she had closed the deal. It was the biggest notch on her acquisitions belt to date. He'd continued his sales pitch. "Neither of us likes to lose, and neither of us allows emotions to cloud our judgment. We both understand that while the employees or citizens of whatever business or property we acquire may not think a Land's Edge acquisition is in their best interest, we know in the long run it is." Kim didn't completely agree with that. She'd had a few tinges of guilt here and there, but the golden pot at the end of the rainbow had more than soothed her conscience. Nick had smiled and raised his glass to her. "I think a merger is in order."

She'd stared at him, not fully understanding his

intentions. "I propose a professional and personal merger, Miss Michaels. I want you to work exclusively for me." She'd opened her mouth to protest, but he'd stopped her. "Bring me Evergreen, and become my VP of acquisitions here at Land's Edge and my partner in the social world as my wife."

Dumbfounded, she'd stared at him. It was what she'd always dreamed of—being a managing partner in a Fortune 500 company. Power, wealth; the world would be hers for the taking. He smiled that famous let's-close-this-deal smile of his and continued with his sales pitch. "Like you, I have no yearning for children, and like you, I understand that love is not the glue to a successful business. We understand that success is built on hard work and dedication. It's about keeping your head screwed on straight and keeping all emotion out of the equation. If we both enter this merger understanding there is no love expected, then there will be no expectation of it, and in that, no hurt feelings."

"Sex?" she'd blurted out.

He'd nodded, and his crystal-blue eyes had twinkled as he'd scanned her from the tip of her Jimmy Choos to the top of her blond head. He'd smiled, and while it shouldn't have, it had made her skin warm. Nick Gold was a powerful, dominant, handsome man. She had, on more than one or two occasions, fantasized of dressing up as Little Miss Secretary and having her way with him on his big marble and teakwood desk.

"I think I could accommodate you in that department."

"But—?"

He held up his hand. "Listen, Kimberly, I know there will be times when you're traveling, when we haven't seen each other in weeks, perhaps months, and you will have urges." He set his empty glass on the tray of a passing waiter. "By all means, feel free to indulge when and where you can." He honed those clear blue eyes back on her and squinted. "But please, keep it clean. The last thing I want is an annoying STD from one of your boy toys."

There it was: an offer on the table. A professional and personal merger, from which, as far as she could see it, she had everything to gain. She hadn't needed any time to consider the proposition. They'd shaken on it then and there. An hour later he'd proceeded to fly off to Moscow for a month. He hadn't bothered once to contact her. She hadn't even tried to convince herself that maybe in time they would fall in love. She didn't need love. She wasn't into the warm fuzzies. In fact, those gushy warm fuzzy people annoyed her. Especially those women and men who gushed over babies, like theirs was the only baby ever to be born. If they only knew how ridiculous they looked.

Long before Nick's proposal, Kimberly had resigned herself to the fact that she was done with emotional entanglements. Sex, sure, when the urge struck, and that wasn't often. She knew she sucked in the picking-out-decent-guys department. She picked losers or, like the guy last night, pretty boys. Pretty boys who couldn't keep their dicks in their pants. Yeah, it was kind of amazing when she thought about it. On the one hand, she could dissect and disseminate a financial statement, breaching even the most diligently protected property for acquisition while knowing in her gut she was right, but damn if she could trust herself when it came to men.

Except Nick. She had no delusions. She had money now, but as Mrs. Nicholas Montgomery Gold, she would have more money then she could ever spend. More than that, though, the doors to the world would be open to her. Nick had hinted just the other day that after Evergreen was procured he had his heart set on an island in the West Indies. The only problem was that it had what appeared to be a thriving economy and solid political structure. Kim smiled. That wouldn't stop either of them from finding a way to expose the vulnerable underbelly every property had, making it ripe for a buyout. Hostile or otherwise.

As those thoughts went through her head, Kim wondered if her parents would actually show up to wedding number three. They hadn't bothered for either of her previous weddings. Her mother had wrinkled her nose and asked why she was slumming. Kim wrinkled her own nose. Maybe she wouldn't invite her parents—let them read about her marriage in the *Times*! It would serve them right.

Kim settled back into the soft, down comforter and smiled. Last night had been a welcome respite from her life. It would be her last. Because despite Nick's stand on extramarital sex, she knew that once she said "I do," she would not sleep around. She was a lot of things, but she was not going to violate the forsaking all others part of the merger. She sighed, hoping that she and Nick would be as compatible in bed as they were in the boardroom. But she doubted he could come close to the guy last night. What she wouldn't give for just another few hours with him.

"Kimberly!?"

She shot up in the bed, so lost in her thoughts that she had forgotten about Nick! "I'm sorry, what did you say?"

"I said, for the third time, why are you calling me?"

Her rancor rose. "To tell you my flight arrived in Reno as scheduled, but at the moment, this entire county is blanketed under thirty feet of snow. I'm holed up at the Legacy—"

"Find a way out."

"I'm working on it, but I was told the road into

Evergreen won't be open until a day or two after 80 re-opens."

"I don't want excuses."

Grrr. "I'm not giving you any. I'm telling you, *I can't get out right now.*"

"Time is of the essence, Kimberly. Make it happen."

Damn him! "I guess you haven't heard a word I've said. I. Can. Not. Get. Out." His deep, throaty chuckle startled her. She didn't trust his quick mood change. "What?"

"I hear you, but I also *know* you," he replied.

And he did. He knew she would find a way, no matter the cost, to get into Evergreen within the agreed time frame. "I'll get there as soon as humanly possible."

"That's my girl." He hung up.

Kim flopped back into the pillows and slapped her hand over her eyes. Pain erupted behind her eye sockets, and she groaned. Nick would be an ass, then he would turn the tables on her to make her challenge herself to get the job done. While the real Nick—the one she had come to admire—was a prick at heart, she didn't mind him when he loosened up. Of course the real Nick was a cut-to-the-chase man who created oases out of barren wastelands.

He had a knack for revitalizing properties, from a lowly corner supermarket to entire towns. And right now, Nick had his sights set on Evergreen, California, a small gem of a town tucked intimately between the snowcapped Sierras and the elegant and unspoiled shores of Reindeer Lake. With Reno to its northeast and Lake Tahoe to its south, the town had the potential to explode.

She slowly inhaled and exhaled a deep breath. She wanted Evergreen as bad as he did, but for different reasons. And if he was a bastard about getting it, she could be a bitch about it. And bitch she could be. It was her job to unearth and expose the town's weaknesses, as well as its strengths, but mostly she was to find its Achilles' heel. It was how Nick would move in, seize the property, then wave his magic wand.

Kim didn't usually consider the will of the residents in these types of takeovers—and Lord knew some of them had been hostile—but in the end it always worked out. Besides, who could be unhappy when their beleaguered bank accounts plumped up from Land's Edge cash?

She glanced toward the bright window and squinted. She was screwed. If it hadn't been so damn windy she would have hired a chopper to take her into Evergreen. Maybe a snowmobile? She rolled over. Nick didn't like excuses. It didn't matter in the least to him that her wings were clipped.

As she always did when she was irritated, Kim reached to the locket hanging from a gold chain around her neck. It was her only link to the grandmother whose love had fortified her when her globe-trotting parents had jetted off, leaving their only child in the old woman's care. After Gran died when Kim was eight, Kim had been left to a revolving door of nannies.

She jackknifed up in the bed, grabbing at her bare throat. *No!* The necklace was gone. Hastily she tore the sheets off her bed, scoured the carpet, dumped her purse, tossed the bathroom and her suitcase. Nothing.

Kim stood quietly in the room, her eyes squeezed shut. She knew exactly where it was and how it had gotten there. Excitement rippled through her, but trepidation hurried along behind it. It was in room 417, the one where she'd spent a night in sexual nirvana. She swallowed hard. As much as she wanted another roll in the sheets with Mr. No Name Hotty, she was done with dalliances for the moment. She had work to do, and she would need to focus one hundred percent. Knocking on his door and casually asking about her heirloom necklace, which he had most likely ravaged off her throat, was a surefire way to sidetrack her.

But if she didn't go up there? She would never see the locket, and while she was not a sentimental woman, it was all she had from the only person who had loved her unconditionally.

Kim quickly showered and changed.

Two

For a long moment she stood outside door 417, waiting, hand poised ready to knock, when the door opened from the inside. Kim started, and so did the housekeeper on the other side of the threshold. "I need to speak to the man inside," Kim calmly stated.

The robust lady looked surprised but smiled. "He no here."

"He no here as in, he's gone from his room or he left the hotel?"

"He check out."

Heat flamed Kim's cheeks, and she cursed the reaction. At least one of them had had a good time last night. It burned her bad that she now had the unenviable knowledge of what it felt like to be a quickly forgotten one-night stand. For several long moments she stood silently while she adequately leashed her anger. Once again she'd picked a love 'em and leave 'em Don Juan. One would think that after twenty or so years a girl could spy a hit-and-run guy from a distance.

Kim calmed down a little. It didn't matter. She was here for her locket—that was all that mattered. She'd never see that guy again. And besides, she was the one who had slipped out of the room with no intention of going back, while he'd lain there on his back in all his naked glory happily snoring after a vigorous night of sex.

Kim smiled. She'd stood there for a good long time, staring. Her gaze trailing up from the long, thick muscles in his legs to his thighs and up to that bad boy curled up asleep in a soft, downy nest of dark curls. Even asleep he was hung like a horse. His belly was flat and hard and defined. He worked out. A lot. His chest and arms? Long, muscular arms that had held her tightly as her body had quivered and trembled as one wave of orgasm after another had shuddered through her. He had the classic chiseled face of David, though his hair was cut shorter, in a fashionable style that had been completely mussed when she'd finished with him.

She'd moved closer to the edge of the bed and bent down to press one last kiss on those full, sensuous lips of his. Her body warmed. Dear Lord, they'd been dangerous. He'd licked and sucked every inch of her body. When he'd smiled at her, the entire room had lit up. Never in her life had she just closed her eyes and free-fallen. It had been the most emancipating experience of her life. The smell of their sex had hung heavy in the air. Leaving that room had been one of the hardest things she could ever remember doing. But she had had to go. And he hadn't asked her to stay.

Had her necklace not gone missing she would have done everything humanly possible to avoid him like a cold sore. But he'd beaten her to the punch. Kim flinched. Dumped again. The story of her life was really getting old.

"Did you find a necklace in there? A gold chain with a small heart locket?"

"No, *señorita, nada.*" The maid stepped back and opened the door wider, grinning from ear to ear. "You look. But I change the sheets." She gave Kim a knowing smile.

It took Kim all of five minutes to come to the same conclusion the maid had. Her necklace was nowhere to be found. Or. Kim raised her eyes to the quiet, dark ones of the maid. Had she found it and pocketed it? Kim shook her head, not wanting to think the worst, but she had seen some pretty crappy things go down in her lifetime. Most especially in her line of work. It boded well for her to be suspicious, and she was by nature. Nothing personal. She just knew everyone had a dark side, and even good people did bad things. It was her mantra, one she had developed and lived by for years. It kept her safe and it kept her sane.

"Maybe you ask the man at the front desk for it?" the maid offered.

Kim thought about asking the smiling maid to empty her pockets right then and there, but something about her serene smile told Kim she'd look the fool.

"Thank you," Kim said instead, then went directly down to the concierge desk. The tall man behind the counter smiled and held up a finger. He was on the phone. She paced back and forth, debating if she should have demanded that the maid empty her pockets. What if she *did* have it? A desperation almost like a panic attack overcame Kim. *She had to have that locket!*

When the concierge hung up, he gave Kim a smile and his undivided attention. "How may I help you?"

"I'm Kimberly Michaels, room two eighteen. Is there a message, a note, a package, *something* for me?"

He grinned, bent down behind his stand, and stood up with a small white envelope in his hand. He pulled a yellow Post-it from the envelope and looked from it to her.

He cleared his throat and asked, "Could you tell me the room number of the man who left this for you?"

Kim gasped, but her desperation slid into hope. The

concierge's cheeks flushed. "The gentleman wanted to make sure I gave it to the correct lady." He continued to grin and looked at the Post-it, then back to her. "He said I should only give this envelope to a pushy, blond-haired, blue-eyed nymph who smells like springtime and who knows his room number."

Kim swallowed hard and thought her insides would puddle right there on the floor. "Fo—four-seventeen."

The concierge's smile widened, and he handed her the envelope. On the outside, in a bold scroll, was one word: *Cinderella*. Kim's hand trembled as she took it. She hurried to a nearby chair and sat down, afraid her knees would give out. Closing her eyes, she brought the envelope to her nose and inhaled. It was there, barely perceptible, but his spicy scent wafted along the velum. Sliding her nail under the edge, Kim opened the envelope. Folded inside a piece of paper was her gold chain. And scrawled in the same bold handwriting as on the envelope was a note: *If you want what goes to this, call me. 408.555.1043*

Three

"Ricco, take plow four out with Dennis and say a prayer," Peyton Moore directed. He handed Ricco a two-way radio. If Ricco had to guess, he would say Peyton's lips were drawn tight with worry, but he couldn't tell under all of the layers of clothes that Evergreen's mayor and acting maintenance superintendent was wearing. His job covered roads, public property, and animal removal. Evergreen was last on Caltrans' list of places to clean up during a blizzard; if they didn't get the roads cleared soon, they wouldn't get them cleared at all, which would mean another abysmal season for the small town, which lived or died between Thanksgiving and New Year's Day. That would be the last nail in their fiscal coffin.

The blizzard of the year had buried Evergreen. Ricco

was lucky he'd made it out of Reno when he had. Having a four-wheel-drive vehicle had helped. Getting out before they'd closed 80 had helped too, but what had helped more was his badge.

He nodded, pulled on a pair of ski gloves, and climbed up into the behemoth of a snowplow. He turned the key and the big diesels roared to life. He was just as concerned as the other residents were for the survival of the small town that had welcomed him, his mother, and sisters so many years ago, when they'd been on their last leg, but he couldn't help a huge grin now. As a boy he had always fantasized about driving one of these bad boys down Evergreen Promenade, the snow sluicing out of his way in great white snowy waves.

Every year he came home for the holidays and saved the town a few dollars by taking one of the plows out himself. It was the least he could do. He and his family could never repay Evergreen for taking them in when no one else had. He was happy to give what he could.

He grinned wider.

Another fantasy slipped in between his boyhood dreams and his real-life man dreams. That long drink of water last night: he was thirsty for more of her. He could still feel her silky smooth skin against his and her warm breath as she'd gasped and moaned beneath him, coming time after time. Her fresh ocean breeze scent mingled with the scent of their sex had created pure love potion number nine.

His blood quickened as he visualized the shocked look on her face when she'd climaxed the first time, her sultry body hanging suspended in his big hands as she'd gasped for breath while her body had spasmed and twitched. Yeah, it had been poetry in motion, a beautiful sight, one he had never tired of. He doubted he ever would. He loved women too much.

All wide-eyed and dewy, she'd raised up in his arms, pulled his lips down to hers, and demanded he take her there again. He'd been happy to oblige.

He'd been pissed to wake to an empty bed. That had been *his* move. He couldn't remember the last time he'd taken a woman back to his hotel room or his house in San Jose. He usually either found a neutral place to retreat from, or went to the home of his current love interest. And while he loved just about everything about a woman, he didn't like the way they got all clingy after a night of sex. His grin waned. He was more like his old man than he cared to admit, and it bugged the hell out of him.

Despite the ill thoughts of the man who was his father on paper, Ricco managed to smile again. Yeah, the sheets had still been warm when he'd woken up reaching for that firecracker, so it hadn't been long since she'd slipped out on him. He liked to think she'd given him serious second thoughts before she'd bolted. Ricco rearranged his jeans around his swelling dick. Damn if he could get her out of his head, and damn if he knew why. She'd been just another warm body to while away the hours with.

He rolled down his window and called to his ride-along. "C'mon kid, the snow isn't waiting on you." The object of his words bobbed his head and turned back to the man he was talking with. Ricco squinted in the bright glare of the snow. It had been a long time since he'd seen so much snow come down in a twenty-four-hour period. If it continued much longer, Evergreen could kiss a profitable season good-bye. And with that, they would lose what they all had worked so hard for. He scowled. Ezzy had told him about some company wanting to buy up the entire town! And it was a shitty offer with no guarantees for the residents. Why Evergreen? Irritated, he began to drum on the steering wheel, but instead of thinking of the bind the town would find themselves in if the snow didn't let up, he thought of soft, creamy skin and pouty red lips and the naughty things they'd done to him last night, and this morning. . . .

Yeah, if he was honest with himself, he could admit that Cinderella was pretty special. She had opened up like a timid little flower, blossoming for the first time.

She'd been reserved at first, then *bam*, once he'd undressed her and pressed his lips to her throat, she'd come alive under him. It had been amazing to behold the transformation. Ricco rubbed his chest where her nails had left marks. She was no shrinking violet for sure. More like a Venus flytrap.

He patted the left pocket of his ski jacket. He knew she'd call eventually for her locket. What he didn't know was whether he could talk the little blonde between the sheets again.

A thud on the passenger door jerked him out of his thoughts. "Open up, Ricco!" Denny Troyer called over the rumbling diesels. Ricco hit the power locks and the high-school kid hopped in, brushing snow from his shoulders and face. All Ricco could see were two dark eyes and full lips from behind the red-white-and-blue snowflake ski mask. Denny grinned up at Ricco, and Ricco could not help a return smile. "You ready, kid?"

"Yep, let's get this bitch on the road!"

Ricco laughed.

A loud blast of an air horn startled them both. "Maza! Get going!" Peyton shouted from the yard, waving him on.

Ricco nodded and put the Mack into reverse. The caution beeps piped up, warning any who stood too close to move out of the way. Then he carefully backed out of the maintenance yard and onto the main street—Evergreen Promenade to 82 north—and Evergreen's survival.

As the truck rumbled along, Denny asked, pulling off his ski mask, "How long are you gonna be around this time, Ricco?"

"Until the new year, like usual."

The kid nodded, then turned a sly sideways look his way. "What?" Ricco asked, knowing that look too well. It was the same one his mother and sisters got when they were about to fix him up.

"My sister Poppy is back from Cal for a while."

Ricco grinned. Ah, yes—sweet, sweet Poppy. She was tall and sultry, and, if memory served him and half of the men in Evergreen correctly, she had the greatest pair of tits in Nor Cal. But she was twenty-two years old and Ricco liked his women with a little more experience and age. "Denny, Poppy doesn't want an old guy like me."

"That's not what she told me last year. She *really* likes you."

"Well, tell her I really like her too, but not like that."

"What about Felicia?"

Ricco scowled, not wanting to think of his high-school sweetheart. He leveraged the steel snow shovel down to meet the road. The attachment locked into place, barely disturbing the huge truck they were in. Billows of heavy white snow arched up and out of their way. Ricco grinned. Worked like a charm. "Can I drive it?" Denny asked.

"Hell, no! I get my Jones on every time I drive up here when it snows."

Denny frowned and changed the subject. "Mom says we might move."

Ricco continued to grin as the great waves of snow flew out of their way. Yeah, baby!

"Why?"

"Mom says business is drying up. She said the last five years really messed her up, she had to borrow against the house, and if this storm keeps coming, she said she'd have to close up the shop. Poppy wants to go to graduate school, and I'm locked in to Davis this fall. She said she can get a dealer job at the Legacy."

A hard jolt of heat zapped Ricco in his groin at the reference to that particular casino in Reno and the woman he'd spent the night with. Quickly he leashed his rising libido and said to Denny, "I was lucky enough to scholarship. You must have had decent grades to get into Davis. How about a student loan? Payments are deferred until a year or two after you graduate."

"I dunno. I need to talk to my mom more about it. But she said something about a town buyout. Will the town give us money?"

Ricco kept his eyes focused on the bright white of the road in front of them. The wind had died down, and miraculously the snow seemed to be abating. Ricco's belly tightened, and he said a prayer. Maybe there was hope for Evergreen yet. After all these years, he'd hate to see his family pull up stakes and move. His mom was not only the city controller but also a CPA who did ninety-nine percent of all the residents' personal and business tax returns, as well as their books. She employed three full-time assistants. All three of his sisters were financially embedded in town. His oldest sister, Elle, was a physician's assistant at the Urgent Care. His sister Jasmine taught at St. Anne's, the small Catholic school in town. Her fraternal twin, Ezzy, owned and ran Esmeralda's B&B, a high-end inn. If there was no town, there were no jobs, and then no family. *No way!*

"Not the town per se," he replied. "The way I hear it, a fat developer has made an offer to the town counsel to buy up a chunk of the property. They want to redevelop the area into another casino resort."

"Would that be bad?"

"It would for those who love Evergreen the way it is. Bring in the casinos and resorts and we go commercial. We'd have to start locking our doors, Denny, and there's no fun in that."

Denny nodded. As Ricco smiled and turned back to look at the road ahead, he was nearly run off the road by a swerving, out-of-control SUV. It slid past him; in his big side mirror he watched it dive-bomb into a snowbank, then farther down the steep embankment that ran along this part of the road.

"Did you see that?" Denny asked, craning around to look behind them.

Ricco nodded his head and started to slow down to maneuver the plow around. "Yeah, some crazy-ass urbanite who can't read a road sign."

Four

Kim was feeling pretty smug. She might not have the face of a Victoria's Secret model, but she had the tits, and then some. Cleavage and her room key had gone a long way toward getting an SUV with chains and directions out of town. She'd been more than lucky to not come across any of the large plows haunting 80—not until she'd blown past the Road Closed sign leading to Evergreen. The plow wasn't going to chase her, though, and by the time they called CHP she'd be checked into her room at the B&B. She smiled, and when she readjusted her booted foot to the stiff accelerator pedal, it stuck. She punched it to unstick it, but instead she fishtailed, then overcompensated. She screamed and went rigid, trying desperately to maneuver the steering wheel to right her fishtailing car. Her actions had the opposite effect, however; panic and dread seized her, and instead of pumping the brakes, she mistakenly hit the accelerator, losing complete control of her rental. The last thing she saw was the big steel snowplow barreling straight for her. Her life flashed before her, and her heart twisted as the last person she saw was Gran's sweet, smiling face. Then. Blackness.

SHE WAS COLD. HER HEAD HURT AND SHE HEARD A VOICE. A low, smooth voice calling to her to be still, to breathe slow and easy, and not to be afraid. Why was he telling her that? Kim groaned and raised her hand to her head. "No, no, *precia*, stay still," the deep voice soothed.

A sudden warmth filled her belly. That voice. She turned her head from where it rested on something hard. The steering wheel? Was she in her car? Her eyelids fluttered open; slowly she focused. Two deep, espresso-brown eyes with a hint of green striations in the irises stared back. The edges crinkled from what she knew must be a smile. Prince Charming had come to rescue her?

"Hello, Cinderella," he softly said; his warm breath frosted in the air between them. She just wanted to melt into his strong arms and let him carry her away, anywhere but the cold tangled mess that was . . . Kim squinted, then closed her eyes. Where was she?

"Your car went off the road. You're lucky we saw you, or you'd be an ice cube before long."

Slowly she opened her eyes. "Wha—?" She couldn't speak. Her face suddenly felt stiff and frozen.

"Stay still. You hit your head pretty hard. Your air bag failed to deploy. Let's make sure everything is still working, starting with your toes. Wiggle them."

It took her a minute to get her brain to obey the command, but it did. She wiggled her cold toes in her fleece-lined Uggs. " 'K, they wiggled," she said.

He leaned across her. Gently but firmly, he slid his hand up from her ankle to her knee, softly plying and poking her. "Any pain?" he asked, looking directly into her eyes. They were only separated by a few inches. Despite the fact that it was freezing cold and their breaths mingled in a frosty surge and retreat, she felt no pain. Indeed, she felt . . . tingly.

Kim hurried to assure him that she felt no pain by briskly shaking her head. It felt like a bowling ball was crashing against her temples from the inside, and she gasped.

"Not so fast, take your time, princess."

He smiled and moved his hand up from her knee to her thigh, once again gently poking and prying. "Hurt?"

Kim swallowed hard. This time, she slowly shook her head. He deftly moved his hand to her left ankle and repeated his motions. No pain . . . just warm tinglies . . .

"Can you wiggle your fingers?"

She did.

"Slowly stretch out your right arm. Good, now your left."

Once her limbs were cleared, he said, "Take a big, deep breath." She did and smiled. No pain.

He nodded and gently touched her forehead. Kim winced. "Ow."

"You've got a nice egg cooking there. We need to get you out of this car and to a doctor."

Kim shook her head and winced at the sharp stabs of pain, but she soldiered through it. No way was she getting sidetracked. She'd lost precious time as it was. "No, I'm fine. I need to get to Evergreen." And what the hell was he doing here? Of all the places on earth to meet him again.

He grinned. If a thousand suns had just risen, she couldn't have felt more warmed. God, he was good looking. He was one of those very few men—hell, people—who just attracted the opposite sex. Had she been able to bottle his deep, earthy sensuality, she would have been able to retire years ago. Her spine stiffened. It was guys like this that got her into trouble. Guys like this who walked out of her life just as quickly as they walked in. And he was no different. She might have left the bed first, but he'd left the hotel.

He reached across her and unstrapped the seat belt. "This saved your life."

As he helped her out of the SUV, whose grill was planted in a snowbank, all of the surrounding sounds, scents, and sights suddenly came to light. The deep, throaty sound of a diesel engine, the bright glare of the snow, the warm, spicy smell of the man helping her out of the disabled vehicle. She ignored it and squinted up at a man pacing on the shoulder, while several other men stood staring down at them.

Kim continued to look up the steep embankment and swallowed hard. How the hell was she supposed to climb that?

In answer, a thick yellow rope was tossed down to them. Prince Charming made a quick harness out of it and fit it over his shoulders and around his chest, then turned to her. "I want you to get up on my back, like a papoose, and hold on. Can you do that?"

Her eyes widened and she looked from his broad back, up the embankment, then back to him. His deep, dark, chocolate-colored eyes held calm confidence in them. She nodded. She'd climbed the rock wall at the gym plenty of times. Hell, she could haul him up!

"My bags?"

"Someone will get them. C'mon."

He knelt down. Kim reached around his neck and hopped onto his back, the way she had seen other little girls on the playground do with their daddies. He hiked her legs around his waist and held on to them with his left hand, while holding the rope with his right. He called up to the gathered throng of men, and before she knew it, her rescuer started to slowly walk up the embankment with a little help from his friends.

By the time Kim got to the top of the embankment she was embarrassed to her core. She felt extremely uncomfortable under the scrutiny of the half dozen men who were staring at her as if she were some kind of freak.

One guy winced, another squinted and looked hard at her forehead, and several others shook their heads, as if she were the biggest idiot ever to drive in the snow. And if she hadn't had so much pride, she would have to agree. She'd never driven in the snow, and she knew damn well she was lucky to be alive. But they'd never know that. She tried to hop off the broad back she clung to like a baby koala and ended up dangling upside down, her head hitting the back of his knees.

The man standing closest to her rushed to grab her as she fell, just as her savior let go of her. She crashed into the packed snowbank.

"Ow!" she howled. Half a dozen hands reached down to her. Frustrated, cold, and humiliated, Kim swatted them away and scooted back, then stood very carefully. The trees swayed and so did she, but she managed to keep her balance, with a little help from tall, dark, and handsome.

She yanked her elbow free from his grasp and swiped

at the snow sticking to her legs. She wasn't wearing a jacket—just a heavy sweater, jeans, and boots. It was freezing. Cold, wet snow batted her cheeks. She shivered hard, and her entire body felt like one big piece of pummeled beef.

Like a knight in shining armor, the tall guy took off his jacket and placed it around her shoulders, moving her toward a big black pickup truck with the Town of Evergreen's seal on the side. Three tall evergreens surrounded by a lake and a Christmas wreath.

It bothered Kim that she felt all gooey around this guy. He flustered her. She was thirty-eight years old, for crying out loud, not some tittering schoolgirl about to be kissed for the first time. She narrowed her eyes and hugged the heavy ski jacket closer around her. "What is your name, anyway?"

As he helped her into the pickup truck, he grinned and said, "Ricco."

Ricco. She liked the sound of it. She held out her hand and smiled like a goof. "I'm Kimberly Michaels."

He took his glove off, took her hand into his big warm one, and smiled. "Nice to meet you, Kimberly Michaels." He dropped her hand and turned away. She watched in the side mirror as he talked to another man, made some motions with his hands, then pointed to his head and the pickup she sat in. He looked back at her and smiled, and she melted some more. She shook her head and faced

forward. She needed to get a grip. She was practically engaged! She shook her head, then heard a little voice say,
Yeah, like that stopped you last night. Kim sat rigid in the
big seat. Sex was like chocolate—something she craved
every once in a while, got her fill of, then steamrolled over
with other matters.

And the other matter now was getting the dirt on
Evergreen and maneuvering a clean, neat buyout. She
needed to get into town. *Now.*

The driver door opened and Ricco hopped in, chaf-
ing his arms even though he had on a dark, bulky,
cable-knit sweater. His frosty breath swirled around
his head. He pulled off his ski beanie and shook his
head. Kim fought the urge to drag her fingers through
his damp black hair. Instead she focused on the road
ahead. The snow-swamped road. A large snowplow
pulled ahead. As it roared ahead of them, shoveling
tons of snow off the asphalt, Ricco pulled in several
long yards behind the truck to ride in the cleared wake.

"What's your rush to get to Evergreen?" Ricco asked.

Kim's heart jumped at his question. If she told him
the truth, he'd dump her on the side of the road and
radio his buddies to keep going. She shrugged and said,
"What does anyone do in Evergreen this time of year?"

He nodded and kept his eyes on the truck ahead of
them. "You're one of those evasive types."

"I'm not evasive."

"This morning you were."

Kim went rigid, but her skin flamed, and she knew her throat and chest were splotching at that very moment. "No, I wasn't," she croaked.

"Sure you were, sneaking out like that. And now? Answering a question with a question means you have something to hide."

Kim mustered her ire. It wasn't easy. The minute he'd mentioned this morning, the entire night had replayed in her mind in slow, sexy Technicolor. She squeezed her eyes shut. When she opened them, she was more focused. She shot him a hard glare. "I have nothing to hide. People go to Evergreen this time of year to vacation. I'm doing the same."

"At the risk of your life?"

"I lost control, it happens."

"But 80 is closed and 82 has had only one pass with the plows—hardly ideal driving conditions. Why not wait until the roads were cleared?"

Kim looked hard at him and laid it all out on the table. "Just because we had sex doesn't give you the right to give me the fifth degree."

Ricco laughed out loud. "I'd call what we did more than just sex." He seared her with a stare. Kim's skin warmed hotter. She couldn't help it. Dammit.

"Okay, so I had a weak moment. I'd rather not talk about it."

He chuckled again, his voice warm and smooth, like one-hundred-year-old brandy. "If I remember correctly, you had six weak moments."

Her cheeks scalded and she turned to look out the window. It took her a moment to trust her voice, and when she spoke, she enunciated each word as she turned to look directly at him. "It. Was. A. Mistake. And if you have a shred of a gentleman in you, you'll stop reminding me about it."

He stared hard at her, his eyes dark and intense. He nodded and looked back to the road. "If you can forget, I can forget."

Kim crossed her arms across her chest and nearly screamed as her hands brushed her hardened nipples. *Jesus!* Her head snapped back, and she glared at him. "I want my locket back."

"Your locket?"

"Yes, my locket! The one that was on the chain around my neck that came off while we were . . ."

He slowly shook his head. "I'm really sorry, but how can I have something that belongs to you when I just now met you?"

Kim sat back in the hard seat and contemplated this man. She was used to dealing with men, and surely she had had her dealings with pretty boys like him. While that had once presented a problem for her, she had grown and matured dramatically since then. Gone was the needy, clingy girl looking for love from the first hotty who acknowledged her. In her place stood a woman who knew her weaknesses and steered diligently clear of them. Ricco was a weakness.

He might be more disarming, and certainly more intriguing, than any man she had run across in a long time, including Nick, but he was like all of them before him—a man. Like her father. The good-looking charmer her mother followed around like a lost puppy, both of them ignoring their only child. She'd heard the fights, her mother's accusations, then her father's denials. Mother would threaten to walk out on him, taking him for everything he had. Father would sweep her into his arms and silence her with his smooth words and kisses. Until the next time. Kim laughed, the sound short and bitter. Never once during any of those heated arguments had Diana Marie Michaels threatened to take Ian Wycliff Michaels's daughter from him. How ironic. And here she was, chasing men just like her father—a man who didn't want her. And in the end, the ones she was chasing didn't want her enough to fight for her either.

So she'd finally seen the light. No way was she going down that miserable road again. She was Kimberly Ann Michaels, a woman who could and did indulge on occasion but did so clearly knowing that was all it was—an indulgence. Too much of anything made you fat and lazy.

"I left you a message this morning," she replied.

"Bad reception up here."

Kim nodded and decided she would play this guy close to her chest. "Do you live in Evergreen?"

"I did."

"What were you doing out with the snowplow guys?"

"Plowing the roads."

"So if you don't live in Evergreen, why were you on the snowplow?"

"Does everyone have to live where they work?"

"No. I suppose not. So you're a road maintenance guy?"

"Is there a problem with that?"

"No, no problem at all."

He grinned. "In your fantasy, what did you think I did?"

Her skin warmed some more and she squirmed in her seat. Ricco laughed. "C'mon, Cinderella, tell me."

She didn't have the courage to tell him she'd fantasized that he was the town sheriff come to rescue her from the town robber baron. And that once he'd laid eyes on her, he hadn't been able to resist her charms and had risked all to take a side trip with her to his room.

"I don't fantasize."

"Liar."

Jesus! Was she a freakin' open book or what? What the hell happened to her cagey barracuda demeanor?

"So what if I am."

"What are you afraid of?"

Her head shot back. "What kind of question is that?"

"Something scares you. Is it intimacy? A relationship? Love?"

Kim unfolded her arms and turned toward him. "Are you married?"

He snorted. "Hell, no!"

"Have you ever been in love?"

He shrugged. "Maybe."

"How can you *maybe* be in love?"

"If I wasn't willing to forsake all others, I guess I didn't love her that much." He turned that sizzling grin on her. "Have you been married?"

She sat back into the seat and looked straight ahead. Tall ponderosa pines and evergreens lined the small highway into Evergreen like silent sentinels. The wind blew them to and fro; their pointed tops nodding toward them as if giving permission for them to pass.

"Twice."

"Ouch."

"Yeah, both of them guys just like you."

"I guess old habits die hard."

That stung. Kim didn't bother with a retort. Her head throbbed, and she was suddenly very tired. "Please drop me off at Esmeralda's B&B at Candy Cane and Evergreen Promenade."

When his face lit up like a Christmas tree, her antennae shot straight up. "What?"

"Nothing. It's a nice place. Best in town."

"Of course it is, that's why I'm staying there."

"Yeah, I took you for one of those high-maintenance types. What do you do for a living?"

"None of your business."

He nodded. As they entered the quaint town, Kim perked up. She felt like she was in the Swiss Alps, with a dash of Norman Rockwell tossed in to spice it up. Snow covered the roads. Residents were out shoveling, and they waved their mittened hands and smiled as they drove by. It was a gem amongst the High Sierras, and as they continued farther down the road, Kim felt a warmth she had never experienced before. She shook it off. They rounded the center of town, which circled around a skating rink and a huge gazebo decked out to look like a large manger scene, and she twisted and turned to take in all of the sights. She saw Esmeralda's pass by them on the left, where it overlooked the frozen Reindeer Lake. "Hey, you just passed Esmeralda's!" She winced as a jagged spear of pain jabbed her in the right temple. Gingerly she touched the lump there and hissed in a breath. The road ahead seemed to tip to the left before righting itself.

"I'm taking you down to the Urgent Care first. You need to have your head checked out. You were unconscious when I got to you."

She didn't argue. "My head hurts."

"The doc will give you something for it."

Kim nodded and suddenly felt very tired. "I don't remember skidding off the road."

"I watched you. I'd give you a perfect ten for form and speed."

Five

EVERGREEN URGENT CARE WAS JUST A LITTLE FARTHER down the road, at the end of town. Ricco looked over at Kim as she fought off fatigue. He doubted she had more than a minor bump on the head, but he didn't want to take any chances. A few minutes later he pulled into one of only four cleared spots in the snow-covered parking lot of the small medical center. He cast a glance at his passenger before he killed the engine. She was hunched over, her head resting in her hand.

He came around to Kim's side and opened the door to help her out. She opened up like a Siamese attack fish, flinging his hand away. She stumbled out of the raised truck and stalked past him, stumbling in the snow. He had half a mind to let her face plant in it, but he grabbed her elbow and hauled her backward, the inertia slamming her against his chest. He let out a loud whoosh. Her soft curves tensed against him, and as he hurried to right her, his hand grazed her right breast. Kim straightened, her blue eyes narrowed, and Ricco grinned, lifting his hands in surrender. "That wasn't on purpose."

Kim turned and, with a much more maneuvered stride, made her way to the front door of the mini ER.

"Oh, my God! Ricco!" Trina Vey screamed, startling the two elderly folks sitting in the small waiting area. She hurled her little self from her chair behind the receptionist's desk and jumped right into his arms. Ricco laughed and gathered her to him, spinning her around. "Ricco! You're home!" she cried. Just then another shriek came from the doorway leading to the examination rooms.

"Ricco!" Ricco grinned and set Trina down only to find his oldest sister, Elle, in his arms. He hugged her long and hard, then pulled back from her and grinned wider. Elle took his face in her hands and planted a big kiss on one cheek, then the other, then she pulled him to her again. Of all of his sisters, she was the one he could talk to the easiest. Maybe it was because she was the oldest and had had her share of heartache. "It seems you go for longer and longer these days."

"I do it on purpose. Your welcomes were getting lame!"

"Hah! If I didn't have to share you with every other woman in this town, maybe I wouldn't be so lame!" She grinned, her perfect smile dazzling. It was good to see her smile. She had too much to frown about.

"How's my boy doing?" Ricco asked.

Her face lost its humor, and a sudden frown creased the worry lines in her face. "He's twelve and thinks he knows everything. How do you think? He needs his father, Ricco."

Ricco pulled Elle close to him and kissed the top of her head. "I know. I'll speak with him."

"He couldn't sleep last night. He can't wait to see you. It's been too long."

Guilt washed over Ricco. Maybe it was time for him to come home. "You tell him I'll see him tonight, and he'd better have some answers for me. He's not too old for me to take him over my knee."

Humor returned to Elle's face. "I'll pay good money to see that. The boy needs a good swift kick in the butt."

A soft cough beside Ricco reminded him why he was there. "Oh, hell, Elle, I have a patient for you." He pulled Kim forward. "Kimberly Michaels, she was driving the Indy 500 along 82 and she forgot about the snow. She crashed and burned."

Elle turned dark brown eyes up to Kim. "You've got quite a shiner growing there." She looked to Trina and said, "Get her signed in and send her back ASAP."

"I don't have my wallet with my insurance info in it," Kim said.

Elle smiled, took her hand, and patted it. "This is Evergreen, Miss Michaels. We treat anyone who is hurting, with or without insurance information. Just sign the treatment and release part and fill in your name and address, and we'll fix you right up."

Ricco watched Kim do the necessary paperwork, while Trina made cow eyes at him. He grinned back. He loved coming home, and when his three weeks were up he always felt the same torn feeling. The boy in him wanted to stay and pretend it was Christmas all year long, but the man in him thirsted for adventure. Maybe one day he'd have it both ways. But until then? His gaze swept the petite blonde next to him. He liked the way her hair hung loose and thick down past her shoulders. He remembered all too well the way his hands had fit around the smooth cradle of her hips. The way her full breasts had plumped up when he pressed his lips to them, their pink tips pebbling under his tongue. Her ice princess act didn't fool him. It might have if he hadn't experienced firsthand the heat he'd stoked in her.

"Ricco!" both Trina and Elle said.

He shook his head and focused on his eldest sister. "Yeah, sure, what do you need?"

Elle scowled and put her hands on her hips, and he

watched Kim watch the interaction. "I said I'll take your friend back now."

"Oh, yeah, sure."

Trina popped up and slipped her hand along his arm, hugging it to her ample breast. He cocked his head and took a closer look. Trina had added something since the last time he'd seen her. She grinned up at him and said, "Do you like them?"

He watched Kim flash him a scowl as Elle led her into the exam area, shutting the door behind them. Ricco grinned down at Trina. "I thought they looked pretty good the way they were."

She smiled and pressed her new girls more firmly against him. "I know you like full-figured women, so I—"

Ricco shushed her with two fingers to her lips. "I like all shapes and sizes, and I told you, you're my best friend's little sister. That puts you on the When Hell Freezes Over list." He patted her arm and removed it from him. "What happened to you and Lance?"

Trina wrinkled her pert little nose and said, "He's at Davis with his sheep!"

Ricco grinned. "So he got into the vet program, did he?"

"Yes, and he told me to wait for him. I doubt that will happen."

Ricco chuckled, "Tri, he's less then two hours away, and he wants to come back here and practice."

"Jimmy says there isn't going to be a town after this blizzard. My mom is driving into Reno three times a week as it is. She's at the Legacy, and even then she said we might just have to sell the house."

"We're getting the roads cleared, Tri, the tourists will come and spend just like they do every year."

"The last few years they came too late." She sighed and went to her desk, where she began to enter Kim's information into the computer.

"How was the Thanksgiving trade?"

She looked up and smiled, then looked back to the form. "The usual, but we both know it's now or never, do or die."

Ricco looked toward the door where Elle had taken Kim and nodded. "Do or die." And he had a bad feeling.

"Tell me what happened, Miss Michaels," Elle urged after she took Kim's blood pressure.

"I was driving in from Reno, and I guess I was blinded by the snow. The next thing I remember, I was in my car in the snow and Ricco was there."

Elle shone a light into her eyes at an angle and nodded. She poked and prodded around her head. "Any headaches, nausea, vomiting, dizziness?"

"I have a hell of a migraine right now, and coming in here I felt a little dizzy."

"Did you lose consciousness?"

"Ricco said I was out when he got to me."

Elle jotted notes into a file and nodded. Without looking up, she asked, "Is that how you met Ricco?"

"He-I-ah—" Kim couldn't tell this woman, who was obviously the mother of Ricco's twelve-year-old son but, by the lack of a wedding band, not his wife, that she'd spent a hot and heavy night with him at the Legacy. As Kim thought of the absurdity of the situation, her rancor rose. He was just like every other Don Juan out there. But worse. He had a kid! And to think she had contemplated giving him another spin for shits and giggles.

"That's okay, I know how he is. I get the same response all the time."

Kim looked up at the woman's calm face. "And you don't have a problem with that?"

Elle shrugged and took out a little hammer from her white jacket pocket. "Relax back. I'm just going to lightly tap your knee to check your reflexes." As she tapped Kim in the right knee, Elle said, "Ricco's affairs don't bother me."

Kim squinched her eyes. "I'd kick his ass!"

Elle laughed. "I used to be able to kick Riccito's ass. But now if I tried, he'd kick my ass."

"Why do you call him 'little Ricky'?"

Elle stiffened and hit Kim's left knee a tad bit harder then she had the right. Kim's reflex nearly kicked her in the chest. "He's named after his father."

Kim nodded and decided by Elle's change in tone that she should stay away from the subject. Instead she got to work on the reason for her visit to Evergreen. "So, are you the only doctor here?"

"I'm a PA. Dr. Juarez is the regular doc. We had to let Dr. Newman go."

"Did he do something wrong?"

"*She* wanted more action. This last year there's been a slow, steady exodus from Evergreen."

"Why?"

Elle shrugged and put a thermometer in Kim's mouth. Just as it beeped, Elle nodded. Satisfied with the read-out, she answered, "Bad weather five years in a row, but mostly panic. The general economy is on the verge of recession, and when that happens, people stop spending. We live and die by holiday cheer. Kind of hard to keep a second doctor on when there's no cash to pay them."

"What will the town do?"'

Elle sat down and jotted more notes down in the folder. "Some fancy-ass developer has made an offer to buy the town lock, stock, and barrel. Like that's going to happen."

"Was it a good offer?"

"Doesn't matter. This town is held together by more than tinsel. We've weathered a lot worse over the years and we're still here. I have no doubt we'll weather this storm as well."

Kim nodded. Well, that answered her burning question. Did the town have the heart to fight for themselves? The answer was plain. "Well, I hope it all works out."

Elle smiled. "Have no doubt. Now, Miss Michaels, you have a slight concussion. I could send you to Reno or down to Auburn for an MRI, but you look fine, and the headache will subside. I'll prescribe something for that. In fact . . ." She scooted over to a cabinet and opened a drawer. She pulled out a few samples and handed them to Kim. "Here. The apothecary isn't open right now. Jules'll be down at the lake this time of day, ice fishing. I'll give you a prescription for more, though. Where are you staying?"

"Esmeralda's B&B."

Elle grinned. "Excellent choice. Put some ice on that lump and take one of these when you get to your room. Make sure to rest. If anything begins to feel worse, call me. If I'm not here, Ricco can find me."

Kim took the packet and thanked her.

As she walked back into the waiting area, she found Trina, along with two other young women, hanging on Ricco's every word. Their gooey cow eyes made Kim want to smack someone. Ricco looked up, smiling when he saw her. She scowled. What a Casanova! He slept with her, then flirted outrageously with these women while the mother of his child looked on. And she didn't mind?

What the hell kind of place was this?

He looked past her to Elle, who had followed her out. "Will she live?"

"She'll live. Take her over to Ezzy's and get her tucked into bed." Ricco lit up and nodded, coming toward Kim with his hand extended. Kim slapped it away. "Don't touch me," she hissed.

"Can you give her some of those nice pills, Elle?"

"The pills I gave her will do the trick."

"Great. Thanks." He winked and said over his shoulder, "I'll see you at dinner tonight?"

"Wild horses couldn't keep me away."

"Good. And tell 'Tonio he'd better watch out."

She laughed, "Are you kidding? That boy has been counting the minutes!"

Kim stalked past Ricco to the door. She flung it open, pushed through the hard chill of the air that hit her like a wall, and walked to the city-owned pickup. She just didn't get it. Philandering lover and father of your child comes home, flirts with women under your nose, and you don't have a problem with it? A sudden creepy feeling overcame Kim. Were they polygamists? Did he have other women and children around town? Ricco opened the door for her, but she didn't give him the chance to help her into the cab. Instead she glared at him, daring him to touch her. He backed off.

They drove back to the B&B in silence. As he parked, then made to get out of the cab, she stopped him with a hand on his arm. Looking directly at him, she said, "I need to make something crystal clear to you, Mr. Maza. I want no further interaction with you. On *any* level. And I expect you to respect that."

Ricco sat silent. His dark eyes widened incrementally in surprise, and his full lips tightened, barely noticeable. She could tell he was not happy with her mandate. It was probably the first of his life. "I want your word you'll forget we ever met."

He nodded. "You've got a deal." He opened the door, shut it, then walked up the cleared stone steps to the log-cabin-style B&B. Kim shoved open the door and followed him.

The minute she entered the warmth of the inn, the familiar scent of baked ginger assailed her senses. She smiled. Big. Gingersnaps. Her favorite cookies. Every year, as a special treat at Christmastime, Gran had baked them for Kim. Her mother had always told her they would make her chubby, but Gran had shooed her mother and father away the few times they'd stuck around, telling them both to stop nagging the child.

As if some type of weight had been lifted from her shoulders, Kim felt her muscles relax. The tension eased from her body as the comforting memories took over.

"Ricco, you're home!!" Another high-pitched female scream. Dear Lord, this was getting ridiculous! Kim closed the heavy oak-and-beveled-glass door behind her and stepped all the way into the open entryway.

"Ezzy!" Giggles and kissing sounds erupted from down the hall, followed by a crying baby. Oh, great, another one of his kids? Kim walked farther into the inn and looked down a short hallway, where Ricco turned with a very pregnant, petite, red-haired woman in her mid- to late-thirties in one arm and a toddler in the other. He was grinning ear to ear.

She was in the twilight zone.

"Kim, this is Esmeralda." He hugged the beaming woman to him and dropped a kiss on her forehead. He lifted the little girl, all decked out in pink and white, and planted a big kiss on her cheek. She giggled and reached her chubby little hands to his face. Ricco smiled like a proud papa. "And this is my big girl, Krista!" He nuzzled the baby in the belly, and she screamed in delight. Esmeralda smiled and smacked at Ricco, then waddled toward Kim. "I'm so happy you made it. Elle called and told me what happened to you. You're so lucky." Kim looked down at Esmeralda's right hand. No ring.

She scowled up at Ricco and was about to tell him he was a creep when Esmeralda said to him, "You need to go see Antonio. He's missed you, and Elle is having fits about it." She turned back to Kim. "C'mon up to the room I prepared for you. The fire is warming it up, and

Denny just brought your purse and luggage from your rental. It's over at Santa's Workshop. Ben's already called the rental company. I can't believe even with chains they let you take that out in this storm. I thought 80 was closed." Her incessant prattling soothed Kim in a weird, staccato way. She supposed when she went to the bathroom the entire town would know in a matter of a few minutes.

Before going up to her room, Kim looked over her shoulder to Ricco, who stood cooing at the little girl in his arms. He was completely oblivious to Kim. The baby was blond and had her mother's hazel eyes. Neither Ricco nor Esmeralda had blond hair. Maybe somebody had come around while Riccito had been tomcatting around somewhere else. Served him right.

Kim grinned and let out a big, long breath when she opened the door to her lodgings. She could not have asked for a more comfortable amenity-laden room. This was *so* going to do. Taking up the center was a big four-poster bed, carved out of rough-hewn wood smoothed and polished to a satin luster. The thick mattress and comforter were heaped with masses of gem-colored pillows and looked more inviting than her own. She just wanted to shuck her clothes and sink into what she knew would be heaven on earth. A small desk of the same wood was snuggled into one corner, and in the other a stone fireplace crackled invitingly. Up against the other wall was a hewn armoire, whose doors were carved with reindeer and snowflakes. Tiffany-type lamps adorned each of the nightstands. A large alpaca rug covered most of the hand-cut, wide-slat hardwood floor. Kim looked up to the high, slanted ceiling of exposed cedar. A slowly turning, old-fashioned palm fan rotated the warm air. A large picture window overlooked the main street. It was picture perfect. "I love it!" Kimberly gushed. And she did. She could hide in this room forever.

Ezzy smiled and opened a door that led to the more than ample bathroom. An oversized claw-foot tub dominated the black granite bathroom fitted with rustic brass. Thick, fluffy green-and-ivory-colored towels were neatly folded and amply stacked on a brass rack. On the counter a treasure trove of shampoos, soaps, and lotions were hers for the taking.

"There's an afternoon tea, coffee, juices, and soft drinks in the parlor. Continental breakfast is brought to your room every morning, but if you prefer something heartier, I cook a big spread each morning. Just let me know if you'll be down for it. Lunches are light, but at five-thirty we sit down to a country-style supper. We have Wi-Fi, and if your cell doesn't get service, we have free long distance on each of the phones in the house. Feel free to use it. It's unlimited."

Kim sat on the edge of the bed, sank into the downy comforter, then flopped back on it. She was enveloped by thick, soft down. "Oh, my God, Ezzy, this is heaven."

The innkeeper laughed. "I'm glad you like it. I try. There's a cottage in the back if you need me during off hours, or Ricco is usually around, so don't hesitate to holler."

As Esmeralda left her to her solitude, Kim sat up. An emotion she wasn't sure she was experiencing gnawed at her. She had been shocked to discover Ricco had a twelve-year-old son. It felt like she'd been kicked in the gut. She didn't know why. It pissed her off that he and Elle were so nonchalant about it, and that he'd then come down here to be with his other woman! And pregnant to boot. What kind of woman tolerated that? And what kind of man was he? The audacity! And more than that, she experienced a keen sense of jealousy and, last but not least, loss. She still wanted the prick! But not now. No way, no how. He was off limits. And to that end, she felt sad, and gypped. She'd never have another one of those earth-shattering orgasms. Ever. Again. Because no matter how hard she wished or how hard he tried, she knew Nick would not measure up in the bedroom like Ricco had.

She pulled off her boots and set them neatly on the floor. No, Nick would be slow and methodical in bed, just as he was in business. He'd be thorough, he'd be neat, and he'd be clean. No hot and sweaty, down and dirty, twisting-up-the-sheets sex for Nick and Kimberly. He wouldn't perspire, and neither would she. Hell, she might not even muss her hair.

Kim inhaled deeply and caught the warm scent of gingersnaps. A big glass of milk and a cookie or two might help her get to sleep. And she needed a nap. With warm cookies on the brain, Kim followed her nose in her stocking feet.

As she came to a bend of the wide stairway, she heard voices from the back of the house, which she assumed was the kitchen. She walked in that direction but abruptly stopped. "Oh, Ricco, I don't know how much longer I can do this alone. It's too much."

"Shuuuuush, where's my strong girl? The one who knew the score when she agreed to this gig?"

Ezzy sniffled. "I thought it would be different. I can't raise two children alone."

"You don't have to. The family is here."

"Ricco, come home. Stay here. Don't go back. Everything is changing. We need you."

"You know I can't stay. I have responsibilities."

"Your family is your responsibility!"

"Ez, don't do this to me. Not now."

Kim heard her choke back her tears, then Esmeralda said, "You're just like *he* is, Ricco. You can't make a commitment to anyone!"

Kim stiffened, and when Ricco spoke, her body chilled. "Do not *ever* compare me to him." His voice was low, menacing even, but she heard every word crystal clear. The house rattled when he slammed the door closed behind him. She heard him roar out of the driveway, then she heard Esmeralda's quiet sobs. Kim stood frozen, unsure of what she should do. Comfort the woman? The thought of that terrified Kim. She hadn't a clue how to go about it and, quite frankly, touching a pregnant woman gave her the willies, even one as sweet as Esmeralda.

As Ezzy's sobs began to climb in volume, Kim backed away, suddenly feeling sick to her stomach. Anger at Ricco mounted. What a piece of crap! His woman, the mother of one of his children, and about to give birth to a second one, was begging him to stay, and he couldn't be bothered.

Kim hurried up the stairs, and as she topped them, the hallway shifted. She grabbed the rail and steadied herself. She slowly made her way back to her room and dug the samples Elle had given her out of her pocket. She popped one in her mouth and grabbed one of the bottles of water from the ice bucket on a stand in the corner of the room. She took a long swig and stripped down to her bra and panties, folding her clothes neatly and setting them on the nightstand. Then she slid between the decadent sheets and sighed.

Heavy lidded, she started to doze off when she

remembered she hadn't called Nick. She rolled over, not wanting to get out of the bed to dig for her cell phone, which was in her bag on the floor across the room. Instead she picked up the phone on the nightstand and dialed his number.

"Gold."

"Hi, Nick, it's—"

"It's about damn time!"

She blanched at his outburst. Had she not felt so mellow under the influence of Elle's pills, she would have told him to shove his attitude up his ass. Instead she said, "You're such a horse's ass. I'm here, barely. My preliminary report is this place is ripe for a buyout. They probably just need a nudge. I'll call you tomorrow with more details." She hung up despite his questioning voice.

The drugs were already taking effect; she reached to the side of the bed to put the phone back into its cradle but missed. It thunked to the floor. She didn't care. She felt warm and woozy and very safe. Her last conscious thoughts were of Ricco bent over her, his slick, taut body sliding effortlessly into hers as she arched up to meet him, then the crying of a baby and the soulful eyes of Elle looming above them.

Six

HE WAS STILL ANGRY HOURS LATER AS HE DROVE THE BIG Mack snowplow back to town. How dare Esmeralda compare him to their father? How dare she even imply it? He was nothing like Enrique Lucien Maza. Ricco came home nearly every year and spent his vacation with his family if his work allowed it. Enrique had not made it home for Christmas in over ten years. Sometimes Ricco came up for a long weekend. Enrique came up when he needed booze money or a guilt fix. And damn if his mother didn't give it to him every time. For fifteen years, Ricco had not seen or spoken with the man he only considered a sperm donor. Ricco would never forgive him for leaving them destitute in East Oakland all those years ago. After his mother had been mugged, raped, and left for dead, they'd finally left Oakland for good. Evergreen had taken them in and given them what they had never had as a family—a safe place to live, food, work, and no questions asked. Evergreen had been a safe place, where Leticia had been able to work and raise her children. With a grant the town paid for her to return to school. She'd repaid the town by keeping the finances balanced to the penny.

Was it his fault Ezzy's husband, Ray, was back in Iraq? Was it his fault that prick Elle had married had bailed on her and Antonio ten years ago? Next, Jasmine would be blaming him for Don's time away with his new start-up company. Ricco worked hard at his job. He couldn't help the fact that undercover work demanded so much from him. They should understand, especially when he took dirtbag criminals off the streets. After the last conversation with his mother, he'd gone back to regular police work at Montrose. It gave him more time here with the family. Now he was supposed to give that job up too?

Ricco tried to wash away his anger and resentment. He wasn't angry with his sister. He was angry with their father. He was angry he couldn't be everything to everyone in his family. Hell, he could barely be what he needed to be for himself. A lot seemed to be eating at him at that moment, and he didn't like it. He wanted things to be smooth and carefree like they normally were. He didn't like turmoil in his personal life. His job was turmoil enough. He came to Evergreen for peace and tranquility, not family discord. With that, Ricco pushed all unpleasant thoughts from his head and took a big, deep breath to focus on the town.

He was satisfied with the progress they'd made today. By nightfall, 82—the main road into and out of Evergreen off Interstate 80, and the major artery that ran between Reno and Sacramento—was open for business. And no sooner had the Closed Road signs been removed than a steady stream of traffic had begun to head toward his hometown. He was glad, and he was tired. He'd been up since the crack of dawn on virtually no sleep. He grinned as he pulled the big Mack into the city yard, where there was a small area for service vehicles.

He had no complaints about how he spent the evening, and despite Kim's sudden coolness toward him, he had a hankering to get her alone again. He turned the behemoth off and sat for a long minute in the cab, contemplating what exactly it was about Kimberly Michaels that had his dick getting hard at just the thought of her.

She wasn't the beauty queen type. She was, he decided, handsome. But sexy in a classic type of way. Those big baby blues of hers reminded him of a child in their naked innocence. Yet he knew there was nothing innocent about the woman. She was sharp, and well bred. He could see it in the way she dressed, smell it in her expensive perfume, and hear it in her cultured voice.

His taste usually ran to tall, voluptuous, extroverted, exotic women, not quiet, petite blondes. Ricco slid the keys in the visor and jumped out of the snowplow. Since he was the last one in, he walked to his truck and slowly drove back to Ezzy's, dreading another outburst from her. He should stop at his mom's before he headed over for dinner, but he wanted to clean up before he saw her. He knew there would be a huge meal and lots of talk and laughter. He smiled. Despite the recent pressure, he loved coming home, and he loved that his family always welcomed him with open arms as if he'd just come home from work at the end of the day, instead of seeing them sometimes only once a year at Christmastime.

He pulled down the side driveway of the B&B and parked to the side of Ezzy's evergreen-colored minivan. His heart went out to her. Ray was in Iraq, on his third tour, and she was stressed. She hadn't heard from him in a month; that told them he was on some type of covert op. Ricco understood her fear. Two of Ray's unit had come home in body bags.

He saw her light on but decided not to bother her. He'd see her at dinner. Ricco hurried up the back stairway to the second floor and the room he used when he came home. He glanced across the hall to the Vixen suite. Kim's room. He grinned and decided that was a perfect name for her.

Ricco pressed his ear to the Vixen suite door and listened. Silence. If she'd taken what Elle had prescribed, she'd probably sleep through the night. It would do her good. He moved across the hall to his own room—the Dasher suite. Ezzy had a wry sense of humor. Closing the heavy door behind him, he shucked his clothes and boots and jumped into a hot, steamy shower. When he emerged fifteen minutes later, shrill, bloodcurdling screams assailed his ears. He flung his towel around his hips and rushed from his room to the hallway. Kim! He shoved open the door, expecting to find her at the hands of some attacker. Instead she was sitting up in the middle of the bed, her eyes wild, her hair flying, screaming at the top of her lungs, with nary another person or animal around.

A nightmare? "Kim!" he called and moved to the edge of the bed. She continued to scream. He grabbed her by the shoulders and shook her. "Kim! You're dreaming! Wake up!"

Wild-eyed, she stopped and stared at him. "You're okay," he softly said. Her big eyes searched his face for recognition. "It's me, Ricco."

She trembled in his arms. He watched her eyes fill

with tears. At that moment, he saw her as a scared little girl with no one to turn to. His heart warmed and he drew her into his embrace. Kim's sobs wracked through her body, and she clung desperately to him as if she would drown if she let go. He held her, soothing her with a slow, rocking motion, as he had soothed his nieces and nephews as babies.

THE BOGYMAN FROM KIM'S CHILDHOOD HAD COLLIDED head-on with the narcotics she had taken. A wild and terrifying montage of shapes, sounds, and long-suppressed fears had erupted. She'd cried out for Gran, only to realize she hadn't been there. Her screams had been the screams of a wounded animal, betrayed and abandoned, left to the wolves of the world.

The strong arms holding her were those of a man who had children from two different women with whom he was obviously still involved. And she didn't care. Not at that moment.

Keeping her eyes closed, Kim inhaled the spicy man scent of him. His skin was smooth, his muscles hard. She could feel the steady thud of his heart against her right hand. She pulled her head back only enough to look up into his face. His dark brown, green-tinged eyes showed only concern. Her eyes traced down to his straight aquiline nose, then to his lips. They were full and, she knew from memory, soft but firm, and they did things to her that made her warm and wet and hungry. A spark flared between her thighs, and she licked her lips. Ricco bent his nose toward her cheek, and she could feel him inhale her scent. She rubbed her cheek against his nose. Her breasts filled and her nipples tingled. When Ricco's lips brushed against her ear and his arms tightened around her waist, the limited space between them ignited.

Her nightmares were but a distant ugly memory. She was safe in the arms of a man who could take her to the moon, then to the stars. Her muscles relaxed to liquid. He moved her gently back into the mound of pillows. Kim sighed and wrapped her arms around his neck, and it occurred to her at that moment that he was naked.

And what about those kids of his and his women! She stiffened. She felt him smile against her cheek. "I'm not going to ravish you, Cinderella."

"I wouldn't let you."

"You were screaming. I thought you were being attacked."

"Bad dream."

"Want to talk about it?"

Kim moved away from him, shaking her head. "No." She pointed to his bare chest and the damp towel riding low around his waist. The definition beneath was not lost on her. She pointed to him and couldn't resist saying, "Riccito?"

Ricco chuckled and moved toward her. "We both know there is nothing little about Ricky."

Kim wanted to play, to tease, to feel his arms around her again. Realizing that, she realized just how much her life lacked physical human contact. And not just bedroom contact, but simple human contact, like the brush of fingertips against her cheek, or arms wrapped firmly around her, gently rocking her. As all of those thoughts passed through her head, Kim remembered the pregnant woman downstairs and the crying baby. She pulled the comforter tighter around her, suddenly feeling weak and very foolish. She'd almost gone down that road again.

"Please leave my room."

Ricco moved away and tightened the towel around his waist. "I'm right across the hall if you need anything."

As he exited the room, she couldn't help but watch the way his muscular behind moved under the damp terry cloth. When the door closed behind him, Kim sank back into the pillows and exhaled. What the hell was wrong with her? Wanting comfort from a tomcat? Having nightmares about being abandoned? She hadn't had one of those dreams since college. She grabbed the small packet of drugs Elle had given her and read the label. Oxycodone? Jesus. No wonder she was having nightmares. She'd taken this stuff once before, when she'd had a pinched nerve in her neck and had been in so much pain she'd just wanted to cry. Even then she'd only taken half a pill at a time. But, she smiled, it sure helped with the pain. She reached up, touched her forehead, and winced. Okay, so it still hurt, but not like it would have. Carefully Kim made her way from the bed to the bathroom, where she started the tub. A nice hot soak would feel good.

As she luxuriated in the thick silky bubbles, there was a knock on the door. "Miss Michaels?" Ezzy's voice called.

"Come in," Kim called back.

Ezzy stepped into the room and said, "Since you're my only guest tonight, I wanted to ask if you'd like to join me and my family for dinner at my mother's house just two doors down."

Kim sat still in the hot, soapy water. A hard rush of emotion smacked her in the chest followed by a sudden well of tears. No one had ever asked her to have dinner with their family. Not even her two ex-husbands. She wanted to scream. What was wrong with her that she was a sudden puddle of mush?

Hormones. It had to be. "I appreciate the offer, but if it's okay, I think I'll just stay in my room tonight," she replied.

"Are you sure? It's really no problem. We always have a full table and plenty of food."

"I'm sure, but thank you."

"I'll leave a tray for you in the kitchen. If you need anything, I'll be two doors down at eight seventy-three."

"Thank you."

When she heard the door close behind Ezzy, Kim sank farther into the soapy water. She almost called out that she'd changed her mind, but she didn't. She wasn't a people person. She got along better with spreadsheets. Nick was so right when he said they were bookends. She rinsed off, then wrapped herself in a thick, velvety towel to consider her options. She could go downstairs and have dinner alone. Nothing new or exciting there. She ate alone most nights and liked the solitude. But she could bundle up and take a walk around the small town. The meds were wearing off, the dosage having been minimal, thank God.

She dressed in a fresh pair of jeans, a thick fleece sweater, and a different pair of Uggs. These were flat and black suede, with gray suede crisscross ties and white fleece lining. The house was quiet, but her brain coming out of the drug fog was on high alert. She thought of Ricco. She couldn't help it. He bothered her on several levels, not one of them good for business. And the business at hand was to ferret out the town's problems, exploit them, then capitalize on them. She moved to the big picture window in her room overlooking Evergreen Promenade—the main street that ran through town.

She smiled as she watched two kids playing under the warm glow of streetlights in cumbersome red snowsuits. They were throwing big, fluffy snowballs at each other. A golden retriever ran crazily around the kids, barking and trying to intercept the balls. The kids shrieked in joy, the dog barked happily, and Mom and Dad stood smiling to the side. What a pretty picture. Kim frowned. *Not.* Screaming kids and shedding dogs were an annoyance she was happy to be free of. And the snowballs? Cold and wet. She liked warm and dry.

She turned away from the postcard picture and thought of Ricco again. How many runny-nosed little bastards did he have running around this town with his last name? Didn't he care how his absence affected his children?

Her frown deepened, and she shook off the sudden feeling of malaise those thoughts stirred up. The kids would survive somehow. They always did. She was a prime example. Shoving the irritating emotions aside, Kim grabbed her purse and headed for the door. She was going to go downstairs, eat, then hit the town. There was no time for dalliances even *if* the cock of the walk wasn't linked to every woman in the county.

"ARE YOU HUNGRY?" A DEEP VOICE ASKED FROM THE SHADOWS of the entryway as her foot hit the last step of the wide stairway. Kim jumped back, catching her breath.

"Stop doing that!" she groused, collecting herself. Kim

shot the now clad and much too handsome Ricco Maza a glare and pushed past him. His spicy, evergreen-infused scent seriously messed with her head. When he followed her into the kitchen, she was painfully aware they were quite alone in the big house.

As she entered the kitchen, the warm scent of ginger-snaps assailed her nostrils. Her smile was quickly followed by a sad mien. Gran used to make the best gingersnaps on the planet. Kim could still taste them. Warm and just a tad soft before they hardened. And the spices she'd used had been fresh and aromatic. No one made them like Gran. And though they were Kim's favorite, she had not eaten one since Christmas day, thirty years ago.

Ricco pulled the red-and-green checkered cloth from the tray of cookies and snatched up a handful. He me-andered to the fridge and poured himself a tall glass of milk. Like a little boy, he stood at the counter and hap-pily munched. So engrossed was he in his snack that he forgot about her until she cleared her throat. He grinned and offered her the last cookie. "No, thank you," she softly said and moved to the covered tray that Ezzy had left for her on the butcher block table.

Ricco popped the last cookie in his mouth and chugged down the last of his milk. He wiped his mouth on a napkin, then headed for the back kitchen door. "You gonna be all right here by yourself?"

Her head snapped back. "I'm not a two-year-old."

He shook his head. "Lady, I don't know what school you went to, but around here a simple 'yes, thank you' or 'no, thank you' goes a long way." He turned the knob on the door and said over his shoulder, "You have fun with yourself." Then he shut the door soundly behind him.

She sat down and pulled the cloth from the tray. While the fresh-baked biscuits and gravy, chicken, peas, and mashed potatoes should have made her belly happy, she only stared at the full plate. Picking up the fork, she picked at and pushed the peas around on the crowded plate. Gran used to chide her for her food art. Even as a child, Kim had never had much of an appetite. The good part was that she'd never had a weight problem, and even if she had, she was a gym rat. She whiled away hours in the gym.

She dropped the fork, and it clattered against the red-and-white delft plate. She didn't want to do anything except go back up to her room, crawl between the comforter and soft flannels sheets, and sleep for a week. She shook her head. What the hell was wrong with her? It wasn't like her to mope. She needed to get herself out of this funk.

She looked up from the concoction on her plate to the door Ricco had exited, and she caught her breath. He stood staring at her through the window. He shook his head again, and she stiffened. He opened the door and said, "Go get your jacket."

"I—"

"Just do it, Kim, and for once don't argue."

She sat defiantly for a long moment, when he walked past her up the stairs and returned with her big camel sheerer jacket. He tossed it to her. "Come with me."

Slowly she stood, knowing she'd regret it, but a prick of excitement tickled her belly. She shrugged on the jacket and followed him out the back door. "Aren't you going to lock the door?" she asked him.

Ricco turned to look at her, his brows raised in surprise. "We're in Evergreen, no one locks their doors here."

"But—"

He grabbed her hand and pulled her along with him. "No buts."

As they came around the front of the big inn, she noticed that all of the sidewalks were neatly cleared, the snow pushed to the sides. They worked fast. They had to. From the homework she'd done on the town, she knew they had a robust artisanal trade year-round but that the mainstay to the economy was tourism from the week of Thanksgiving to the day after the New Year. Evergreen was a quaint Christmas mecca renowned for its scenic tranquility. And for the annual Christmas parade. While many cities and towns across the country had pulled back from the original reason for the season, Evergreen prided itself on its nativity parade and live nativity scene in the center of town. It was one of the most photographed Christmas scenes in the country. But the last five years of bad weather during the holidays had put a crunch on the little town. They were feeling the pinch. And this year they had done the unthinkable—advertised on national television. It had cost them a pretty penny, too.

If it didn't pay off? Kim grinned. If it didn't pay off for them, then it would pay off for Land's Edge. And she was counting on another deluge of snow to keep the tourists out.

Kim shivered, but it wasn't from the chilly air—it was from anticipation, the rush, the excitement of the hunt, then the kill. She smiled, her mood suddenly lifted. That was what she did, and it was why she was here. To hunt and ultimately snare the town into submission.

She took a deep breath and ignored Ricco's wary eye on her. The air was chilly, but there was no wind and nary a breeze. The moon was waxing and the stars twinkled in the clear sky. Ricco pulled her across the street, and Kim counted no fewer than three snowmen. Gay holiday wreaths and twinkling clear white lights illuminated the houses they passed. "Where are we going?"

"Someplace to eat. It's loud and crowded, but the food is always good and the company the best."

"But—"

"No buts."

Two steps later he turned up a gaily decorated sidewalk to a smaller version of Esmeralda's B&B. This house was built with fresh cedar logs. It had a green copper roof and green shutters. All of the light fixtures were brass, the glass beveled. It was warm and inviting. She could hear the shriek of children's laughter halfway up the poinsettia-lined sidewalk. She balked.

Ricco turned on her, an angry frown marring his handsome face. "I'm starving here!"

She shook her head and stepped back. "I don't do well around children. They, uh, they don't like me, and I don't care for them."

He pulled her along, and she stumbled behind him. "These kids don't bite."

She knew she was making a huge mistake. When the door flew open from the inside and a female shrieked, followed by, "*Papi!* I've missed you so much!" Kim cringed. Great. She was meeting the mother. Ricco grabbed the tall, striking woman up into his arms and twirled her around, kissing her cheeks. "*Hola,* Mama!"

Kim watched the doorway fill with more women and watched as the children squeezed in between the grown-up bodies, their little heads popping out, their eyes wide, the smiles near face-splitting. Kim stiffened. Holy shit! Both Elle and Esmeralda were there, and so was another woman with a kid! Kim backed up. No way. This was too damn weird. And his mother was in on this?

Ricco set the smiling woman down and turned to Kim, his eyes bright, his smile wide. "Mama, this is Kim Michaels. I found her in a snowbank. She's grumpy, doesn't like kids, and says she's here on vacation, which I don't believe, but she's hungry. Can you help her out?"

Kim scowled and tried to smile at the tall, gracious, auburn-haired lady, who now studied her with less than appreciative, deep, hazel-colored eyes. "Of course."

Ricco turned to the doorway filled with kids and women and said, "Well? Come give your *tio* a hug!" A gangly boy of about twelve leapt forward and clung to Ricco's neck like a noose, followed by an adorable (well, adorable if she was into kids) little girl with big dark eyes and thick golden curls. They were joined by another toddler boy and Krista, who squealed as she pressed against the horde that clung to Ricco's legs, arms, and back. *Tio* Ricco.

Heat filled Kimberly's cheeks, and she felt like a complete and utter idiot. These were his sisters, not his concubines. Kim stepped back, as if she'd somehow been intruding on a private moment. A hard knot tightened in her belly. The sisters, all laughing and speaking in soft, melodic Spanish, peeled the kids from their uncle—all except the oldest boy. His dark eyes narrowed her way as Ricco carried him into the house. The boy looked at Kim as if she'd been an unwanted intruder. She felt like one.

The chilled air whipped around her head, lifting her hair, and Kim shivered hard. A firm hand touched her elbow. She started and looked up to the wise eyes of Ricco's mother. "My name is Leticia, but my friends call me Leti," she said.

Kim forced a smile. "I'm Kimberly."

"Welcome, Kimberly, but I warn you. The kids haven't seen their uncle in a long time, and they are very selfish and quite aggressive with his time when he is here. I hope you don't mind."

Kim hurried to assure her it was not. "Not at all. It's not like that between us."

"Are you saying you aren't involved with my son?"

Kim nearly choked. Heat rose in her cheeks. Leti patted her hand. "I don't mean to be so blunt, but you are the first girl he's brought home . . . er, ever . . . and as you can plainly see"—Leti pointed to her smiling son, who was laughing and playing with the children—"my boy has a way not only with the children but the ladies as well. It cannot be resisted."

Kim removed Leti's hand from her arm, then faced her. "Mrs. Maza. I am not romantically involved with your son. I'm here because—" She frowned. "I'm here to relax. And I can assure you there is nothing between us."

Leti smiled, the fine lines around her knowing dark green eyes crinkling. "If you say so."

Kimberly just shook her head. There was nothing between her and this woman's son now, and there sure wasn't going to be any in the future. And it didn't matter what this woman thought. In a week she would be gone and the town a distant memory.

Though she didn't want to be there, the minute Kim entered the abode, *casa* Maza assaulted every sense she possessed, with its warmth, fragrant scents, and laughter. The one sister she had not met, who resembled Ricco like a twin, introduced herself as Jasmine before she ducked back into the cavernous kitchen and continued to chatter with the other women. Ricco wrestled with the kids, the sisters bustled around, setting the long dining room table, happily chatting amongst themselves. A phone rang from a back room, and Leti's animated voice answered. Kim was all but forgotten. And it was okay with her. It gave her the time to look around and absorb her surroundings without being observed herself.

The house, though smaller than the B&B by more than half the square footage, had an open, welcoming feeling to it. Cedar-paneled walls combined with painted drywall and thick woodwork gave the large, open family room an airy feeling. The large river rock fireplace that blazed in the corner drew her with its warmth. Krista screamed and waddled past her older cousin, who chased her on all fours, then she grabbed Kim's leg, ducking behind her. The little hands digging into her calves startled her. Kim stiffened. She didn't like to be touched.

Ricco laughed and came crawling across the thickly carpeted floor, making funny growling noises that sent Krista into a fit of giggles. Kim's blood quickened as she watched this big, strapping man, a man who, with just his lips, had made her feel things she had never felt, play like a big kid. She wanted to scream and laugh and have him chase her, tickling her until she laughed so hard she couldn't breathe. She wanted him to press her down into the thick carpet and kiss her and tell her how beautiful she was. She wanted . . .

Seven

"DINNER'S ON THE TABLE!" ELLE ANNOUNCED. RICCO grabbed Krista up, rescuing Kim from the little girl's clutches. The older boy stared at Kim so intently that she would have sworn he knew her secret. Ricco tousled the boy's dark hair and said, "C'mon, 'Tonio, Grandma's worked all day."

The boy gave Kim a sideways look before he stalked off. She looked up to Ricco, who watched her watch 'Tonio. "I don't think he likes me very much."

Ricco smiled and shifted Krista in his arms. " 'Tonio isn't very happy with the world right now. It's not you."

"When was the last time his dad came around?" she asked. Ricco's eyes narrowed. "Elle mentioned it at the clinic," she hurried to explain.

"Ricco!" Elle called. He stepped aside and motioned for Kim to pass. He pulled out a chair for her near the end of the table and handed Krista off to her mother. After Kim sat down, Ricco sat in the empty chair at the end of the table next to her. His mother sat at the other end. The sisters and their children filled in the sides. It occurred to Kim that at that moment, he was the only dependable male in the family.

Once the kids were settled and the din of voices lowered, Leti said, "Antonio? Would you say grace, please?"

The boy looked as if he was about to defy his grandmother, when Ricco coughed. 'Tonio's cheeks pinkened, and he dutifully put his head down and folded his hands. Kim bowed her head and folded her hands, feeling extremely self-conscious. She hadn't said a prayer since she was eight, and then the only one she'd known had been the one Gran had taught her to say before going to sleep.

The table grew quiet; even the younger children remained silent as they waited for 'Tonio to speak. The boy cleared his throat and began, "Lord, thank you for bringing my uncle Ricky home, and please make him stay. Bring Uncle Ray home from Iraq, and Uncle Donny home from his new business. And keep my father far away from me! Amen."

"Antonio!" Elle said. The boy shot his mother a glare, and Leti put her hand on her daughter's arm. "It's okay, Elena. It was a good prayer. Most of it, anyway." She looked down the table and smiled at her son. "Maybe we could see more of you in the future?"

Ricco smiled. "Duty calls."

Jasmine piped up, "Your family is your duty."

And with that the floodgates opened, and Ricco was deluged by the females and the little people of his family to come home and stay put. Finally he raised his hand and said, "Can we please eat?"

Leti nodded, and the family dug in. More conversation erupted. "Ricco, are the roads cleared?" Leti asked.

He nodded as he scooped up a large mound of fluffy Spanish rice. He put half of it on Kim's plate and the other half on his. "Clear as glass. Evergreen is open for business."

"Let's hope the regulars get the news and we get a rush of fresh faces," Jasmine said. "Enrollment at the school is down thirty percent."

"I have several guests coming in tomorrow and, God willing, a few walk-ins. I'm booked for the week of Christmas and through to the New Year," Esmeralda contributed.

Leti nodded and passed a platter of yummy-looking chili *verde.* Ricco passed around the salad bowl, filled with sliced avocado, tomatillos, white onion, and cilantro mixed with fresh greens, corn salsa, and blue tortilla strips, tossed in what smelled like a lime and *pico de gallo* vinaigrette. Her nose followed the casserole of enchiladas. Then a bowl stacked high with tamales. The aromas were wonderful, and the conversation enlightening. Her appetite suddenly voracious, Kim dug in. But she never once forgot why she was there. "Has there been a problem with tourists?" she casually asked.

As one, all the adult eyes turned to her and stared as if remembering her presence. She didn't mind; she'd grown used to it as a child. Elle nodded and answered, "We've been cursed with bad weather the last half of December for the last five years. The last few years have been the hardest. It's caught up with us. Bad weather has kept the tourist trade away. The only way into and out of Evergreen is on 82. Regular snow is not a problem, but when it keeps coming down we can't remove it fast enough, and when they close 80, it's the kiss of death."

"Is the town in trouble?"

Leti smiled, and it wasn't a happy gesture. "We've had rough spots before and weathered those. We'll weather this one as well."

"Mama's the town controller and a private CPA. She knows who owes what and to whom, and if she says Evergreen will pull out of this slump, then we will," Esmeralda proudly said.

"The Martinez family finally put the marina up and pulled both of their kids out of St. Anne's. Mother Justina is worried and is making cuts," Jasmine said as she fed her little boy a piece of tamale.

"Is your job in jeopardy?" Ricco asked.

Jasmine nodded. "I've updated my resumé."

"For what?" Ricco asked.

Jasmine set down the piece of tamale and looked at her brother. "For your information, little brother, I have a master's in child development. I'm not your garden-variety teacher."

"I know that, Jazz. What I meant was, what is there here for you in Evergreen other than teaching?"

She looked down at her plate, then looked back up to her brother. "Nothing. I'd commute to Reno or move to Sac."

"No!" Elle and Esmeralda said in unison.

Jazz set her fork down and put her elbows on the table. She looked around at her family. "What am I supposed to do, then? Live off my family? Don is never home, and while he makes a decent living, we can't survive on his salary. I need to work."

"We let Dr. Newman go last week," Elle said quietly. She looked at her mother. "I don't know where Dr. Juarez is going to come up with that balloon payment. He can barely make payroll. He hasn't drawn a check in months."

"Dr. Juarez isn't the only one," Leti sighed. She seemed to have lost her appetite. She pushed her food around on her plate.

"What about investors?" Kim asked between bites of tender boiled pork.

Once again all adult eyes turned to her. Leti scowled. "We have an offer from a land developer in L.A. to buy Evergreen lock, stock, and barrel."

"Oh," Kim said, acting innocent. "Is it a good offer?"

"Any offer, good or bad, is not subject to consideration."

"Oh," Kim said, then couldn't help adding, "why not?"

"Evergreen is unique. The people here trust one another. We can and do count on our neighbors, and we know all we have to do is look like we need a hand and it's given without question. This town rescued me and my family over thirty years ago when no place else would. I've seen it happen over and over—families uprooted elsewhere and taken into the fold of this town. Our roots are deep and loyal. There is no other place any of us would rather be than right here. We'd rather commute into Reno or down to Sacramento then give up our homes here. Selling out is not an option."

"But if the money—"

"Not an option." Leti's tone left no room for further discussion.

Ricco laughed. "Leticia Maza is the mama bear of the town. Cross any resident, and you cross her."

Kim understood that on a business level: Fight for the deal. But she could not relate on a personal level;

she had never fought for anyone, nor had her mother ever fought for her. She smiled up at Ricco, then to his sisters. "You're fortunate to have a mama bear."

"What about your folks, Kimberly?" Ezzy asked.

Kim shrugged. "They travel a lot."

"Are they meeting you here for Christmas?"

Kim nearly choked on the rice she'd just swallowed. She grabbed her glass of tea and took a deep swig. She shook her head. "No."

"What *are* they doing for Christmas?" Ricco asked.

Kim shrugged. "I have no idea, probably spending it in Europe, like they usually do."

"Are you mad at your mom?" little Mari, Jasmine's oldest child, asked.

Kim smiled, not sure how to answer the question. "Mari, that is none of your business," her mother lightly chastised her.

Kim took the out. As the conversation moved from topic to topic, several things became crystal clear to Kim. One: Evergreen was in trouble. Two: Leticia Maza was the key to unlocking the financials of the town, the way for Kim to get a detailed road map to a buyout. And three: The Maza family was tight, and if you messed with one, you messed with them all.

"*Tio?*" Little Mari softly said, tugging on Ricco's sleeve. Ricco set his fork down and smiled at the child. Her big brown eyes looked up to him with the innocent wonder only a child could have. "I'm Jesus' mama this year. I want you to watch me."

Ricco smiled slowly, his entire face lighting up. Kim watched, transfixed. Pure love and joy marked every cell in him. Her insides did that weird jumpy thing again.

He smoothed her hair back from her little angelic face and rubbed noses with her. "I wouldn't miss it for the world."

She pursed her little lips and pointed a finger at him. "Promise."

Ricco crossed his heart and made as if to poke his eye. "Cross my heart and hope to die. You know if I say I'm there, I am."

"My daddy says that, but he's gone."

"Mari," Jasmine shushed.

"It's okay, Jazz," Ricco said, smiling down at his niece. "Daddy works a lot, Mari. But he's going to try very hard to be home to see you."

The little girl smiled and reached up for a hug, and her uncle obliged. "I love you," she whispered against his ear, squeezing her eyes shut. And Kim felt her heart constrict.

As the dinner was winding down, there was a knock on the door. 'Tonio jumped up to answer it. No one seemed to mind or think there could be a complete stranger on the other side—or, worse, a criminal. "Grandma! There's a man here."

Leti set her napkin on the table next to her plate and stood. As she walked toward the door, everyone at the table craned their necks to see who it was. You could have heard a pin drop when Leti's stunned voice whispered as if she had seen a ghost, "Enrique."

Ricco was up so fast that his chair flew backward and crashed onto the floor. All three sisters gasped and came to their feet. Krista whimpered, Mari shushed her, and little Donny blinked his big brown eyes like an owl. His little chin quivered, and he looked as if he was ready to belt out a scream. Kim braced herself. But more formidable than the little boy's imminent eruption was the Maza siblings. As a unit, the four of them marched toward the door.

"What the hell are you doing here?" Ricco angrily demanded. Kim stood and shushed the children, who stared at the door wide-eyed and frightened.

"*Mijo*—" an old man's voice beseeched.

"Don't '*mijo*' me! Get the hell out of here!"

"Ricco!" Leti said, her voice high and strained. "Do not speak to your father like that."

Incredulous, Ricco looked at his mother. He pointed to the well-dressed man who leaned heavily on a wooden cane. "This man is no father of mine."

Leti put her hand on her son's arm, her eyes beseeching him to comply. Ricco's eyes hardened to stone. His jaw tightened, and whatever words he wanted to say he held inside. His gaze shot past his mother to Kim. "Get your jacket, we're leaving."

Kim hurried to do just that. Quickly, she thanked Leti and the girls for dinner. She gave Ricco's dad a quick glance and almost blanched. There was no way to deny that he'd fathered the tall, angry man waiting at the door for her. Enrique, a handsome man with an incredible aura of pride swirling around him, was Ricco in thirty years, but he wore the pall of a death mask. His aristocratic face was a series of sunken planes and angles. He was pale and drawn. He looked ill. No, Kim decided, he was past ill. This man was dying. Despite that, he was well dressed and held his head high with pride, even if his dark brown eyes held years of regret in them. He nodded to Kim and smiled. Ricco kissed his mother and sisters, then grabbed Kim by the hand and drew her past the man he refused to acknowledge, and out the door.

The door closed behind Ricco, and she heard shrill female voices erupt inside the house. Ricco did not hesitate in his step.

Eight

Ricco's long, angry strides made it difficult for Kim to keep up. She noticed, though, that instead of heading back to the B&B, they were going in the opposite direction, straight to the heart of town. The air was colder and the wind had picked up, but the atmosphere was clear. The snow had stopped before dinner. She looked up and gasped. The deep purple sky was filled to bursting with stars. They twinkled brightly, and the combination of the stars, the wispy scent of evergreen, and fresh air was exhilarating, despite the angry man who drew her behind him like a sack of dirty laundry.

"Ricco," she breathlessly said. "Slow down."

Abruptly, he did, and she knocked into his side.

Absently he righted her before she fell. He didn't let go of her hand, and in a sudden, shocking awareness, she realized she didn't want him to. His warmth and strength, even if he wasn't aware of his gesture, made her feel wanted. She shook that off, and with it, she pulled her hand away. He scowled down at her as if just realizing he'd been holding her hand but was glad she'd made the break.

"Sorry," he mumbled, then began to walk, looking down at her to see if she could keep stride with him.

"Was that your father?" she softly asked. Kim felt Ricco's body stiffen beside her even though they had no physical contact. His stride increased in pace. She sped up to keep up.

And for reasons unknown to her at that moment, Kim said, "I know how it feels." He slowed and scowled down at her, still not saying a word. Old hurts swelled in her chest, pressing into her heart, a heart she had kept closed to intrusion. Yet she had a need to connect with this man, to let him know he wasn't the only kid who'd been deserted by a parent. And, she told herself, she was going to be in Evergreen for the next week, and Ricco's mother was the gateway to her report for a buyout. Who better to get close to than the woman's only son she doted on?

Kim hurried to explain. "I gather your father wasn't around much?"

Ricco grunted a response.

"My mother and father were absentee parents too. My grandmother raised me until she died. Then it was a revolving door of nannies."

"Do you have siblings?"

She shook her head. "I call myself the Trust Fund baby. Without the baby, my mother didn't get the trust fund."

Ricco glanced down at her then looked ahead. They were approaching the ice rink. Several couples and small children frolicked on the smooth, shiny ice. Low holiday music piped across the space. A large bonfire burned on the other side, and she could see several people huddled around it.

Impulsively Kim grabbed Ricco's hand and said, "C'mon. I've never ice-skated! Teach me!"

He resisted. She pulled him toward the rink. "C'mon, Ricco, teach me."

He stood dug into the sidewalk, his dark, stormy face unyielding. Kim smiled and tilted her head. She pouted and pressed herself against the long length of him. At the contact she felt his body stir. "You know you want to."

He stood stalwart. She persisted, and much to her surprise, she found herself enjoying this lighter, flirtier self. And if it got her the information she needed, she was game. Besides, it wasn't like she wasn't attracted to the guy. If she wasn't careful, she could find herself twisting up the sheets with him again. Her body lit up at the notion.

When Ricco refused to budge, Kim resorted to a little reverse psychology. She released his hand and skipped past him toward the rink. She knew he'd follow her, if for no other reason than the fact that he'd feel some sense of responsibility for making sure she was returned safe and sound to the inn. Not that this town was threatening in any way. It was Christmas paradise, and she felt as light and carefree as she had when Gran would take her out on the town.

The fact that Kimberly didn't have a cent on her didn't matter. The smiling lady in the rental hut just told her to drop off the two-dollar rental fee the next time she came by. Kim sat down on a warmed bench and pulled off her five-hundred-dollar boots, fretting about where she could put them so no one would steal them. The nice lady from the rental hut just a few feet away smiled and said, "No one will bother your things."

Kim smiled and put on the skates, tightly lacing them. As she stood, she nearly lost her balance. She grabbed the edge of the rink and was thankful for the thick rubber matting that led to the ice. She glanced over her shoulder to where she'd left Ricco. He stood, silently watching her. He hadn't moved an inch. Her belly somersaulted. She felt his pain. Really, she did, but she'd learned to compartmentalize it. It made life so much more manageable. And frankly, being emotionally unfettered cleared the way for complete focus on her job. And she loved her job. The thrill of the hunt was better than sex any day. Well, except the other night, but that was an anomaly. Seriously, it had been one of those all-of-the-stars-in-alignment nights.

Gingerly Kim put her right foot onto the ice. She gripped the edge of the rink wall and put her left foot out. The right foot pushed forward, she flexed backward to compensate, and her left foot went flying out from underneath her. She hit the hard ice with a loud whoosh. She lay stunned and breathless for a long moment. She opened her eyes to see several concerned faces peering down at her.

"Are you okay, lady?" a teenaged boy asked.

"I think so," she answered. As far as she could tell the only thing stinging at the moment was her pride, and, well, her behind. The boy extended a hand and she reached for it. As he pulled her up, her skates went willy-nilly and she fell back onto the ice, this time bringing the kid with her.

She lay flat on her back, sprawled out like she was going to make a snow angel, with the kid sitting on her stomach. He hurried to move away, apologizing profusely. A dark shadow moved over her, and big, capable hands lifted her from the ice, setting her aright on her feet. Kim looked up to see Ricco's hard face above hers. Heat infused her cheeks. His eyes, not as hard as his face, twinkled just a smidge. "You're going to kill yourself and everyone else on the ice," he told her.

Carefully, Kim grasped the edge of the low wall and scowled up at him. "No, I'm not!" She turned to grab the wall with her other hand, misplaced her weight, and found herself once again on her back, this time staring up into two very amused dark brown eyes.

He stared at her for a long moment before those sensual lips of his broke into a smile. "Yes, you are." He extended his hand and hauled her up against him. He wrapped his left arm around her waist, and, in a slow glide, he pushed off, holding her to him. Like he was an NHL star, he moved with the grace of a pro along the ice. The slow, long glide guided by his long, hard body made her think of other long, slow slides.

He was so big and so strong, and so adept on the ice, that she couldn't have fallen had she tried. He held her easily and maneuvered them effortlessly around the small rink. Her feet made weird directional changes even as she tried to guide them, but Ricco kept her close to him. His spicy personal scent, mingled with that of their surroundings, was heady stuff. Kimberly looked up to him, but his eyes were focused ahead, his jaw set. While he had gone where she'd wanted, he was in his own little world.

"Earth to Ricco," she said. He glanced down at her and slowed. He stopped then, pressing her back against the rail.

"I'm not very good company tonight."

She smiled and liked the way he kept his body close to hers. When she pressed into him, he cocked an eyebrow. "What happened to the spitfire who wanted me to stay the hell away from her?"

Kim shrugged, then smiled big. "I thought Elle was your girlfriend and Tonio your son. The way you acted when you saw Ezzy, I assumed the same thing with her and thought you were a twisted bastard."

He threw his head back and laughed. She smiled, liking the way it sounded. Thick, hearty, and full of amusement. He shook his head. Taking her right hand in his, he sobered somewhat and said, "Rest assured, I don't have children squirreled away—or their mothers. I'm fairly certain there are no little Rickys running around out there." He slowly drew her away from the railing. She hesitated. "I won't let you fall," he softly said. And she believed him.

He slid his arm around her waist and brought her up against his side. Looking up at him, she smiled. Ricco grinned back, and something deep inside of her shifted. He pushed off. In a slow, easy circle, they moved across the ice. The chilly air against her skin and the freeing effect of the movement made her feel footloose and fancy-free. She looked down at Ricco's black skates; she moved her feet in time to match his, and just like that, with a little help, she was skating.

"Oh, my God! I'm doing it!" She was skating! "Let go!"

Slowly Ricco unreeled her from his side. She tightened her grip and looked up at him. As the word no escaped, she felt her feet go out from underneath her. Ricco did a slick half circle move and grabbed her up to him before she hit the hard ice.

"Not so fast, Cinderella. You have to crawl before you can compete in the Olympics."

She hung onto his shoulders, and she felt his body stiffen. His eyes darkened. Her body warmed. She wanted him to kiss her, she wanted to experience the thrill of him again. When he moved away from her, even though he didn't let go of her, a sudden rush of embarrassment assaulted her. Her spine straightened and she twisted her hand out of his, and fueled by the power of a woman solidly scorned, Kim managed to make it around the rink not once, but twice, with no help from Ricco.

When she came to a victorious final lap, stopping at the rail near where she had originally started and fallen just thirty minutes earlier, several bystanders clapped. Ricco's big body swished up beside her in a rooster tail of shaved ice, just like the hockey players did when they turned on a dime. She glowered up at him. "Show-off." He grinned and helped her off the ice.

As they sat beside each other on the warmed bench, Ricco said, "You didn't do too bad for a virgin."

Kimberly sat up from wrestling with the tight laces on her skate. "I beg your pardon?"

He shook his head and said, *"No te espume, chocolate."*

She scrunched up her nose. "What does that mean?"

He grinned and bent down to pull off his skates. He had big feet. He had big hands. She swallowed hard; he had a big something else too.

"It means, 'Don't foam up, chocolate.' "

She peered at him. He cocked a brow and bent down to loosen up her laces. "In real easy terms, Cinderella, it means, 'Chill out.' "

"Don't call me Cinderella."

"Why not? You earned it."

He pulled off her skates. She let him. His fingers were long and strong, and they felt good on her. "Because I left before you could?"

He smiled and moved his head closer to hers. He reached a hand to her face and pushed back her unruly hair from her cheek. He lightly touched her bump. It didn't hurt anymore. "I admit, I would have left, but not before saying good-bye."

Kim swallowed hard. "I'm sure you have one-night-stand etiquette down to a science. But since you were my first, I was a bit unclear on the procedure."

Ricco moved back and handed her a boot. "These are really nice."

She yanked it from his hand. "Thanks." Once she put her boots on, Kim picked up her skates. Ricco reached out and took them from her. "I covered your bill."

She narrowed her eyes. "I can—"

He put his hand out to shush her. "Buy me a cup of coffee tomorrow."

She brought it down a notch. "Fair enough."

As they walked to the rental hut, the woman smiled up at Ricco with that doey-eyed look every woman seemed to reserve just for him. She had to be older than him by fifteen years. Ricco grinned back as if she'd been the only woman on the planet. "Thanks, Margie."

"Any time, Ricco." Then Margie smiled at Kim and said, "You have the best teacher in town. He's been skating like Wayne Gretzky since he was six years old."

Kim offered an awkward smile. "Lucky me," she said, then moved past them both. The warmth and sincerity of these Evergreen people was downright creepy. *Who acted like that?*

Ricco caught up to Kim as she walked toward the inn. "That was kind of rude."

She turned and he nearly crashed into her, but he caught himself. "Look, you Evergreen folks have your way, I have mine. Sorry if I don't get all warm and fuzzy like every freak up here."

"Since when is simple common courtesy freakish?"

"Since everyone in this town is like a Stepford person!"

Ricco laughed, but the amusement was thin. "Granted, the folks here are a bit isolated, but it's by choice. Three weeks out of the year the same people flock here to get a taste of these Stepford people. It makes them feel human again. It gives them the courage to go back to their conveyor belt lives, where they interact like robots and drones. Don't knock it until you try it, Cinderella. Pollyanna life for a week or two, especially during the holidays, doesn't hurt anyone."

She nodded her head. "Is that why you come up here?"

"My family is here. Those Stepford people you find so contemptuous took my mother, my sisters, and me in when no one else would. They didn't ask for anything in return. We owe far more than we can ever repay."

"Is that why you were clearing the roads?"

"Among other things, yes."

"What about the buyout offer?"

He started to walk toward the inn. "Land's Edge can offer the moon, but the town will pass."

"How can you say that? If the offer is strong—"

He stopped and turned her to face him. He put his hands on her shoulders and bent down, then said slowly and firmly, "Evergreen is not for sale. Now or ever."

"But—"

"No buts."

For a long moment Kim stood still, wanting to thunk this guy in the head. She wanted to warn him that she and Nick were batting a thousand when they put their heads together and decided they wanted to acquire a property. Losing was not an option, and giving up was unheard of. If the town of Evergreen dug in, for each day they resisted the price would drop, and in the end it would be Land's Edge getting the deal, not the residents of this quaint little Christmas town.

Ricco nudged her forward. They walked in silence for a few minutes, but Kim couldn't let the subject die. "It's suicide to stay if the town is sinking financially. Why not grab a few bucks and start up somewhere else?"

Ricco stopped and let out an exasperated breath. "There is no option because there isn't another place like Evergreen in California. Because families have been here for generations and have no intention of splitting up."

"What's so special?"

His brows rose, and he turned her back to face the rink, which had thinned considerably since they had stepped on it. The gazebo beyond was softly illumined in white lights. The homes, inns, and stores that fronted the main drag were gaily decorated, the warmth and invitation blatant. "That! And the people who reside behind each and every door in this town. You will not find a more honest, genuine, easygoing group of people anywhere else on the planet. There is no crime here. No strife here. There are roots here. We're a family. A family who sticks together through thick and thin. It will never change."

"If it's so great, why don't you live here year-round?"

He stared down at her for a long minute. The tight muscles in his jaw flexed. "It's . . ."

"It's what?"

He shrugged and gestured for her to follow. "I need more."

"But Evergreen has *everything*," she sarcastically countered.

"It will for me one day. But now isn't the day."

His words ended on a final note. Instead of entering the inn from the front door, Ricco walked her along the back to the kitchen door. Ezzy looked up from the cleared table, where she sat going over what looked like a shopping list. A baby monitor sat inches from her right elbow. Her eyes were puffy and red. Kim quickly excused herself and moved down the hallway, but she hovered over the railing as she very slowly walked up the stairway. She told herself she wanted to hear something that might help her land Evergreen, but the truth was, she wanted to know what had happened after they'd left.

"Ricco," Esmeralda softly said.

He was having none of it. It burned the hell out of him that his sisters would swarm around their father and his mother would cuff him for speaking out, and after all he had done! Or in Enrique Maza's case, *not* done!

He put his hand up. "Do not mention his name in my presence."

"He's dying, Ricco."

His gut jumped, but the shock and the very fleeting feeling of regret were hammered down by his anger. "Good riddance."

"How can you say that? *He's our father!*"

Ricco set his fists down on the table across from her and slowly said, "He's a fucking sperm donor, Ez. Accept that fact. He doesn't give two shits about anyone but himself. Why the hell do you think it was so damn easy for him to walk away time after time? Hell, he was gone almost ten years during one stint! He's here because he wants something. And if you all are so blind to him, then you live with the fallout. But leave me out of it!"

"Ricco!" Esmeralda cried, reaching for her brother.

He jerked his arm away from her. "He's a shitty

husband, a shitty father, and a shitty man, and I can't for the life of me understand why the hell we're even having this conversation."

"I want us to be a family, Ricco, for once!"

"He made the choice for us a long time ago, Esmeralda. Our family exists without him."

He strode past her to the hallway and looked up the stairs to see Kim frozen in her tracks. His anger soared. "Did you get all of that, Miss Michaels? My father is a drunk and a deadbeat dad, and I can't stand the thought of him. My sisters and mother think he's some saint come home." He moved up the stairway and stopped beside her. "Are you happy now? Evergreen isn't so perfect after all." He moved past her then, to his room, where he slammed the heavy door shut. He shucked his clothes and put on his sweats and running shoes. He needed to get away. He felt like he was being slowly strangled. His mother, his sisters, his nieces and nephews. They all wanted a piece of him, and it seemed the more he gave, the more they wanted, and if he continued to let them, there would be nothing left for himself.

As often happened when he felt the yoke of emotional encumbrances tighten around his neck, Ricco bolted.

An hour into his run he still felt the yoke around his neck. Anger, resentment, and hatred boiled in his heart, and the angrier he became with his sisters and his mother for even talking to the prick, much less welcoming him back with open arms, the angrier he became with the man who had in Ricco's mind been nothing but a sperm donor. He hated the fact that he shared the same blood, the same DNA, and the same looks as Enrique Maza. He classified the man in the same genre as the scumbags he arrested. Ricco picked up his pace. There was no way on this earth or in his lifetime that Ricco would ever accept the man on any level except for the piece of shit he was.

As he hit the north end of town for the fifth time, Ricco took solace in the fact that in a couple of weeks he'd be back on the streets in Montrose, where he faced his enemy head-on and the only emotional entanglements he'd be forced to face were those of victims. And even then he could turn himself off. While he was empathetic to their feelings, he was rarely sucked in. Too many times they'd turned on him, especially the women who'd been abused by their boyfriends or spouses. He'd shown up to many a call from a battered woman, only to be attacked by her when he hooked up the piece of crap who used her for a punching bag. He shook his head and kept running—from what, he wasn't sure—but he didn't look over his shoulder to find out. Instead he kept his eyes focused ahead and ran.

Nine

FROM HER WINDOW, KIM WATCHED RICCO RUN AWAY FROM
the inn as if the bulls of Pamplona were breathing fire down
his back. He was a paradox to her. On the one hand, he
seemed to dote on his family. He was so loving and warm
with his mother, his sisters, his nieces, and nephews, but
when they wanted more from him, he resisted. And boy,
did they want from him. All of the men in the family were
gone. Ricco was here, and they expected him to step up
and fill each pair of shoes. That was asking a lot. She could
totally understand why he only came up once a year.

She nodded to herself. She could relate. Sort of. It
wasn't like she had ever had anyone who'd wanted
something from her. Except her parents' money. In
college there had been guys who, when they'd learned

who her parents were, had wanted to get all up on her. But they'd never really wanted it bad enough to stick around. Ken, her first husband, was a prime example. So was Giorgio, her rebound husband.

It didn't bother her that her parents never expected any emotional interaction from her. If she was honest, neither did she. It made life real easy. It was why she'd agreed to marry Nick. He couldn't hurt her.

So maybe she and Ricco weren't all that much alike after all. Well, except they both wanted to keep free of the type of encumbrances that required an emotional commitment. It was, she supposed, why he liked to come home for a few weeks a year. He could get his fill, then leave.

Since it wasn't too late, Kim decided to give Nick an update call. She didn't want to do it from the inn phone, however, so she slipped her jacket back on and went out front to catch a signal. She scowled. One bar. She moved down the street a bit and picked up another one. A little farther and she picked up three. That would do. As she pressed the speed dial, she found herself wishing she didn't have to speak with him. His curt manner was beginning to really annoy her.

"Gold."

"You know damn well it's me, why do you have to answer like that?"

"Are you PMSing or something?"

"What the hell is that supposed to mean?"

"Since you landed in Reno you've been bitchy."

"I thought that's what you loved about me."

"What I admire about you is the fact that you don't allow your emotions to get involved. Can you keep it that way?"

"You know what, *Gold*? Maybe you can find yourself another boardroom and bedroom partner."

"Kimberly, what's *wrong* with you?"

"Nothing, I just think you're rude."

"Would it make you feel better if I told you I miss you?"

"Maybe."

"And that I'm looking forward to your return?"

"Really?"

"Really."

Kim smiled and felt some of her aggression ease. "This place is ripe for a takeover."

"Talk dirty to me, baby."

Kim laughed. "As we already knew, the last five years have been fiscal busts. The weather has been a detractor. This place is nestled in the Sierras, and the snow pack has been dense. But last year they went out on a financial limb and purchased a fleet of snowplows that if manned properly can have the roads cleared in a snap. I expect by tomorrow I'll be seeing a lot of traffic. But the really interesting thing is, the city council voted last year to take out a loan against the property the city buildings are on, as well as the buildings themselves. They lent that money to the residents whose businesses have foundered. Not only that, they pulled out money for all of those prime-time television ads. I got the impression from a conversation this evening that a balloon payment is imminent."

"How much?"

"I'm not sure, but if I had to hazard a guess, I'd say in the neighborhood of a few million."

"That's chump change."

"To us, yes. To this town? It would be like cutting a main artery. I'm going to do some digging and find out who holds the notes."

"We can up the offer."

Kim walked down the street, her eyes alert. The temperature had dropped and the breeze had picked up. The streets were quiet. A coyote howled off in the distance. "I'm not sure if money is the answer here, Nick. This town is weird. The people are so nice and friendly and warm and helpful, it's freaky. Like they're Stepford people."

"As in fake?"

"No, quite the contrary. There is no crime in this town. No one locks their doors at night. I haven't seen a cop. I think they have their own little department. Probably Andy Griffith and what's that deputy? Opie?"

"No, Opie was the kid. Barney Fife."

"Well, whatever. I bet if someone broke the law around here, the town would have a party for the poor dope and forgive him so long as he promised never ever to do it again. The ladies would bring a fruitcake and hot cocoa to seal the deal."

"You're making me sick to my stomach."

"Yeah, it's pretty nauseating." Kim stiffened. She heard a woman's voice in the background, then Nick shushing her. "Where are you?" she asked him.

"My office."

That didn't surprise her. "Who's there with you?"

"Gina. We're working on the Napa deal."

Ah yes, the Beauchamp Vineyard buyout. A piece of cake. So why was Gina there? A little voice gnawed at Kim's subconscious. She ignored it. Besides, if what she suspected was really happening, was what she'd done with Ricco any different? No, it wasn't, but at least she wasn't fucking her CFO's secretary.

"Well, you two have at it. I'll call you with an update when I have more information." Kim hung up. And wanted to throw the phone into the gutter. Instead she squeezed it until her hand hurt. She turned and headed back to the inn. Her cell vibrated. She looked at the number. Nick. It occurred to her that she really didn't care what he had to say. Let him and Gina have their fun. When she and Nick were married, the bodacious little brunette was history.

She could deal with Nick's affairs, but she would be damned if he was going to be boinking the secretary under Kim's nose and having everyone at Land's Edge knowing about it. He told *her* discreet? She expected the same from him. And with that, Kim's thoughts turned to the man who would be sleeping just across the hall from her. Her body warmed, and her breasts swelled. She wanted him. She wanted another night like the night in Reno. She wanted to fall asleep on that wide, muscular chest and wake up there. She wanted him to take her over and over, and speak those sexy Spanish words to her and make her feel as special as Cinderella.

When she entered the quietness of the inn she knew instinctively that Ricco was not back. She also knew he'd be gone for hours. He was in excellent shape, and she bet he could run a marathon no sweat. Her bed had been turned down, and a low fire burned in the stone fireplace, warming the room and giving it a soft glow. She liked it. Taking her time, Kim washed her face, cleaning up the sink as she finished. Then she slipped on a pair of hip-hugger flannel pj's with a cropped flannel top. She made sure all of her clothes were neatly in their place and the bathroom was tidy, the soiled towels in the hamper, nothing out of place. Okay, so she had some OCD going on. Big deal. It was a godsend, with her business. Had she not been so organized and ready to jump at any given scenario, she would not have been where she was. She liked things neat and orderly. And to be in complete control. Otherwise her life was left to the whims of others.

Before sliding beneath the soft comforter, she glanced around the room to find everything in its place. She let out a long breath and slid beneath the soft downy comforter. It had been quite a day, and she was tired. Closing her eyes, she let her mind go blank. Soon she drifted off to sleep.

She didn't know what woke her, but she instinctively knew someone was upstairs. For several minutes Kim listened to the sounds of the house and the low crackle of the fire. Off in the distance, the mournful howls of coyotes drifted across the lake into the little town of Evergreen. There was no traffic, no industry sounds, just the soft lulling sound of nature.

A creaking floorboard outside her door alerted her to a presence. If she'd been anyplace else on earth, she would have been on high alert—afraid, wondering who was outside her door and if they had any nefarious intentions. But not here. Kim knew who was standing outside her door. She wanted to call to him to open the door, to come in, to take her to that place he'd taken her to the night before. But she lay still until she heard the soft click of his door shutting. In the quiet of the house she heard the far-off sound of water running. She smiled. He was in the shower.

Her smile broadened as she thought of how shocked he would look if she slipped in with him and worked him into a lather.

The water stopped. Her heart thudded against her chest. And suddenly she wasn't tired. Kim slipped from the bed and walked to her door. Before she could change her mind, she opened it and stepped across the hall to the Dasher suite. Perfect moniker. She knocked.

When the door opened, she caught her breath. Ricco stood tall, wet, and naked save for the towel wrapped around his waist. He didn't seem surprised to see her. He smiled a smug little half smile and stepped back from the door, giving her complete access. She glared up at him. Damn him! Was she that predictable? Or did every woman he'd encountered come to his room looking for some love? She shook her head. She didn't want love, she wanted to shoot to the stars again. But that wasn't why she was standing there. She held out her hand, palm up. "I'd like my locket back."

He grinned wide. "That couldn't wait until tomorrow?"

Maybe it could, but she was feeling lonely too. She put her hands on her hips and just slightly thrust her chest his way. She knew she looked good. She had the body of a twenty-year-old, and firm boobs. Big firm ones. Ricco's gaze traveled down her body and back up to her face. "You know you're playing with fire, don't you?"

Kim smiled and leaned against the doorjamb. "Well, be careful, cowboy, or you'll get burned."

Ricco threw his head back and laughed. "Come in, the draft is cold."

Hesitantly she entered. His room was a replica of hers, except his had more of a hunting theme. And whereas she was neat and orderly, Ricco was . . . not. His duffel bag sat gaping open on the floor near the armoire. Clothes were hanging out, as if he had been digging for something to wear. She had neatly hung her clothes and refolded her other things painstakingly into the bottom drawers. His bed was mussed, and she . . . stopped before she got into trouble. And looked up, and away from Ricco. Several trophy heads adorned the walls. An eight-point buck and a doe on one wall, a trout and a bass on the other. A large deerskin adorned another wall. The fire in the corner burned bright, and Ricco's bed was as big and comfy-looking as hers. His eyes followed hers to it. "Why are you here?" he asked. His voice was lower, if that was possible. The timbre had shifted. To . . . predatory. The damp towel rode low around his waist, and Kim found herself wanting him to drop it and get dirty with her. She'd never considered the male body all that spectacular, but Ricco changed all of that. He was tall, muscled, and perfectly proportioned.

She swallowed and said, "I told you, my locket."

Squatting in front of the fireplace Ricco tossed a few

small logs onto it. The muscles in his back flexed with the movement, and the fabric of the towel clung to his ass, outlining in great detail what was beneath. Her blood began to warm and her mouth was dry. "How many women have you slept with?" she blurted out. She bit her bottom lip regretting the outburst.

Ricco looked over his shoulder, and the devil could not have looked more sinful. "I have no idea. How many have *you* slept with?"

"Women?" she squeaked.

He grinned wider and stood facing her. Lord help her, but her eyes dipped, and what she saw made her catch her breath. He was aroused. He stepped toward her. She stepped back. "Yes, women," he whispered as he continued to move toward her. She swallowed again and felt the hard wooden plank of the door against her back.

"I, never, uh—none."

"Men?"

She could count them on one hand. Two had been her husbands; two had been short-term relationships, and the last one, her recent and only one-night stand.

"Enough."

"Enough to what?" He pressed closer to her. He slid his right hand along her neck, his fingertips barely touching her skin, before sinking deep into her hair. Cupping the back of her head in his big hand, he pulled her up toward him. His lips hovered over hers. Her body trembled and her breasts were suddenly heavy.

Their gazes held. His, dark and fiery; hers, she could only imagine. Heat flushed across her chest, and Kim knew it was splotchy. "Enough to be enough." She licked her dry lips. His dipped down to her cheek, and he softly brushed his lips across her skin.

"What do you want?" he softly demanded.

Before she could answer, his lips traveled lower, to the curve of her jaw, then lower, to her neck. He kissed her there, his teeth lightly raking across her jugular. She arched into him, hissing in a breath. His other hand slid up her arm to her neck, and he pressed his chest against her aching nipples. Kim closed her eyes and melted. Her body went liquid. Warm and wet, she flushed for him.

RICCO'S HEAD SPUN WITH THE HEADY SCENT OF HER. Some exotic scent mingled with her own natural scent promised a wild and wanton ride. It's what had attracted him to her in the first place. She'd walked past him in a crowed hallway at the Legacy, and when he'd seen her later that night, he'd been drawn back to her like a hummingbird to nectar. He hadn't been able to help himself then, and he couldn't help himself now. He wanted nothing more than to take her to his bed and sink into her warm, wet voluptuousness.

"You smell very fuckable, Miss Michaels," he murmured. As he said the words, his dick filled to capacity. She moaned and arched against him. He could feel the wild beating of her heart against his chest and the delicate tremble of her limbs. His lips trailed down her neck to the curve where it met her collarbone. He nibbled the ridge there. He let his right hand slip from her hair to her shoulder, then to her breasts.

She moaned again and rolled her head back against the door, pressing her chest into his hand. She had great tits. Big, and full, with rosy nipples that plumpened, begging for his attention. He had no idea how many women he'd made love to over the years—he wasn't one to keep count. What he cared about at that moment was the woman in his arms and how she made him so hard he ached.

Kim pressed her hands against his bare chest and pushed him slightly away. Her sapphire-colored eyes had deepened to almost black in her passion. He grinned. Even in the firelight he could see the red splotches that covered her chest. He'd noticed it before, and for some reason, for all of her little control issues and bluster, the splotches made her more vulnerable to him. He traced a finger across the swell of her breast, where there was a bright red blotch. "Do you always get polka dots when you're aroused?" She smacked his hand away, but she didn't move away from him.

Indeed—those full, pouty lips of hers turned up into a slow, sexy smile. "Keep looking at me like that and your entire body will go up in flames." The heat from his body, combined with the dampness of the towel around his waist, which was coming dangerously close to falling off, sweltered up the air, thickening it around them. He pressed his hard-on against her belly. "You're saying pass go and collect two hundred dollars with those big blues eyes, Cinderella . . ."

She leaned into him. "I haven't decided if it's emotional suicide to get into that bed of yours again or carnal suicide not to."

Ricco grinned and his blood quickened. He moved his hands down her body to her waist, then slid his hands down between her flannel pj's and warm skin. Her body moved beneath his hands, giving its own permission to proceed. Slowly he pushed them down her thighs. Kim's eyes widened, and he saw the rush of heat behind them. Her bottom lip trembled and he could not resist tasting it. He kissed her, his lips sipping her first. Then, feeling her body respond, he pressed more intimately into her. His tongue swirled across her lips, his hands pressed into her skin, and her tits drilled into his chest. He was swept away in her sweet, hot response to him. He wanted to taste all of her. She was sweet and musky, and, like a bee, he wanted more of her honey. "Cinderella, I promise not to turn into a pumpkin," he whispered against her lips. He felt her entire body loosen.

"No strings?" she breathed, her warm breath caressing his cheek.

"No strings," he answered, wondering if he could keep that promise.

"No awkward good-byes?"

"No awkward good-byes."

"I'm leaving in a week," she whispered.

His dick flexed. "I can do a lot of damage to this sweet body of yours in a week." He nipped at her bottom lip and said, "I'm leaving in three weeks if you decide to come back for more."

"Okay," she breathed.

"Okay," he repeated.

He slid his hand farther down her belly. Her hips rocked softly against him. "Jesus, Kim," he hoarsely said. She was so soft, and so warm, her skin like pure silk. His fingertips brushed across her soft downy mound, where heat sweltered from her body like a furnace. He wanted to push her pants down to her ankles, to get down on his knees and take her into his mouth. He wanted her to come against his lips, in his hand. He wanted to sink so deep into her that he would be lost forever.

With only a week to savor this work of art, Ricco followed his thoughts. He dropped down to his knees pulling her pajamas with him. She hissed in a breath. "What are you doing?" she rasped, her voice throaty and full of desire. Her thighs trembled. He parted them at her knees. Using one hand to steady her, he used his other to spread her full, luscious lips.

"I'm going to have my dessert," he said against her flaming skin.

THE SOFT PERCUSSION OF HIS WORDS CARESSED HER full lips as effectively as if he had touched her. Kim closed her eyes and let herself go. Ricco's tongue slid across her sensitive nub, and she nearly swooned. Her knees shook, and had he not held her, she would have tumbled to the floor. She dug her fingers deep into his thick hair. It was still damp from his shower. "Ricco," she breathed, barely able to speak. His lips brushed against her mound, and his thumb traced slow, agonizing circles around her creamy clit. Her chest rose and fell swiftly as she tried to catch her breath. Her excitement, her anticipation of what he could do to her nearly suffocated her. "Go slow, and—" She cried out and undulated hotly against him. He slid a thick finger into her and at the same time, took her clit into his mouth and gently suckled her. Kim knew at that instant she was going to die of sensory overload right then and there. Digging her fingers into his hair, she pressed his head against her. His finger slowly slid in and out of her, and each time he slid deep into her, he tapped that sweet spot that made her come undone.

Kim pressed her back hard against the wooden door, afraid that if she didn't, she'd crumble to the floor. Her hips rocked in slow, deliberate unison with Ricco's voracious mouth and expert hand. It amazed her how her body went on instant alert. It was as if it knew what was going to happen and was preparing itself for the event. Her skin was hot, her blood thick, infusing her nerve endings. Every sense was on heightened alert. Ignited and ready to burn. She felt the orgasm build from deep inside of her. She felt the flash, then the catch. As a fire would with a rush of hot air, the waves built at a frenzied pace.

The sensory overload of him in her and around her was almost too much for her to bear. A hard sob lodged deep in her throat. The crest rose, and the sluicing sound of her juices as she drenched his hand and his mouth was so carnally sensual that it embarrassed her. But she didn't care. All that mattered to her right at that exact moment in time was Ricco and her G spot. The wave crashed, it slammed, it destroyed everything in its wake before receding, only to come back and crash again, and again, and again.

Kim cried out and her hips undulated wildly, Ricco's hand and mouth expertly riding out her orgasm. She gulped for air. In a wild, wanton gesture, Ricco pulled her down to him, his mouth glistening with her on it, and kissed her.

"See how good you taste?" he said, then licked the inside of her mouth, giving her more of herself. He twisted her around and pressed her into the thick alpaca rug. His towel had come loose and she dug her nails into his ass. He growled and nipped at her bottom lip. "I hope you have another one of these," he said, then ripped her flannel top down the front, exposing her breasts to the simmering air. A wild, wanton abandon overcame her, and she felt truly free of herself. She could, she decided, take all of him for as long as he was willing to give her this next week. And hope that it would be enough to carry her through the rest of her life. She stiffened as a fleeting thought of the life she had chosen sprang up into her mind. She shoved it away. She would live now in this moment for as long as she could.

He must have sensed her hesitation. Ricco moved slightly up from her, his dark eyes searching her face. "What's wrong, princess? Having second thoughts?"

She swallowed hard. No one had ever called her princess, let alone any other endearment. Ricco had a way of making her feel special, as if no other woman existed for him. Her chest swelled, and in a sudden realization, she knew that if she wasn't careful, she might be the one who would break the rules.

His dark eyes held hers, fire burning hot in them, as

he waited for her to give him the signal to continue. His erection was thick and hard against her thigh. Only his towel separated her from him. He lowered his lips to the tip of her nose and lightly kissed it. "I'm about to explode, sweetheart."

She closed her eyes and relaxed back into the soft fur. Ricco did not spare a millisecond. His hot mouth ravaged one hardened peak, then the other, and his hips pressed hotly into her. She opened up for him, her skin and body burning as hot as the flames in the fireplace eating up the dry logs.

With his foot he slid her pajama pants farther down her legs. Warm air rushed between her legs, then his hand brushed across her hot mound. She arched into him, her back coming off the floor, her breasts spearing into the air. "Ricco," she begged, "take me there."

He slid his arm around her waist and pulled her up toward him. As he did, he moved against her, the wide tip of his penis pressing her slick folds for entry. "Princess, I don't have a condom."

Kim squeezed her eyes shut and wanted to scream. "I-I don't either!" He pressed his forehead against hers and softly chuckled. "It's not funny!" she cried. "Why don't you have one?"

He pressed her back onto the thick fur. "If my memory serves me correctly, I used up my stash on some nymph in Reno the other night."

Heat flushed her chest. She reached down to him and nearly recoiled at his hard heat. "My God, Ricco. Does that hurt?"

He pressed into her hand. "Like a mother. Make it go away."

Kimberly smiled, and for the first time in her life, she felt sexually confident. This man had a raging hard-on, not for what her parents could do for him but because she turned him on.

Releasing him, she twisted out from underneath him and pressed her hands to his chest, pushing him back into the fur rug. Her body followed his, leaning full against him. Her lips reached for his and he pulled her down to him, encircling her with his long arms. The heat of the fire scorched their skin, but neither one minded. Indeed, their own fire was hotter. Her hand slid down his hard belly to his full cock. He was thick and full and hard as stone. She so desperately wanted him inside of her.

Kim wiggled against him, brushing her swollen, moist folds against the fleshy tip. Ricco hissed in a breath. "Kim—"

"I just want to feel you for a minute. Just—" She pressed herself against him, and when he entered her, they both went rigid, sucking in a deep breath. Kim moaned and moved ever so slightly against him. He filled her another inch. She closed her eyes when he grabbed her hips and squeezed, preventing her from impaling him farther. But he couldn't help himself either, and his hips pressed up and he moved another inch deeper.

They froze, suspended like that, connected as one, wanting more, desperate to be as fully connected as two humans could be. Him only inches inside of her, her liquid muscles clamped like silken vises around his throbbing shaft. Just as she thought she had overcome the initial rush of an orgasm, it rushed up, blindsiding her. Her body jerked, as if she had been struck head-on by a truck. She cried out, overcome with such intense sensation that she nearly crashed against him. Impaled only by half of him, she jerked and writhed on him. Ricco cursed, his fingers digging deep into her skin, holding her back from impaling him more fully. His hips jerked as she writhed against him, and she knew he was at his limit.

He pushed her off of him and in one fell movement rolled over onto her, his hips thrusting against her belly. Then he came all over her. To her utter astonishment, she didn't mind. In fact, the opposite was true. She looked down at his glistening seed pooling on her flat belly and into her belly button and smiled. Now that was a testament to the man's self-control.

He rolled onto his back next to her, his great chest rising and falling as quickly as hers. Long moments passed before they caught their breath. Ricco rolled over, took his towel, and wiped her belly clean. "Jesus, Kim, next time I might not be able to hold back."

She rolled over and up on an elbow and smiled at him. In the firelight, his bronze body glowed like a Spartan warrior's. "I'm sorry, that was pretty selfish of me." He grinned up at her and pulled her down to cuddle against his chest. She resisted. Too intimate.

He pulled back and looked at her. "Are you going to disappear now?"

"No, I just—"

"Just what? After that, you can't stay here for a few minutes?"

She moved back and shook her head, wanting separation. Wanting it, because if she had a choice, she'd climb in bed with him and fall asleep with her head on his shoulder. And that was not going to happen. Sex was one thing. Anything postcoital was not an option.

She stood and hurried to pull her pj's back on. Ricco stood as well. He grabbed a pair of shorts from his duffel bag.

She pulled the shredded pajama top on, trying to cover her breasts. It was useless. As she moved to the door, he said, "Answer one question for me."

Kim hesitated with her hand on the knob. "Maybe."

"Why do you run away?"

She opened her mouth to tell him she wasn't running

away. She was . . . just leaving. "I don't know," she honestly said, then hurried from his room before he could ask her more uncomfortable questions.

RICCO STOOD FOR A LONG TIME STARING AT THE DOOR, wondering at the woman who'd managed in just two days to make him question his own behavior. Something about her pulled at him—an underlying vulnerability she tried to hide but he saw as clearly as if she'd been waving a billboard banner. She had deep emotional scars, and he found himself wanting to unlock the wild woman that he knew only revealed herself in the throes of passion. She was like a child with a new toy. For crying out loud, she admitted she'd married twice. Were her ex-husbands idiots? She was a passionate woman who walked around like an ice cube, keeping the world at bay.

His dick twinged. "Down, boy. You'll get another turn." He hoped.

Suddenly feeling hungry, Ricco slipped his flannel pajama bottoms on. Taking the stairs three at a time, he trucked into the kitchen and raided the refrigerator. As he sat down to a mixing-bowl size of Cap'n Crunch, the back door opened and a haggard Esmeralda stepped through.

"What are you doing up so late?" Ricco asked, his earlier anger at her gone. She set the baby monitor down on the butcher block island and turned to him.

"I couldn't sleep."

He could see the glint of tears in her eyes. He started to stand, but something—pride maybe, or maybe it was hurt feelings—stopped him. He wasn't going to play both sides. If it came down to a choice, then by God she'd make it. And if it were his old man? Ricco pushed the full bowl away, suddenly not so hungry. He couldn't bear it if one of his sisters chose the bastard over him.

"You have a big day tomorrow. You better take something."

"I can't, not with the baby."

He eyed the Cap'n Crunch with Crunch Berries. It had been his first and favorite cereal. He pulled the bowl back toward him and spooned a big bite. As he chewed, he nodded. Esmeralda walked toward him and stopped two feet away. Her eyes brimmed with tears. He shook his head, set his spoon down, and stood up. As he opened his arms, she moved into him and broke down. For a long time he just held her and let her cry. If it had been anyone other than his sister, he would have hightailed it out of the room, but he'd spent his life cleaning up their emotional messes. Because it had never been directed at him, he'd been able to handle it.

After several more minutes, her sobs trailed off. He smoothed her long hair from her face and kissed the top of her head. "I love you, Ez, you know that. Let's not fight over him anymore, okay?"

She looked up, and fresh tears sprung up. "Uh-uh, no more tears. He's not worth it. Go back to bed." He kissed the top of her head again, turned her, and gently pushed her toward the door. When it shut behind her, he sat back down and ate his soggy Cap'n Crunch with Crunch Berries and thought of ways he could discreetly get his old man to leave town and never come back. Maybe he should pay him off? But he'd be back for more. Nah, he'd have to stand his ground and let the old man hang himself a final time. He'd stand back and pick the pieces of his family back up, as he had done too many times before. And he would tell them that there would be no more next times.

Ten

Kim didn't bother changing. As she had at the Legacy, she kept Ricco's scent close. On its own, it was potent. Mixed with her scent, then adding their sex, it was heady stuff. Each time she inhaled, he encompassed her, and she felt like he was right there beside her. Her body was still rosy and plump from his lovemaking. She pressed her hand down her belly, then between her legs. She flinched. Still warm and moist.

It was not over with Ricco Maza.

She bit her lip and lay back into the cold sheets. What the hell had she just done? Fantasizing about an affair with Ricco was one thing, but actually doing it was another thing entirely. When she'd gone across the hall, she'd really just wanted her locket. Okay, and maybe a little company. But she'd had no intention of any contact. Maybe some conversation or something, but not sex!

She groaned and pummeled the pillows. What was wrong with her? Was she addicted to sex now? Was she like every other woman in the world who'd gotten a taste of Ricco Maza? Wanting more. And some more after that? Good Lord, she was as doomed as the rest of them. No moss grew on that rolling stone.

Something vital had changed in her over the last forty-eight hours. She wasn't sure what it was, or how it would affect her from here on out. She just knew that what had been acceptable to her two days ago no longer was. And it wasn't about Nick, she realized. Screw him. The way she was feeling, she didn't want what he was offering. Not when she knew what it could be like.

Shit! Was she going through a midlife crisis? Was she losing her edge? How the hell long was this going to last? Did she need to buy a red sports car and indulge in whatever caught her fancy?

No, that wasn't her. She was Kimberly Ann Michaels. She wore Chanel and Yves St. Laurent and drove a classic 600 SL. She smiled. But she also wore red Jimmy Choos and recently discovered she liked hot, messy, no-holds-barred sex. She rolled over and sat up in the bed.

Yeah. She liked hot, sweaty sex. A lot. And she was going to have some more of it. And she was going to get it out of her system before she left this town. It was, she decided, just a chemical reaction to a man. She'd never thought it was possible for her, but she couldn't argue the facts. And the plain fact was she and Ricco had an attraction that was, at its very least, basic carnal. Anything more was not an option. He was Casanova and Don Juan rolled into one. She was and always would be a one-man woman. Anything other than sex with no rules with Ricco was an emotional train wreck waiting to happen. And she did not do emotions. But she apparently did great sex.

Kim closed her eyes. *Oh my God.* Her body sizzled as she relived the moment she'd writhed against Ricco and he'd held her hips from impaling him more. The pure eroticism of having but not having had driven her insane. It had been the same for him. Most men would not have had the self-control he did. He must really not want kids. She cooled. Neither did she. Until last month, she hadn't even been on the pill, since she had been a monk for the last few years. The only reason she was at the moment was that she wasn't sure if somehow she and Nick would end up in bed. She didn't want to take any chances. The last thing she wanted was a child. The thought terrified her.

Kim snuggled deeper into the covers and closed her eyes. Instead of sticky-fingered, poopy-diaper-smelling kids, Kim thought of the man across the hall and let his lingering scent rock her gently to sleep. More than a few times she woke in a sweat, gasping for breath, dreaming of his body doing naughty things to hers.

LIKE A WELL-FED CAT, KIM YAWNED AND STRETCHED under the smooth warmth of the flannel sheets. She smiled before she opened her eyes. Her first thought was of big warm hands stroking her. She rolled over and pressed into the mattress. The morning sounds slowly infiltrated her sex-infused dreams: the slow sound of traffic, the dull drone of water running off in the distance. She turned to face the window; since it caught the western sun, she wasn't blinded by the morning sunlight. She slid from the bed and meandered over to the window. The small town glowed like a Swarovski crystal beneath the bright morning sunshine. It was a glorious morning. She stretched and smiled, her body warming. She couldn't wait to see Ricco. She should have realized then she was in trouble, but she had always managed to control herself. *And*, she told herself, she was in the driver's seat with the Latin playboy, not the other way around.

Excitement thrummed through her veins. She wanted to see Ricco again. She wanted him to touch her. She wanted to touch him, smell him, feel his long, muscled body against hers. Like last night in the ice rink. Yeah, she liked the anticipation of him—not just the sex, but him as an individual.

She was also excited to get out on the town and get her own unbiased opinion of it.

Quickly she showered and dressed. Grabbing her purse, she headed downstairs. The minute she opened the door to the hallway, voices assailed her from downstairs. Esmeralda's friendly voice rose above the din, and every so often she heard Ricco's deep, throaty voice. She walked downstairs and literally ran into a crowd of people, all of them with luggage, in the salon.

Kim caught Esmeralda's excited eyes across the room. Esmeralda smiled. Kim smiled in return. Behind her, her brother looked up from the phone in his hand, and he smiled too. Heat rushed into Kim's cheeks. Her smile widened. Esmeralda looked from Kim and turned around to find her brother grinning like an idiot. She looked back at Kim and scowled. It was easy enough to put two and two together.

Ricco bent back to the telephone and gave the person on the other end directions. After he hung up, he grabbed two suitcases beside the couple in front of him. "Mr. and Mrs. Schafir, right this way." He walked past her, brushing his elbow against her breast in the process. The contact nearly toppled her. Kim held her breath and looked up to find Ezzy's knowing eyes watching. Kim was glad for the conversation and the activity; she could hide in it. She watched Esmeralda manage the hordes, calmly checking them in.

Ricco came down and took the next couple up, along with their luggage. In the corner behind Esmeralda, Kim heard the whimper of a baby. Krista? Esmeralda smiled at the older couple she was checking in. Krista's wails were clearly beginning to grate on everyone's nerves. Esmeralda excused herself and tried shushing her with her binkie, but the baby was having none of it. Ricco was off on an errand, and Esmeralda seemed for the moment to look a bit desperate. She walked toward Kim with the baby. Kim looked behind her to see who Ez was looking at, but she saw no one. When she turned back around, Ez grabbed Kim's purse and tossed it behind the desk. Just as Kim was about to tell her to be careful with her three-thousand-dollar bag, Ez thrust the screaming kid in her arms. "Kim, I need you to take her into the kitchen or up to your room and rock her. Just keep an eye on her for a few minutes until I get everyone checked in."

Kim's heartbeat jumped to a marathon pace. She stepped back, shaking her head, putting her hands behind her back. "Uh, no, sorry, Ez, I don't do babies."

Ez grabbed Kim's right arm, brought it around, and thrust the screaming Krista against her. Then she grabbed her left arm and wrapped it around the baby's back. "Five minutes," she said, then walked back to the waiting throng.

Kim held the baby out at arm's length. Krista screamed

louder, her face turning fire-engine red. When it seemed the rug rat's lungs were filled to capacity and no sound came forth, Kim panicked. She carefully jiggled the baby. It gasped for breath, and Kim watched, horrified, sure she was going to self-suffocate. Then Krista let out another shrill scream and Kim about dropped her. Her hands shook and panic overcame her. What the hell was she supposed to do with it? "Rock her," Ezzy calmly said from across the room. Horrified, Kim looked up with the baby still at arm's length, as if she'd had a case of kiddy cooties, and walked gingerly down the hall to the kitchen. Screw the rocking chair. There had to be a kid seat somewhere where she could set it down. Frantically she looked around, but she found nothing suitable for a screaming, slobbering baby. And there was no rocking chair. *As if.*

"Shush, Krista, shush now," Kim pleaded. It seemed to only infuriate the baby more. When the back door opened and Ricco walked in, Kim hurried toward him with the baby in her outstretched hands. "Take this kid!"

Ricco put up his hands. They were full of dirt and wood chips. "No can do."

"But I don't know what to do," Kim cried, panic and fear closing in on her.

He moved past her to a door. He opened it and pulled out a bentwood rocker. He pushed it toward her with his boot, then said over his shoulder as he strode past her, "She doesn't bite. Figure it out."

As Ricco moved to the front of the inn, Kim stood alone in the middle of the large kitchen, holding sixteen pounds of screaming, snotty humanity. She jiggled the baby again. She cooed at it. She attempted to sing to it. Yet it continued to cry. She sat down on the edge of the rocking chair with it still at arm's length and began to awkwardly rock. Her back was so rigid that she thought it would snap in half. That would do neither her nor the baby much good.

"Shushy, little baby," Kim tried to soothe. She looked wildly around for a bottle or a cup or *something*. It screamed louder. It was getting that deep red color again, and Kim knew Krista was going to pass out from lack of oxygen. And then what? She'd get blamed for the baby passing out? When Krista refused to settle down, Kim finally did the unthinkable. She brought it closer. And jiggled it a little. "Krista," she sternly said, "you are being a bad baby. Please stop crying."

The baby's cries lowered half an octave. Kim smiled and jiggled it some more. The baby grunted. "Okay, you don't like that. Do you like this?" Kim made a funny face. Krista stopped crying and looked cagily at her. Kim smiled, then stuck her tongue out at the baby. Krista's bottom lip trembled. "No, no don't cry again. Be a good baby."

She brought it closer, so close she could smell it. It smelled good. Sweet. Like baby powder. Not so bad. Krista grabbed a hank of Kim's hair and put it in her mouth. "No, no, don't eat hair. You'll get a fur ball. Then you'll have to go to the vet, and drink cod-liver oil, and that's never fun."

She brought the baby closer, so that now she was pressed to her chest. Krista reached out a wobbly hand to the fur fringe of Kim's three-hundred-dollar sweater and tried to eat it. "No, that's fur. Remember no fur balls?"

Krista yawned. In a move that stunned Kimberly to silence, Krista rested her little blond head on the rise of Kim's left boob. Kim smiled and looked down at the little face. Her big blue trusting eyes looked up at Kim and smiled. Kim swallowed hard. How . . . sweet. The baby's eyelids fluttered, and she stuck her fist in her mouth and started to suck. Instinctively Kim found herself rocking slowly back and forth. She brushed the baby's hair from her cheek and inhaled the sweet scent of her. This wasn't so bad. Krista grabbed more of Kim's hair with her other hand, as if it had been a security blanket. Kim didn't pull it away. Instead she softly cooed and sang a soft lullaby. When Krista's little breaths came slow and even and Kim knew she was asleep, she couldn't resist kissing the shiny golden head. She turned slightly in the chair, adjusting her body more agreeably to the baby, happy with herself for mastering the baby test. She stopped short when her eyes caught and held dark brown ones. A funny look crossed Ricco's face before he smiled and extended his arms to Kim to take the baby. She backed up in the chair and shook her head. "Go get your own baby," she said. He smiled and that look crossed his face again, but he moved past her and out the back door.

Kim continued to rock the baby, who continued to sleep soundly. As she looked down at the angelic face, Kim smiled. It amazed her that this little piece of humanity trusted her. The innocence of a child. Kim sat back and closed her eyes. It seemed a lifetime ago when she'd been innocent of anything. Everything she did, she did with purpose, and in many cases she didn't care who or what was in her way. If she wanted something, she simply set about a way of acquiring it. She was able to sleep at night because she honestly believed that money made people happy. She had yet to meet a single happy poor person.

Land's Edge was padded and willing to pay a fair sum for property it coveted. And Nick coveted Evergreen. The setting was perfect for the super resort casino he wanted to put in. He'd been working with several local tribes and had hammered out a highly profitable management contract. The locals would get their cut, but Land's Edge would come up smelling like a rose. She wanted to get out over by the lake and see where they could clear forest for helipads. There was no way they could get even small aircraft in here. The approach from the Sierras was too steep. But passenger choppers? Flying out of the Bay Area, Sacramento, and even Reno would be a snap.

Yes, Evergreen had promise, and Kim was going to bag it and hang it up on her trophy wall, just like one of those dead deer heads on Ricco's bedroom wall. The baby shifted, and suddenly she smelled something that wasn't baby powder. "Oh, gross."

Lucky for all parties involved, Esmeralda bustled into the kitchen just in time. She plunked Kim's Chanel bag down on the table, and Kim happily handed her the little stinker. "She needs her pants changed."

Esmeralda smiled and took the sleeping child. "Thank you, but I sent Ricco back to get her. What happened?"

Kim shrugged. "I had it covered. He took off a while ago."

Ez's brows wrinkled, then she smiled. "Oh, it's his turn at the North Pole."

"North Pole?"

"Yes, Santa's Workshop and all that up at the pavilion. The kids from the Truckee Detention Center come up every year."

"Detention center as in juvy?"

Krista stirred in her mother's arms, and she was starting to smell pretty ripe. "Yes, it's really sad actually. These kids are young, eight to twelve, and they have the souls of old men and women."

"Then why haul them up here for something they know is fake?"

"Because if we touch just one with the spirit of Christmas, then it's a success."

Kim rolled her eyes. "Give the kids some candy and an iPod and they'll be happy."

Esmeralda cocked her head and rearranged Krista in her arms. The baby was wide awake now and sucking her fist, staring at Kim. At least she wasn't crying. "For some that works, but kindness and a little time do too."

Kim grabbed her purse from the table, moved toward the back door, and said, "It might here, but not where I come from." She forced a smile. "I don't mean to come across as cavalier, but in my world, it's every girl for herself. No one looks after you better than you do."

Esmeralda smiled serenely. Kim didn't trust it. It was one of those I-know-something-you-don't-know kind of smiles, but Kim wasn't going to argue that Ez didn't know how it was in the *real* world. She lived in this Christmas globe. Nothing got in and nothing got out. "I'll see you later—I'm going to head out and play tourist," Kim said instead.

Ez smiled and opened her mouth to say something else but decided against it. Hand on the doorknob, Kim put her other hand on her hip and cocked a brow. She might as well hear the speech now so that next time, she could remind the innkeeper she'd already heard it. "What?" Kim asked.

"Thank you for taking care of Krista."

"That's not what you were going to say," Kim replied. Esmeralda's cheeks flushed. And Kim understood. "If you're going to give me fair warning about your brother, you're too late. We're both adults. I'll be gone in a week, and we'll both move on."

"Just like that?"

Kim nodded. "Just like that."

"Just sex?"

Kim laughed. "With your brother, it's just *great* sex." She laughed again, genuinely amused by the embarrassed look on Esmeralda's face. "Hey, you asked."

As she stepped through the kitchen door into the crisp winter air of Evergreen, Kim stopped on the stoop and inhaled it deep into her lungs, then slowly exhaled. She smiled, not so much at the pristine landscape surrounding her but at the conversation she'd just had. Two days ago, anyone sticking their nose into her business would have been soundly slapped. She'd always had the stay-the-hell-away-from-me look, which had always worked like a charm. People only approached her if she allowed them to approach. But innocent Stepford girl Esmeralda wasn't sophisticated enough to see her repel shields go up. Esmeralda and her family just assumed everyone looked out for everyone else. It didn't occur to them *not* to be concerned for another's well-being and then act on the concern; no doubt Esmeralda would have if Kim had allowed her to interfere. Kim scrunched her brows a little, confused. Because, well, if she was really honest with herself, the really weird thing was, Kim was okay with it. And she guessed it wasn't because Ez was trying to protect her brother—it was because Ez had genuine concern for Kim. A first. But what the sister did not understand was that Kim had perfected the art of walking away. There was no need for worry.

She shook her head and stepped down the few steps to the driveway to walk toward the center of town.

As she made her way, she allowed the cool, crisp mountain air to sink deep into her lungs. And while she wasn't quite used to the altitude, she had no complaints. The sun shone, the air was clear, and the snow glittered brilliantly beneath it. The town lay before her, a jewel in a white, puffy wonderland. She hugged herself and debated whether she should grab her jacket, but she decided against it. Her bulky mohair-and-fox trimmed sweater was enough. Besides, she'd warm up walking around.

As it seemed to be the custom of this crazy town, every person on the street smiled and said hello. To perfect strangers. After the first half dozen smiles and chipper greetings, Kim decided she'd better get with the program. This place probably had a law against those who frowned. So, when in a dorky Christmas town with Stepford people and themed shops, do as they do. Smile and act like you gave two shits about the person next to you.

She had to admit that the shops were quaint in a weird little way, and the names unique. Away in the Manger was a cute little boutique stuffed with baby and children's clothes. Next door was Jingle Bells. Kim was impressed—not easy, with her high-end taste. Not only were there imported brass, glass, and bronzed bells from all over the world but there was also inlaid crystal, porcelain, and fine bone china. Five Golden Rings, the jewelry shop next door, had stuff that would give Harry Winston and Cartier carat envy. She couldn't help stopping at Mistletoe Florals. She loved flowers; they were the one thing requiring care that she indulged in. And it wasn't like when she forgot to water the flowers they felt any pain—she just tossed the pot or dumped the vase and bought fresh.

She smiled and bent to inhale a fresh spray of evergreen and hothouse gardenias. Bright baskets of poinsettias and Christmas cactus adorned the benches out front. Bows of holly, evergreen, and pine festooned with big red velvet bows and bright shining Christmas ornaments hung from brass straps out front.

Kim popped into Figgy Pudding, the local tea shop, and smiled. The subtle aromas of baked savories swirled around her nose, beckoning her deeper inside. Hunger gnawed at her belly. She was immediately greeted by a little old lady who looked like Mrs. Claus and had the costume down pat, even to her black leather lace-up granny boots. "Good morning," Mrs. Claus chirped. "I'm Madison Studebaker. Everyone calls me Maddy."

Kim couldn't help return a smile. "I'm Kim. And it is a beautiful morning, Maddy."

"It's always a beautiful morning in Evergreen. Would you care for a spot of tea?"

"Yes, yes, I would. English breakfast, please, and a blueberry scone?"

The shopkeeper smiled, bobbed her head, and got to it. While Maddy bustled behind the half partition, brewing the tea, Kim asked, "How has business been?"

Maddy looked up from her chore and smiled a big toothy grin. The fine lines around her cheery brown eyes crinkled. She pushed back the red-and-white fabric cap on her head. "It could be better. But the Lord always provides. This season looks like a bumper crop."

"Even with the blizzard?"

"Those boys worked twenty-four-seven until the roads were cleared. The forecast is showing a few inches here and there. We laugh at a few inches."

Kim bit her bottom lip. She'd laughed at a few inches in her time as well.

A few minutes later Maddy emerged with a teapot wrapped in—you guessed it—a Christmas-themed cozy. She set it down in front of Kim, who had sat down at a small table covered with a holly-green-and-gold brocade tablecloth. The bell on the front door tinkled, and several ladies strolled in. Kim could tell by the way they were dressed and the way they looked around they were not native to the town. Maddy bustled over and introduced herself. As she was seating the group, another flock of ladies strolled in.

"Bella," Maddy called to the back of the shop. Another elderly gal—Maddy's twin—scurried out. The old lady smiled. "She's older than me by one minute," Maddy told Kim, and Kim smiled back. It occurred to her that the ache in her cheeks was from all that smiling. She rubbed them with her fingertips.

As she enjoyed her tea and blueberry scone smeared in lemon curd and clotted cream, Kim watched and listened. A half hour later, when she was ready to go, Kim opened her wallet and realized she had no cash. She'd parted with all four hundred dollars when she'd bribed the rental car guy. Kim shrugged. Plastic worked.

"Machine's on the fritz, cash only today," Maddy told Kim at the register.

Kim's cheeks warmed. How embarrassing—she couldn't spring for tea and a scone! "I seem to be out of cash at the moment. Where is the nearest ATM machine?"

Maddy patted her hand and said, "Just come on back before you leave town and pay me."

Bewildered, Kim nodded, thanked the sisters, and left the bustling shop. As she stepped back onto the wooden boardwalk, Kim stopped. Stunned, she could not believe her eyes. People crowded the promenade and the streets. Merchants and shopkeepers were out and about, hawking their wears. Santa's elves worked at several workbenches along the way, sawing, nailing, and painting children's toys. The sounds of jingle bells and Christmas carols and the aroma of pine and roasted nuts filtered through the air. People smiled, laughed, and bustled along, happy and carefree.

Amazing. Kim stood speechless for a long moment and wondered how the hell Land's Edge could stop Christmas. *In a freaking Christmas-themed town.* Because *this* town was fair to bursting with tourists, and the merchants' cash registers were cha-chinging loud and proud. Kim walked down the street toward the pavilion. A long line of children and adults hovered around. She moved closer. She could see reindeer, eight of them decked out in bright, polished-brass, jingle-bell harnesses attached to a sturdy gold-and-red wooden sleigh. In it, a very tall Santa laughed and *ho-ho*ed while telling a Christmas story to a group of enthralled children. Wide-eyed, their necks craned back, they hung on his every word.

Kim moved closer, drawn to the spellbound group. When Santa looked up, she stopped in her tracks. His dark eyes creased under his red velvet and white fur cap. He *ho-ho*ed and turned his attention back to the children, whose eyes never left his face. Kim noticed several women who stood close to him and who looked like they were about to melt. Kim moved closer, intrigued by this Santa the women had flocked to like the children. As she approached, his deep voice became clearer, and she recognized it immediately.

Ricco. Playing Santa. Her skin warmed and she had a vision of her sitting on his lap telling him all of the naughty things she wanted to do to him for Christmas. Silently Kim watched, mesmerized by his deep voice, the ease with which he told the story, and the confidence he had handling the children. They, like their mommies, who swarmed like bees around a flower, hung on his every word. Kim quietly lusted. Fantasies of him coming down her chimney and filling her stocking as she slid that suit off of him, baring that hard, sleek body of his, had her squirming where she stood. She really needed to go buy some condoms.

As Ricco finished his story, the mommies pressed upon him. He raised his head and caught her stare. He grinned and stood. Damn, he was big.

Santa's helpers, a teenaged boy and girl in elf costumes, maneuvered the mommies and their kids for pictures. Kim continued to watch in quiet amazement.

How did those women know it was Ricco? Dumb question. She'd known at twenty yards. How could she not have? His sex appeal oozed over the area like some pheromone-infused gas. At that moment Kim was grateful that she was marrying a man who did not attract women like honey attracted bees. She had a jealous streak that ran a mile wide. It was ugly and it drove her nuts. It hurt to always be wondering who your hot guy was with. And while women were attracted to his power, they didn't puddle around him. Nope. Nick was a good, solid choice. Until then, though? She smiled and caught Ricco's grin. He would do very nicely.

As she turned, a man in a dark hoodie rushed right at her. When their eyes met, he slowed to a hurried walk. Her gaze dropped to the large Louis Vuitton satchel in his hand. She had the same bag. Instinctively, she pulled her own bag closer to her side. Her eyes lifted back to his. His narrowed. Was that hostility in those dark eyes? For a moment she felt right at home. Then he slammed into her on purpose and tried to yank her purse from her. She had two hands on it, though, and yanked it back. He took off running. Kim hit the ground with a whoosh, landing flat on her back. The earth was hard, damp, and cold. Furious, she hurried to stand, when a red-and-white blur raced past her. Holy shit! Santa was after the purse snatcher! She watched Ricco charge after the guy, catch up, then tackle him. It was over in a blink. Kim, along with everyone else, ran after them. By the time she got there, Ricco had the guy in a choke hold and subdued.

What the heck? Should she call the cops? Did they *have* cops in this freak town?

"Step aside, folks, step aside," a deep voice commanded. Kim turned to see what she thought was, thank God, the local cop. She was surprised he wasn't sporting a Santa cap and bearing gifts. Instead, the man, about her age, wore a white Stetson (of course), an officious forest-green-colored shirt with the town's seal stitched on the right breast, jeans with a big 'ol silver belt buckle, and black leather cowboy boots. Over his shirt he wore a heavy chamois-colored leather-and-fleece jacket that did a pretty good job concealing the gun in his shoulder holster. Yay! A cop with a gun! She felt right at home now.

Ricco yanked the assailant up by his throat and hauled him around, then effortlessly maneuvered him back to the ground, planting his knee in the bad guy's back. The cowboy tossed Ricco a set of handcuffs. Before she realized what he was doing, Ricco had the guy cuffed.

He hauled the subdued bad guy up by the handcuffs, forced him to turn around, and shoved him toward the cop. "He's all yours, Jimmy."

Jimmy grabbed the guy—a kid really, maybe twenty or so years old. But not a very nice-looking one. There was nothing innocent about his dark, beady eyes or his pockmarked face. He was shaved and had what looked to be some type of tattoo wrapped around his neck. It was hard to tell under his dark, baggy clothes. "Now, why did you have to go assault that nice lady and take her purse?" the cowboy cop asked. Did he really expect an answer? The guy was no doubt an addict. "We don't do that here in Evergreen. We haven't had a problem in five years."

Well, duh, Kim thought. *That's why he's here. This place would be like shooting fish in a barrel.* Gangstah paradise. Sleeping with your doors unlocked? Indeed! She had triple dead bolts, surveillance cameras, and an internal, as well as external, alarm system. Nobody was getting into her place unless she wanted them there.

The punk yanked away from Jimmy but Ricco stepped up, grabbed him by the shoulder, and whirled him around. He pulled his beard down and got real close. "Mess with Chief Connor, Puke, and you mess with me." Ricco yanked him hard against his chest. "And while he likes to play PC, I don't."

Kim watched Ricco morph from naughty Santa to badass Santa, and she wasn't sure which turned her on more. She shook herself. Literally. What the hell was wrong with her? It occurred to her at that moment that at thirty-eight she was peaking sexually. It probably had something to do with her ovulating as well. Thank God they'd been safe last night. And that reminded her. Condoms. Must buy condoms. A girl could never be too careful.

She shook her head again to clear the cobwebs and watched Ricco shove the criminal back toward Chief Connor. "Do you need any help with him?" Ricco asked.

Jim smiled and shook his head. With a firm hand on the bad guy's handcuffs, he tipped his hat with his right hand to the gathered throng. "Just a minor scuffle, folks, go on back to your fun." He pushed the thug ahead of him and disappeared into the mass of people.

No sooner had the crowd let out a collective sigh of relief than another commotion drew their attention. A blacked-out black Suburban drove screeching at breakneck speed down the promenade, running up onto the overflowing sidewalks. Terrorized, pedestrians jumped out of the way; many fell to the ground, their packages flying into the snow. Ricco growled and took off after the vehicle as it sped out of town. As the SUV disappeared, he slowed to a jog, then stopped altogether. She watched him pull his cell phone from his pocket and dial.

Kim rushed to the elderly couple closest to her as they floundered in the snow. "My God, are you all right?" she asked, bending down to a sweet-looking blue-haired lady who must not have weighed more than one hundred pounds dripping wet. "Mar, are you all right?" the wiry older gentleman next to her asked. Before he could turn over and see that she was not hurt, his hand flailed as he tried to locate her. Kim helped him stand, then they both helped his wife up.

The little old lady's face was pursed and pinched. Her dark blue eyes flashed in fury. She looked like hell on wheels. "Larry, if I were twenty years younger I'd go after the little bastards myself." She flashed Kim a smile. Impulsively Kim flashed one back and wondered what the hell was going on in Christmastown.

"They *were* bastards. Driving like that. They could have killed someone," Larry grumbled, brushing snow off his wife, then himself.

"Everyone okay?" Ricco's deep voice asked from behind her. All three of them turned to face him. He was breathing heavily, perspiration flushed his face, and his Santa coat was open, revealing damp muscles under his white wife beater. He touched his hand to Kim's shoulder. "You okay?" His dark eyes swept her from head to toe, and she assured him she was fine.

"I got a partial on that sonofabitch," Larry said.

Ricco grinned. "Somehow, Larry, I knew you would."

"Larry still thinks he's walking a beat," Mar offered to Kim.

"A beat?"

"He was a cop in Oakland for forty years. Can't seem to get it out of his system."

"What was it?" Ricco asked.

"California plate, One, Ida, Sam," Larry said.

Ricco repeated it. "I'll run it down. I'm sure there aren't too many black Suburbans with that beginning sequence. We'll find out who owns it."

"Twenty bucks says it comes back stolen," Larry said.

Ricco nodded. "I wouldn't bet against you on this one, Larry." He touched Mar on the shoulder and asked again, "Are you sure you're all right, Mrs. Zubreck?"

"I'm fine. It'll take more than a couple of asshole joyriders to mess up my day."

Kim grinned, and so did Ricco. She liked the old lady's spunk.

The sound of "Jingle Bells" jerked Kim out of her

conversation. It was her cell phone. She hurried to dig it out of her purse and glanced at the LED. Nick. She smiled at the couple and at Ricco. "I have to take this call. Excuse me," she said politely, then moved out of hearing distance and answered. "Hello."

"Good morning, Kimberly," Nick said. He sounded fat and sated. He and Gina had probably had a private party.

"Hello, Nick," she answered coolly.

"Is the weather as cold up there as your greeting?"

"Oh, *sorry about that*, but this little town seems to be in the midst of a crime wave at the moment."

"Crime wave? I thought they didn't have any crime."

Kim let out a long sigh. "Well, I guess the word got out to the crooks that Evergreen was ripe for the picking."

"What are the cops doing about it?"

"What cops do."

After a significant pause Nick said, "I miss you, Kimberly." Kim went still. Okay, what had brought that on?

"I—ah, I miss you too."

"I was hoping you would say that. I think it's time we got to know each other a little better. I'm coming up."

Eleven

AT THAT PRECISE MOMENT KIM KNEW EXACTLY HOW IT felt to be on a plummeting elevator. The bottom just fell out of her stomach. She glanced over at Ricco, who was making quick rounds of the people who'd narrowly escaped becoming roadkill, compliments of the Suburban.

"I don't think that would be a good idea right now. I'm making inroads here. I want to keep working my angle."

"No one has to know we're together."

"*I'll* know."

There was a long, uncomfortable silence. Kim was about to fill it in when Nick said, "I'm getting the impression you don't want me up there, Kimberly. Why not?"

She shook her head and began to pace. "I told you, Nick. I work best alone. You'll sidetrack me. I want to do what I need to do to close this deal and be back in L.A. next week. Your being here will delay that."

"Why not take a few days for ourselves?"

Kim pulled the phone away and glared at it as if it had two heads. Who *was* this person? Not the Nick she knew. "Okay, Nick. Spill it."

"Spill what? I want to see my fiancée. Is that so hard to believe?"

Oh, so now she was his fiancée? Yesterday morning she hadn't been. "First of all, I am not your fiancée. Yet. And secondly, yes, it is hard to believe. Why your sudden interest in me?"

He laughed. She felt as if the walls of a small room were closing in around her. She glanced back toward Ricco, who was coming straight at her. Shit.

"Look, Nick, I have a meeting with the mayor in ten minutes. I'll call you later and we'll discuss. Okay?"

"All right, but I'll expect to hear from you after your meeting."

"Okay." She flipped the phone closed and turned to smile up at Ricco just as he stepped beside her.

"Everything okay?"

Her smile stiffened. "Peachy." And she felt like a rotten apple. Lying did not come naturally to her, and although she had to sometimes shade the truth when it came to business, she always did it with great hesitation. She might be in the business of hostile takeovers, but she did it aboveboard and honestly. Nevertheless, she told herself that while she had an honest physical addiction to the man standing beside her, he was also the key to her gleaning information she would not otherwise be able to access without him. Only so much was public record. She ignored the baby twinge of guilt poking at her conscience.

"I need to go down to city hall and give Jimmy the partial license plate and tell him what happened," Ricco said as he looked down at her and brushed back the hair from her face. The instant his fingertips brushed her cheek, she warmed. And damn if she didn't feel all weak at the knees. Ricco Maza did things to her she didn't realize she was capable of. Her cheeks flushed and her gaze caught his, then held. The world seemed to pass them by at that moment. Sound quieted, the breeze halted, and there was no temperature. There was just him.

He moved into her. He gripped her chin and tilted her head back. Bringing her face up to him, he lowered his lips. "I stopped at the apothecary," he whispered.

The earth beneath her feet shifted. "I hope you bought them out," she whispered back.

His lips brushed across hers, and she went liquid. "All ten boxes."

Kim laughed, melting against him. "Is that all they had?"

Ricco slid his arm around her waist and pulled her to him. "I told Jules to order more."

Kim's cheeks flushed hotter. "Ricco! When he sees me with you, he'll know!"

He grinned down at her. "He'd know just by the way I look at you."

Kim looked up at Ricco and smiled. Yeah, she could fall in love with him. Hard and fast, just like every other woman who crossed his path. But she was smarter than that. Emotions screwed up everything. So why go down that road when she knew exactly where it would lead?

No, thank you.

"I'm going to rent a snowmobile and go down to the lake and into the surrounding forest," she told him.

Ricco scowled. "There's a lot of snow out there. It's dangerous."

"How about horses?"

"Worse."

"Well, I'll take my chances with the snowmobile. I won't go far, and I have a locator on my cell phone if I get lost."

Ricco shook his head, then pulled her along with him. "If you can wait a couple of hours, I'll take you."

She considered his offer but thought it would be

better if she went alone. If she looked too nosy, he might get suspicious. "If you don't mind, I'd like some time to myself."

"Suit yourself," he said, his voice clipped.

As they walked through the crowded Santa's Workshop area, Kim saw another Santa in the sleigh. This town didn't miss a beat. "Who's that Santa?" she asked.

"That's Peyton. His side job is mayor."

"Oh, really? I'd love to talk to him."

"Do you always talk to mayors when you vacation?"

"Well, I'll admit I'm doing a wee bit more than vacationing while I'm here."

Ricco chuckled, his humor restored. "Tell me something I don't already know."

She had to hurry to keep up with his long strides. "Oh, really? What do you think I'm doing here?"

He glanced down at her and said, "Spying."

She nearly stumbled. "Spying? What on earth for?"

"You tell me."

"I-I'm not. I have a client who's interested in purchasing some property here. I wanted to get away for the holidays, and it seemed like the perfect solution."

As they weaved around the congested boardwalk Kim didn't miss the turned heads that Ricco's open Santa jacket caused. He'd stuffed his Santa cap in his pocket, and his beard hung down around his neck. And he hadn't worn a padded belly. With the jacket open, revealing the thick black leather belt cinched around his narrow waist and his chest clearly defined under the white wife beater, his tousled hair and his sure stride, he was so worthy of a total neck crick.

"So, you're a real estate agent?"

Kim grinned and looked up at him. "Yeah."

Ricco nodded.

"So what should I tell my client? Is Evergreen in trouble?"

He scowled and glanced down at her. "Maybe."

Evergreen City Hall was a monument to lumberjacks everywhere. It was an impressive two-story building that fit right in with the rest of the town. The only thing alerting anyone to its official status was the seal of Evergreen on the beveled glass of the wide double doors.

Ricco held one open for her. The inner sanctum bustled with activity. It appeared from the signs carved into wooden plaques that this building housed the town's courthouse, police department, city officials' offices, and anything else associated with the mechanics of running a town. Kim noticed a county recorder office annex just down the hall. There was a small courtroom to the immediate right of them, where a deputy stood by to screen for weapons.

"Detective Maza, how's it hanging, man?" the big redheaded deputy said, stepping toward them. He grinned, and Ricco grinned back.

Detective Maza? As in a cop, Detective Maza? After the initial shock of the information, it made perfect sense. The way he'd gone after the purse snatcher, then the crazy driver. Apprehension spiked along her spine in a slow stomp. He could very easily run her name and find out more about her than she'd like him to know. Maybe he already had? She decided then and there it would be what it would be. She wasn't doing anything illegal. Maybe unethical in some people's eyes, but you couldn't go to jail for that.

"Jethro," Ricco said, extending his right hand, "it's going to be 'Sergeant Maza' in a month, and since you asked, it's hanging a little to the left."

Kim rolled her eyes. Guys were so crude. "I didn't know you were a cop," she said.

Ricco continued to grin and shrugged his shoulders. "You didn't ask."

Feeling naughty, Kim raised up on her tiptoes and whispered in his ear, "Do you have handcuffs?"

Ricco's grin nearly split his face. He turned slightly to face her, and his warm breath caressed her cheek. He slipped his arm around her waist and pulled her against him. "Yeah, as a matter of fact, I do."

Kim shivered. The man had a talent. The talent to make her itch for him. "How good are you with those handcuffs?"

"Pretty good. Wanna find out?"

Kim tilted her head back, locked gazes with him, and slowly nodded.

Jethro coughed, then said, "My mama always taught me to introduce attractive women to single available men."

Ricco pulled Kim forward. "Kimberly Michaels, meet Jethro Modine."

Jethro extended his hand. "My name is Jeff. Glad to meet you. How long will you be in town?"

"About a week." She looked up at Ricco and flashed a smile. "Maybe a little longer, depending . . ."

Ricco grinned down at her and squeezed her hand. "On what?"

She nudged into him. "Things."

Jeff cleared his throat. Ricco and Kim looked at him, and Jeff looked down at Kim. "If you get tired of having to fend off every female that walks past this guy, I'm here every day until five. I might not have his looks, but I know how to treat a lady."

Kim laughed and said, "I'll keep that in mind, Jeff."

Ricco laughed too, but his tone was not nearly so amused. "You must be getting old, Jethro. Cuz you'd remember I don't share."

The underlying possessive tone in Ricco's voice caught Kim by surprise. She'd heard it in many men, but never in reference to her. And though she considered herself a modern woman, she kind of liked feeling as if he would fight another man for her.

"I remember." Jeff looked down at Kim and winked. "I'm just saying . . ."

Ricco took Kim's hand and drew her through the metal detector. "I'm just saying too."

As Ricco pulled her along the short hallway to the police department offices, she made mental notes of each office and what she could glean from them. When they came to the PD offices, Ricco opened the door and held it open for her. She stepped through. A pretty, buxom blonde who was on the phone at the front desk looked up. She squealed and dropped the phone, nearly climbing over the desk to leap into Ricco's arms. Kim stiffened and rolled her eyes. This was getting ridiculous.

"Ricco! When did you get into town?" the blonde squeaked like a Kewpie doll.

Ricco smiled and allowed the little bombshell to kiss him full on the lips, but when her lips lingered, he gently pushed her away. He grinned sheepishly at Kim and had the decency to blush. "Um, Brit, I'm here on official business."

The perfectly proportioned and maintained blonde clung to Ricco like a lingering virus. She totally ignored Kim. She ran a red nail down Ricco's chest to his belly, but when she went farther, he grabbed her hand and pleaded, "Brit."

Kim had the overwhelming urge to dig her hands deep into the woman's thick blond hair and rip it out in great clumps, but she resisted. She had never fought over a man, and she would not start now. Ricco reached out to draw Kim closer, but she stepped back and shook her head. "By all means, don't let me interrupt."

Brit turned around and narrowed her big green cat eyes. She kept her hand possessively on Ricco's chest and cocked a perfectly arched brow. Kim smiled a saccharine smile in return.

Ricco extracted himself from Brit's clutches and made a quick introduction. The women nodded to each other.

Moving past the awkwardness of the situation, Ricco said, "Is Jimmy in his office?"

"Yes, he just booked a purse snatcher! Can you believe that?"

"We were there."

"Why is everyone so shocked about a little mugging?" Kim asked.

Ricco and Brit looked at her, surprised. "Evergreen has no crime," Brit indignantly answered.

"None? Not even petty theft?"

Ricco shook his head. "Nada, zilch, never."

Kim whistled and shook her head. "How is that?"

"Up until today, the only folks who visited were the kind who wanted to celebrate the reason for the season with their families and get away from crime and punishment," Ricco explained.

"Well, between the purse snatcher and the jerk who tried to reduce the population by a few, I'd say you're having a regular crime wave." Kim almost laughed at the absurdity of it. Amazing the town would get so uptight about two incidents. And given the fact that no one had really been hurt, they'd been minor incidents at that.

Kim pursed her lips, and the baby pang of guilt was a little stronger this time. If they thought it was bad now, wait until the resort and casino came to town. Life would not even remotely resemble their current Norman Rockwell Stepford town. She looked up at Ricco. "As a cop, how can you be so naive?"

His face sharpened. "Hardly naive, Kim. I've seen things you would never dream of in your worst nightmare, but here? In Evergreen? We live and die on the honor system. The town gets in an uproar if one of the kids pinches a candy from Sadie's Emporium. It just doesn't happen."

"Okay, I get it, but—"

"No buts. You have to drive to get to us—we're between the sierras and the lake. One way in and one way out. We're remote for a reason."

"But how, over all these years, have you had no crime?"

"We've had a spot here and there, but nothing like this. That thug who swiped that purse was not from here. And he wasn't visiting, either. He came with a purpose. I suspect the dude driving the Suburban was with him. It stinks to me."

"Do you think the word is out about Evergreen being an easy mark?"

He shrugged, then frowned. He turned to Brit, who had gone back to her desk and hung up the phone. "Any more from Land's Edge?" Ricco asked her.

She shook her blond head and smiled at him. "No, but Pey was sure pissed when they made the offer. He's still grumbling about some big-ass outfit just thinks they can walk in here, slap down a few bucks, and buy off the town."

Ricco nodded. "Can't say that I blame him." He looked down the hall and said, "I have some info for Jimmy." He squeezed Kim's arm and said, "I'll be right back."

She opened her mouth to say she wanted to come along, but she thought better of it. She supposed he'd say no so that he could do his cop thing in private.

Before Ricco had completely disappeared down the hall, Brit said, "He never stays."

Kim turned, not prepared for Brit's solemn tone. Catty, sure, but solemn? "I'm sorry—?"

Her full pink lips turned down in a melancholy frown. Her big green eyes looked evenly at Kim. "He's like his father. Can't stay in one place more than a month or with the same woman for more than two nights."

Kim didn't know what to say. "I'm . . . um . . . sorry it didn't work out for you two." Sort of. Okay, not really. 'Cause if it had, she'd be minus several orgasms at the moment and not eagerly anticipating more later.

"Don't be sorry. We all grew up with Ricco and know how he is. Of course all of us girls hoped we'd be the one to make him want to hang up his hat. But he only comes around this time of year. Then poof, he disappears until the holidays roll around again."

Kim wondered about something. "Okay, I get he's got a severe case of wanderlust, but if you don't mind me asking, if he's jilted every girl in town at least once, why do you all go crazy over him when you see him?"

Brit smiled a dreamy smile and hugged herself. "Have you been to bed with him?"

Kim's cheeks flushed. Brit smiled knowingly. "How can you not welcome him back with open arms? We all want more." She sat back and closed her eyes, as if imagining Ricco's hands and mouth on her body. Kim warmed thinking the same thing. "And besides, he's always such a gentleman in the end. We all know going into it what it's about. Our bad if we get all clingy. Ricco hates that."

Kim began to feel like a number. Not that she hadn't known it to begin with, and not that she didn't plan to walk away first, but . . . "Just who has he slept with in this town?"

Brit smiled and shrugged. "The easier question is who *hasn't* he slept with?"

"Not as many as you think, ladies," Ricco said, coming down the hall. He gave Brit a look that said, *"Naughty girl."* She blushed and practically puddled on the floor.

He grinned that million-dollar-Hollywood smile of his, tipped an imaginary hat Brit's way, took Kim's hand, and dragged her out of the office.

She didn't know whether to laugh, cry, punch him, or shove him into the nearest closet and have her way with him. "Don't believe everything you hear, Cinderella."

"Oh, trust me, Prince *Charming*, I take everything I hear with a grain of salt."

He squeezed her hand and smiled down at her as they passed Jeff, who watched them with a smirk on his face. A funny jumpy feeling rolled around Kim's belly. Kind of like she was nervous or afraid or her adrenaline was spiking. It was an oddly exciting sensation and one she only felt when she was swooping in for the final strike in a takeover. She'd never experienced it with a man before. And she wasn't sure she liked it.

As they exited the building to the bustling center of town, Kim looked up at him and said, "Even if it were all true, we know we're both turning into pumpkins in a week, so what's the big deal?"

Ricco stopped and let a smiling, happy family pass by. His eyes focused on Kim and he smiled, but not one of those dazzling killer smiles. This one was . . . pensive.

"I think, Cinderella, you're all bluff."

A shot of adrenaline juiced through her. "I guess you'll find out soon enough I never bluff when it comes to the bedroom."

"I guess we're on the same page there. Neither do I."

And his words hurt.

Twelve

"Are you still interested in that snowmobile ride?" Ricco asked as they made their way around the wooden promenade.

Kim thought about it for a minute. Yes, she was, but she decided she didn't want to go alone. A guided tour would be better suited to her motives. And who better than the resident town stud? But she couldn't muster the courage to tell him she'd changed her mind. What if he rejected her? Too much time together did that.

"I am, but right now I think I'll just look around town. Maybe tomorrow."

Ricco stood looking down at her for a long moment. "It's kind of hard to get lost around here." He pointed toward the center of town. "The promenade makes a big circle around the ice rink and central park and the gazebo, with the side streets off every block or two. Ezzy is at the southern end, Sierra side, right now we're at the northern end, Sierra side, but if you get turned around, ask any shopkeeper for directions back to Ezzy's and they'll point you in the right direction."

Kim nodded. Okay, so he was ready to part ways. So was she. Their interest in each other was relegated to a mattress, condoms, and no clothes. Anything more and things could get messy. And she was all about staying squeaky clean. She was glad she hadn't asked him to go out on the snowmobile. She'd hire a guide.

"Great, well, thanks." She stepped backward, away from him. Ricco stood staring at her, his face unreadable. "I'll see you later? Maybe?" she managed to ask. He nodded, his face blank. Okay, she was really digging herself into a hole here. "Look, I totally get it if you want to just say *sayonara* right here."

He cocked a brow, leaned against a wooden post, and crossed his arms over that wide chest of his. "Do you?"

Kim opened her mouth to say their time, great as it was, had come to an end, but when her body flared at just imagining the things he could do and had done to her body, she slowly shook her head. "Uh . . . um . . ."

Ricco unwound those long limbs, and his lips broke into that dazzling smile. He pushed off the pole and said, "Let's keep our options open then?"

"Sure," she squeaked out.

"Then I'll see you later." He turned and walked down the boardwalk, and she watched, speechless, as every woman, from the blue-haired grandmother types to teenaged girls, turned around to watch him in that naughty Santa suit of his, sauntering down the street as if he'd been the cock of the walk. Her belly did that jumpy thing again. "Jesus." She was losing it.

For several long minutes Kim stood there in the cold, staring after Ricco until his tall Santa-suit-clad body disappeared into the throng. She looked around, expecting to see every eye on her, laughing and pointing an accusing finger at her and giving her a number to pin on her back.

She felt like she had as a child, watching her parents leave yet again, wanting desperately to call them back but knowing they had no use for her.

"Did my son pull his Houdini act on you so soon?"

Kim jumped and turned to face Leticia Maza. The woman was taller than Kim by a good six inches, and though her face was serious, her green eyes held compassion in their smoky depths. "It was mutual," Kim responded.

What Leticia did next shocked Kim to the core. She took her hand and pulled her along, walking with her as a mother would a daughter. "Enrique is, as you know, the youngest of my four children. He was raised by women who adored him. We gave him everything he wanted . . . and when we resisted?" Leticia threw her head back and laughed. The sound was warm and deep and resonated with love and pride. "When we resisted, that boy knew just how to twist us around his little finger." Leticia patted Kim's hand. "I admit, I am to blame."

"But why doesn't he ever stick around?"

Leticia's step faltered, and Kim steadied her. "Though Ricco's father was not around very much, the one lesson my son learned was never to stay in one place with one woman too long." She patted Kim's hand and smiled at her. "He isn't even aware of what he does. He just does it. He's always been that way."

"Why are you telling me all of this?"

Leticia shrugged. "I thought you might want to know it isn't you. It's him."

And for some reason that made Kim feel better. They continued to walk along the bustling boardwalk. The sights, sounds, and smells of the little town mingled into a warm welcoming hodgepodge of feelings and vibrancy. Leticia made no movement to release Kim's arm, and oddly, Kim didn't want her to. She'd never had the benefit of a mother who took the time to discuss feelings, much less strive to allay her fears.

"Is your husband ill?" Kim asked. She didn't know why, but she wanted to know.

"Yes. He has come home to make peace with his son."

"How does Ricco feel about that?"

"You saw his reaction."

"I can't say that I blame him." The minute the words left her mouth, Kim regretted them. She was a hard case in business, but she didn't mean to be to Leticia. "Sorry."

"Don't apologize. It's true. But Enrique doesn't have much time, and I know if Riccito doesn't make his own peace with his father, he will always regret it."

"But what if he's already removed himself emotionally? Why go there?" She'd done it. And had no compunction with regard to zero contact with her parents. She hadn't spoken to them in three years. The last time was when her aunt Tilly had passed away. The meeting had been extremely unpleasant, and most uncomfortable. What was the point of making peace when there was nothing there? She completely understood Ricco's refusal to see his father. The man had deserted him and his family—not once, but repeatedly. She looked at Leticia.

"Why didn't you divorce him?" Kim's eyes bugged out of her head. She slapped her hand across her mouth. "Sorry, I . . . this town has made me say and do things I don't normally do."

Leticia smiled and stopped in front of what looked

like a saloon. "I'm meeting the mayor for lunch. Would you like to join us?"

Would she? "I'd love to."

As they entered the 1850s-style saloon, it took Kim's eye a minute to adjust to the dim light of the room. While it was on the main promenade, she recognized it as the place the locals came to hide.

And who should be leaning up against the bar chatting happily with a beautiful redhead? None other than Mr. Ricco Maza. Gone was the Santa suit. Now he was clad in black leather cowboy boots, snug-fitting Wranglers that did naughty things to his ass, and a sweater that was supposed to be bulky but hugged his muscular chest and arms. He smiled at his mother, and when his gaze rested on Kim, he scowled. Wow, the guy moved quick. "Ignore my son, Kimberly."

Kim forced a smile. "You have a son?"

Before Leticia could comment, Ricco strode up, gave his mother a hug, and kissed her on the forehead. He nodded at Kim and said, with his arm slung around his mother's shoulders, "Pey's been waiting for you. He'll be right back." He set Leticia down at a round table and turned back to Kim. "Are you hungry?" he asked.

"I invited Kimberly to have lunch with Peyton and me. You're welcome to join us," Leticia informed him.

Ricco dragged a chair from the small table next to them and pointed to the one near Kim, saying, "Have a seat." When both Leticia and Kim were seated, Ricco sat as well. The tall redhead strolled up to them with an overconfident and overexaggerated swivel of the hips, pad and pen in hand and a big, shit-eating grin slapped across her big glossy lips. Kim resisted the urge to roll her eyes. Despite the redhead's obvious intentions toward Ricco, she didn't seem concerned about Kim as competition. Indeed, let's-be-friends vibes oozed from her bombshell body.

"You want your regular, Leti?"

"Of course."

Kim didn't bother to look at the menu. She just looked at Ricco and asked, "What's good?"

He grinned and said, "Everything."

Kim flushed and said, "I'll have what Mrs. Maza is having."

Once the order was taken, Peyton came in and was introduced to Kim, but it was almost as if she wasn't there. The conversation turned hushed and dire. The town was in trouble. Big trouble. She did everything but scribble notes on her napkin.

"That dang Land's Edge is coming in with another offer. I told Jerry we weren't interested, but he managed to get Donna and John's attention."

"Why on earth would the Tomlinsons be interested in talking sellout?" Ricco asked, anger lacing his words.

"Because," Leticia began, "the nursery is going under.

With the snow, their utility bills have been outrageous the last four years."

"Mistletoe doesn't pay that good," Peyton added.

"Why don't they go solar?" Kim asked. "The feds and the state are offering huge rebates as incentives. A sixty-thousand-dollar setup after rebate is less than thirty grand, and the fed offers some really attractive low-cost and very long-term financing."

All three sets of eyes stared at her, and she wondered why on earth she'd offered that tidbit. It was her job to capitalize on the dire straits of the residents, not help them out.

"They're already mortgaged to the hilt," Leticia said. Then she added, "I hope you understand that what we discuss here does not leave the table."

Kim's eyes widened innocently. "Of course," she hastened to assure her, then raised her eyes to Ricco's dark ones, which calmly regarded her. She felt her cheeks flush as she looked away and asked, "I'm confused how your system works. How does this Land's Edge even get an offer presented to the powers that be?"

"It goes before the city council for a vote. Both of the Tomlinsons are part of the six-member council board. Leti and I, as well as Chief Connor and Ray, Esmeralda's husband, are also on the council," Peyton explained.

"So you speak for the town then?"

"Yes."

"Is the offer bad?" Kim asked.

Peyton nodded and bit into his roast beef sandwich. Kim toyed with her chicken salad. Her stomach was getting jumpy again, except this time it wasn't because of Ricco. "It wasn't great, even if we were in the market to sell out. But we're not."

"Why does this company want Evergreen?"

"Casinos."

Kim's eyes widened. She knew damn well that Nick had given no indication of a casino in the buyout proposal. "Are you sure?"

Peyton nodded and set his sandwich down. "I'd swear it."

"But you have no proof?"

"I don't need it. The local tribes have been making noises for years. They want a piece of the casino pie. Can't say that I blame them, but what will happen is, they get the casino, then contract it out to be managed. And that leaves Evergreen in a lurch."

"How so? It sounds like a windfall to me."

"Hardly, Miss Michaels. If the casinos come to town, we turn into the Las Vegas version of Christmas. We happen to like the no crime, small town, family value system we have going here. We live by what this country was founded on, and the casinos will take that away. No thanks."

"But what if you can't make up this year what you've lost the last five years?"

He pointed to the big window and to the board-walk beyond. Tourists continued to fill up the space. "Look outside. Once 82 opened, the masses poured in. It's Christmas for us. Literally and figuratively. People love coming here. We are the reason for the season, and there is nowhere else you can feel it like you do here. We are charmed, Miss Michaels. And so long as we keep that charm, we keep our trade, and we keep our homes."

"So long as the weather holds and we don't give guests a reason to leave town, we'll weather the storm," Leticia added.

Peyton wiped his mouth with a napkin and then pushed his plate away. "Exactly. We must keep up this level of occupancy through New Year's. Anything less?" He shook his head. "And we're sunk."

"We had two incidents today," Ricco said.

Peyton nodded. "I heard. A mugging and an erratic driver?"

Ricco nodded and finished his hamburger. "The Suburban was deliberate. I got a partial. But the only Suburban in the state with that beginning sequence was reported stolen in Fremont yesterday."

"How coincidental is that? A mugging and an ass-hole driving a stolen truck down the middle of town?"

Ricco shrugged. "We were due. But I think we need to keep a heads-up. With as many people as we have in town right now, there could be more. Hell, for all I know, someone let the secret out. We need to lock our doors."

"Ricco, the only time I lock my door is when I go to Auburn," Leticia said.

"Mom, make it a habit. The real world is getting closer to Evergreen every day."

"But—"

"No buts. Be smart and be safe. Lock them."

The conversation turned to the Christmas parade and Leti's excitement over having her granddaughter play the Virgin Mary. Peyton asked Kim what she was doing in Evergreen, and she explained, "I'm having a bit of a working vacation."

"What line of work are you in?"

"Real estate. I have a client who's interested in a property here or in South Lake. When I leave here I'll head south and see what I can see."

"If your client is looking for peace, quiet, serenity, and nice folks, Evergreen is your place. Reindeer Lake is beautiful year-round." He smiled and continued, "You will not find a more naturally beautiful landscape anywhere in the world. Summertime, this place is green and lush, and that lake is teeming with fish. And during the holidays? Well, you can't find another place as warm and as welcoming. If you don't already know, our Christmas parade is world renowned. Three years ago we were featured in *Living* and *O*. This year *Town & Country* is coming in for next year's Christmas edition."

"You have a lovely town, Mayor," Kim honestly said.

"Pey?" said a short, stout woman of about fifty, barging her way into their conversation. "I just got the new offer from Land's Edge. It's less than what they offered last month!"

Kim sat up straight. Another offer? What the hell was Nick doing? Peyton scowled, and Leticia caught her breath. Ricco said, "What do you want, Donna? A shocked reaction? No one is selling out regardless of what is offered."

Kim cleared her throat. "Do you mean another offer as in *today* another offer?"

All sets of eyes looked at her. "I'm just curious. From a business standpoint, I don't understand the developer's reasoning behind it," she defended.

Donna's head bobbed like a chicken. "Yes, the amended offer just came in twenty minutes ago."

"Maybe he heard about our little crime wave and wants to bank on us running scared," Ricco said sarcastically.

And Kim knew that was exactly it. She was going to wring Nick's neck! How dare he maneuver behind her back!

"It doesn't matter. It is what it is," Donna said, then turned back to Ricco. "It's easy for you to be so cavalier, Ricco—your life isn't tied in to the economy of Evergreen. Mine is." She looked to Peyton and Leticia, her eyes pleading. "My balloon payment is due the thirty-first! I have two kids in college and a grandchild with special needs. I'll take seventy cents on the dollar."

Leticia stood and patted the woman on the shoulder. "Donna, don't panic. We're at capacity right now."

"Maybe for all of you, but I couldn't afford to ship more than a short crop this year. I have nothing left!"

Peyton nodded slowly and said, "Donna, we're meeting tomorrow afternoon in the back room. Come talk to us then. So long as everyone who relied on the tourist trade can come up with their balloon payments, maybe we can work something out for you." He looked at Leticia. "Can you talk to the investors? See if they can rework the terms?"

"I work investors all the time," Kim offered. "Who holds the notes?"

Leticia and Peyton exchanged a look. "It's a private consortium."

Kim nodded and pushed a little harder. "Most of the money I work with is private money." She gave the mayor and Leticia her best trust-me-I-can-help-you smile. "I'll be in town for another week at least. Holler if you need anything."

Leticia smiled, then patted Donna again. "I'll go right now and make a phone call."

And with that, Kim was left at the table with Ricco, in a very uncomfortable silence. And just as uncomfortable was the growing guilt in her belly.

"So, what exactly are you looking for, for your client?" he asked.

She didn't miss a beat. "Waterfront property."

"Have you been down by the lake?"

"No, I'd wanted to do that."

Ricco stood, pulled a few bills from his wallet, and tossed them onto the table. "C'mon, I'll take you down there. There isn't another one like it on earth."

Kim stood but said, "Would you excuse me for a minute? I need to go to the little girls' room." Not waiting for an answer, she hurried to the back of the saloon. Once in the single-stall restroom, she pulled out her cell phone and hit Nick's number.

"Gold."

"What the hell are you doing?"

"Why, hello, sunshine."

"Don't patronize me, Nick. When did we talk about amending the offer?"

"I took advantage of our opponents' fear." He chuckled. 'C'mon, baby, I'm surprised you didn't think of it first."

The fact that he was right didn't make her feel any

better. She shook her head and paced the tiled floor. She was allowing her emotions to get in the way. "You're right, but do me a favor—let me know next time. We've always worked as a team, and I don't like being left out in the cold."

"Then let me come up there and warm you up."

"I told you, no. I'm making headway and I don't want you breathing down my neck."

"If I didn't know you as well as I do, Kimberly, I'd take offense at that."

"Well, then it's a good thing you know me so well."

There was a knock on the door. "Look, I have to go. I'll check in later." She flushed the toilet and washed her hands and smiled to the lady doing the pee-pee dance outside the restroom.

Ricco watched Kim soak in the pristine beauty of Reindeer Lake and the surrounding tree line. Even blanketed in snow as it was, the raw beauty of the view was breathtaking.

"My God, Ricco, this is gorgeous! No wonder everyone braves the snow for this." She walked down the wide, cleared sidewalk to the edge of the lake. The sun had begun its descent over the western horizon, and the rays skittered across the icy snow of the lake, giving it the brilliant kaleidoscope of a prism. To their left, not more than fifty feet away, a small herd of reindeer pawed through the snow, searching out grass. They weren't at all bothered by their human presence.

Ricco moved down to stand behind Kim. He resisted reaching out and touching her shiny blond hair. His resistance to her was so strong that he retook two steps. She bothered him. A lot. For several reasons. She was smart. She was sexier then all get-out, with a passion for him that matched his for her, but underneath all of her fire-breathing bravado she had the vulnerability of a lonely child. Something about her called to his soul, and he didn't like the way it made him feel.

He didn't like not being the one to set the pace and the rules. He didn't like being beaten to the door. That was his move. She turned around and smiled, her deep blue eyes dancing in merriment. "How can you leave this place?"

"Easy."

Her smile dipped, and her finely arched brows nudged together. "Why can't you stay here?"

He shrugged and moved past her to the edge of the frozen lake. "I don't stay anywhere very long."

"To make sergeant, don't you have to stay put?"

"I'm not taking the promotion."

"Why not?"

He shrugged. "It keeps me tied down. I like to spread out and work task forces."

"You can't run forever, Ricco."

Her words surprised him. He turned to look at her.

He was going to tell her to mind her own damn business, then a few more things to push her out of his way. But her concerned eyes stopped him cold. "Who says I'm running?"

"No one has to—it's obvious. Different girl every day, different town to call home. I'd say you have some big commitment issues."

Yeah, he did. So what?

Ricco turned back to the lake and pointed down to the reindeer that had moved farther down the gently sloping fringes. "See the reindeer?"

She moved to his side. "I didn't know they were indigenous to California."

"They aren't. Old Kris Kringle, and, yes, that was his legal name, brought a few down from Alaska. When he passed away some forty years ago, the town didn't have the heart to see the small herd in a zoo, so they let them go. They stayed, they propagated, and the rest, as they say, is history."

"Are they tame?"

"No, but they aren't aggressive, either. They stroll into town more often than not, minding their own business. The town does own a small herd we use for the Christmas parade."

"No animal rights people come up and hassle you?"

"Hell, no! Those deer are treated better than most kids."

"What would happen to them if the town sold out?"

"I'm getting real tired of hearing that term. Evergreen might be a little hard up for cash at the moment, but we'll get over the hump. We always have."

Kim opened her mouth to reply, but a crisp shot rang out, splitting the serene silence of the lake. Instantly their gazes darted to the small herd, and they both watched in horror as a reindeer fell not more than fifty feet from where they stood. Several tourists who had also come down to the lake screamed and scurried for cover.

Jesus! Could the day get any worse?

Thirteen

"Son of a bitch!" Ricco cursed, grabbing Kim to him. Another shot cracked through the crisp, cold air, whizzing past so close to them that Kim heard it zip into the snowbank only a few feet from where they stood.

Ricco pushed her down into the snow face-first, covering her with his body. "Don't move," he softly said.

Ricco turned on top of her, and she could tell he was looking back toward the tree line where the shots had come from. The sound of a snowmobile racing away alerted them. Ricco rolled off her and jumped to his feet. He pulled his cell phone from his pocket and started to run into town. "Get the hell out of here. Go back to the inn!" he yelled at Kim over his shoulder.

She jumped up and didn't bother brushing the snow

from her clothes. She glanced at the downed reindeer and scanned the shore for others. Seeing none and not knowing the first thing about reindeer first aid, she hurried after the others who were running for cover. When she reached the street, she turned back to look at the tree line where the shots had come from. The white snow nearly blinded her in its brightness. For a long time she stood, squinting, hoping to catch a glimpse of something, anything, and it occurred to her that Evergreen was under siege. And she was afraid for the town, and she was afraid for Ricco and for herself. And this time she would not tell Nick.

She turned and ran as fast as she could to the inn. As she did, bedlam broke out in waves around her as word spread. The shots had been clearly heard by those lakeside and by those close by on the sidewalk. Everyone who had ducked down by the lake kept running. Parents grabbed their children close, shielding them and hurrying to safety. Shopkeepers came out from their shops and hurried the tourists inside, soundly shutting their doors.

By the time Kim made it back to the inn, the streets were deathly quiet. Word had gotten around quickly.

RICCO, PEYTON, AND JIMMY SPED OFF INTO THE TREE line on supercharged snowmobiles. Evergreen, though never riddled with crime, was always prepared for search and rescue. And right now they had a poacher to find. Or, Ricco thought, worse. Did someone have bad aim? Had he or Kim been the real target? Or maybe someone else nearby? They sped down into the valley, then up into the tree line where Ricco was sure the line of fire had come from. Sure enough, they came up on fresh snowmobile tracks. They followed them just into the tree line and stopped. There, glittering in the receding sunlight, on top of the hard crust of the snow—as if laid for the express purpose of discovery—were two .308 brass casings.

Jimmy pulled up on Ricco's right, Peyton to his left. Jimmy pulled up his goggles and pointed to the casings. "How nice of the shooter."

"No shit." Ricco looked down into the lake valley at the fallen reindeer so close to where he'd stood with Kim. She could have been killed! He watched the beast struggle to rise in the deep snow. "Bastard!" Ricco cursed and pulled his two-way out. He alerted a number.

"Go ahead, Ricco," Elle's voice came across the static airwaves.

"Elle, call Doolittle. We've got a downed reindeer lakeside just past the west boathouse."

"What the hell is going on? Someone said shots were fired downtown?"

"Not quite. Some asshole decided to take some target practice on the herd." He looked at Jim and Peyton and said to them, "I'm following the tracks, you stay here and collect the evidence." He put the two-way back to his mouth and said, "Elle, Pey'll give you further instructions. I'm going after the asshole."

"Be careful, Ricco!"

Ricco gunned the big Arctic Cat, and, in a rooster tail of snow, followed the tracks of the slimy bastard into the tree line.

Fury encompassed him like a fist that was strangling him. What the hell was going on? A mugging, a crazy-ass driver, and now some random shooting at the herd? In one day Evergreen had seen more felony crime than it had in the last fifty years combined. Hell, the worst thing that ever happened in Evergreen was old Mrs. Mulvaney's deaf, dumb, and blind dog, Raggedy Anne, getting run over by one of the teenage boys.

Ricco gunned the Cat, following the clean trail, and in less than ten minutes he came to the edge of the only road from 80 into Evergreen. He hopped off the Cat and yanked his helmet off. There, in the snow, were tire tracks—by the looks of them made by a truck with all-terrain tires. He followed the wet tracks. No trailer, which meant they'd loaded the sled on the back of the truck. A flatbed? No, not enough tires. Whatever it was, they were headed north.

He considered calling CHP, but they'd laugh their

asses off when he told them to put an APB out for a poacher.

Instead he radioed Jimmy. "He got away."

"Where are you?"

"About two miles north of town on 82. Looks like he parked here, unloaded the sled, did his deed, then hightailed it back. He didn't have much time on me. Put a call in to CHP and ask them to be on the look-out for a truck hauling a sled. At least we can get an ID on the prick and turn him over to the game warden."

"Will do."

Ricco tucked the radio back into his jacket pocket. For a long minute he stared at the road. Something was up. Three incidents in one day was too coincidental. Either someone had taken an ad out to harass Evergreen for the hell of it, or there was a motive behind the skirmishes. Who, and why?

As he rode back to town, his mind wandered, his intuition peaked, and his anger simmered. While he didn't live in Evergreen and hadn't since he was eighteen, he considered it home. His mother and sisters and their families called it home. His friends and their families called it home.

His father flashed in his mind, the way he'd seen him the night before, and Ricco's gut tightened. Knowing the man was there, he'd avoided his mother's house. And he had nothing to say. If what Ez said was true—that their father had come home to die—then so be it, but Enrique Senior had never considered Evergreen his home. Ricco opened up the throttle, and the Arctic Cat lurched forward.

He wanted the old man gone. Knowing his father was too selfish to be the man he should be, it was easier to hate him for the man he was. As he broke the tree line, Ricco could make out a small group of people down by the edge of the lake. He set his jaw when he recognized Kim among the gathered group. Hadn't he told her to go back to the inn? He nearly ground his jaw to dust when he recognized the man she was speaking to. Enrique.

Ricco let off on the throttle and debated whether or not to engage or remain unengaged. His sister Elle made the choice for him. She looked up and saw him, then waved him over. Kim, his father, and his mother looked up as well. On the ground between them was the downed deer.

He pulled up and killed the engine. For a long time his gaze held Kim's. He'd told her to go back to the inn. Why had he thought she'd listen? She was the most exasperating woman he'd ever come across. She was stubborn, opinionated, too smart for her own good, and sexier than hell.

Visions of her naked and sweaty, writhing uncontrollably beneath him, had him on the rise. Mentally he shook himself. His gaze caught hers again as he walked toward the group, and he scowled. Kim's full lips quirked at the edges. Once again the urge to throw her down into the snow and get naughty with her fueled his anger.

Refusing to acknowledge the man standing next to her, he moved past them to the downed deer and caught Adam Ramirez's eyes. The town affectionately referred to him as Doctor Doolittle. He had an uncanny way with animals; since he was a boy, he'd sworn he could communicate with them. From the looks of the animal, Ricco guessed that it was dead.

"You're just in time, Ricco. We need help to remove the carcass."

From the amount of blood on the snow and the entry location of the wound in the neck, it looked like the animal had bled out. His anger turned up from medium to high.

"Uncle Ricco?" Tonio asked, popping out from behind his mother, "did you get the bad guy?"

Ricco shook his head and reached out to tousle the boy's thick black hair. "Nope, he got away. Maybe CHP will pick him up."

Tonio knelt down by the great beast and patted his face. He looked up at his uncle and squinted. "He was the protector of the herd. What will happen to them now?"

Ricco looked across the lake to where the herd had regrouped. "One of them will step up."

"What happens if one doesn't? They need a dad, a protector."

Ricco squatted down next to his nephew and looked at him evenly. The boy's dark eyes held compassion and the simple innocence of a child who still held out hope that his old man would show up and step up. It killed Ricco that Elle had picked a man just like their father. Tonio didn't deserve it—hell, no kid deserved it.

"Then the uncle will step up and make sure all of the other reindeer are safe."

Tonio's eyes filled with sudden tears, and Ricco's heart swelled in love. Embarrassed, Tonio swiped at his eyes with his sleeve. "I hope so," he whispered.

Ricco squeezed the boy's shoulder and said, "C'mon, kiddo, there's nothing we can do for him now."

Tonio stood and moved toward his mother, but stopped and stared down at the dead deer with sadness.

Ricco looked over to Peyton and Jimmy and inclined his head away from the group. As he turned, he noticed that dozens of tourists had gathered up near the sidewalk. Great.

Ricco, Peyton, and Jimmy walked toward the group. Ricco smiled and said to the gathered throng, "Show's over, folks, go on back to town."

Peyton cleared his throat. With a smile in his voice, he walked ahead of Ricco and said in a more friendly tone, "Just a mistake. One of our townsfolk had an accidental misfire of his rifle. Unfortunately, one of our herd was compromised. Nothing to worry about. Everything is okay."

The crowd moved, but grumbled and they looked over their shoulders at the dead reindeer in the snow. They weren't sure they believed the mayor.

"Nice save," Jimmy said.

"Yeah, nice save," Ricco spat. "What are you going to say when the next incident happens?"

Peyton's head snapped back. As tall as he was, he still had to look up to meet Ricco's gaze. "What makes you think there will be another incident?"

"Do the math. A mugging, a blacked-out SUV driving like a maniac down Main Street, and now one of the herd shot, and it was no casual, oh-I-think-I'll-shoot-a-reindeer shot. This guy had motive and he planned it. And his second shot came too damn close to me! The bastard probably had a driver waiting to help get the sled in the truck. Why?"

Peyton scowled and looked at Jimmy. "Tell him," he said.

Jimmy exhaled and said, "A Sysco truck was hijacked just a mile south of town."

Incredulous, Ricco stood speechless for a minute.

What the hell? "Sysco, as in the main food supplier to the restaurants in town?"

"Yeah."

Ricco swiped his hand across his face. "This is bullshit!"

"You don't have to tell us. No food, no tourists, no revenues."

Ricco began to pace. "What motive would someone have to harass the town?"

"For shits and giggles?" Peyton offered.

Ricco whirled around and speared him with a glare. "I doubt it."

"I think the twenty-first century has caught up with us, Ricco," Jimmy said, all joking aside.

Ricco shook his head. "No, it hasn't. This isn't the real world catching up, this is calculated."

"What are you saying, Ricco?"

"I'm saying the more we hold out against this developer, the more shit happens."

"That's a pretty bold statement," Jimmy said, shaking his head, not fully convinced.

"Bold, but true. I'm going to look into this Land's Edge company and see what I can dig up. In the meantime, we need to be discreet, but watchful."

Jimmy nodded vigorously and said, "Yes, keep it under wraps. The crew from *Town & Country* is due to arrive tomorrow. Another truck is coming in with an emergency food shipment. I plan on meeting it tomorrow morning when it turns onto 82."

"Great, just what we need—a police escort for the food truck. How do you think that's going to look?" Peyton demanded.

"Make it look like you're coming back into town. Easy enough," Ricco said. He glanced over his shoulder and saw his family, along with Kim, walking toward his mother's house. He scowled. He seemed to be doing a lot of that lately. His scowl deepened when he watched her take his old man's elbow and steady him when it looked as if he had slipped on an icy patch of sidewalk. Elle hurried to his aid as well. *Son of a bitch!*

"When did your old man come back to town?" Jimmy asked.

"Too soon."

"Leti says he's dying," Peyton offered.

Ricco turned his anger and frustration on both men. Peyton was his mother's age, and Ricco knew the mayor had a soft spot for her. Jimmy and Ricco had started in the same kindergarten class at St. Anne's and graduated high school together. He considered both of them his friends, and if any man knew how he felt—or, in this case, didn't feel—about the man who'd donated his sperm to his mother's egg, it was these two. "He can go to hell." With those parting words, he stalked off, wanting to be alone.

He wanted to punch something, someone, anything to relieve the pressure cooker that had become his temper. It rarely reared its head, but when he reached his flash point, he always found that an hour with a heavy bag usually did the trick. Except there was more to his anger now than just his father's reappearance after ten years and the calamities befalling his hometown. His libido was in overdrive and he wanted a release. But not just any release—and that, he realized, was the crux of his problem. He wanted Cinderella again. And he knew he'd want her again after that and after that. And he couldn't for the life of him figure out why. And it wouldn't matter if he asked her to stay an extra day or two; she would say no. She was the female version of him. Well, not exactly. Sex to him was like football or boxing. A sport, a physical outlet. Something he did for fun. It raised his endorphins and made him feel good, and, since he hadn't had any complaints lately, he'd have to say he made his partners feel good too. A win-win for everyone involved. Why, then, did he feel like sex with Kim was different?

He jammed his fingers through his hair and decided he didn't care. He'd ride the wave again if she let him and get off the board when the wave fizzled out. He made his way back to the lake edge to find the carcass of the deer being loaded on the back of a flatbed trailer. He yanked on his helmet, then drove the sled back to the city yard where the PD kept their vehicles. He decided to go back to his room, grab some clothes, and go work out.

As he was coming out of his room, he nearly slammed into Kim. She cried out, startled.

"Sorry, I didn't see you," Ricco apologized.

She smiled. He didn't expect that. For some reason he figured she was pissed at him for something. "I'm going to your mom's for dinner. She wants you there."

"Give her my regards. I'm heading to the gym."

"Will you go later?"

"As long as that poor excuse of a husband is there, no way."

"Ricco, he's dying," she softly said.

He stiffened. "I don't give a rat's ass."

"Really?"

He moved in and narrowed the space that separated them. His heart rate kicked up several notches. The velocity of his blood pressure was so intense that he'd have a damn heart attack in the hallway if he kept it up. "Let me explain to you how that man won the Father of the Year award. He deserted my mother, my sisters, and me when I was a baby. That was the fourth time he did it. Each time a baby was born, he took off. We lived in a rat trap of an apartment in East Oakland. I went to sleep to gunshots and woke to roaches crawling over my legs.

"My sister was almost killed when she wouldn't give her lunch money up at school. Later that same day my mother was beaten and raped on her way home from work. When she came home from the hospital, she took all four of us and ran as far from Oakland as she could. What little money she had ran out here, in Evergreen. It took that bastard five years to find her. He came, he took her money, and left. He'd come back when he hit rock bottom, my mother, the good Catholic martyr, took him back each time. I stopped talking to him when I was thirteen. He's a liar, a drunk, and a son of a bitch. He left us destitute, my sister and mother were almost killed, and my mother lives with her assault every minute of every day of her life. And for that, I will never forgive him."

He moved past her. "Now if you don't mind, I'm going to work out and find a quiet place to have dinner. Give my mother and sisters my regards and enjoy your dinner."

Two hours later Kim found him nursing a beer at Maxine's. His face was dark and stormy. And for the first time since she had met him and seen him in a social setting, there were no women fluttering around him. Indeed, they watched him from afar knowing this night he wanted no company.

Kim slid onto the bench across from him. "You missed the best paella ever."

His dark, solemn eyes rose to hers, and she caught her breath. As if she could see straight down to his soul, she felt his pain. "I'm sorry, Ricco."

He shrugged. "Don't pity me, Kim. I'm a big boy."

She nodded. "It's ironic, you know."

He raised a brow. "How so?"

"Here you are, the one constant male in your mother and sisters' lives, yet the one who wasn't is the one enjoying their company while you sit here alone nursing a warm beer."

He snorted. "They can have him. I'll be back next year."

"He won't be here when you come back."

He shook his head, pushed the mug away from him, and stood. He tossed a ten onto the wooden table. "I'm counting on it."

He stood staring down at her for a long minute. She didn't know what to say. He was adamant. And she understood. Nodding, she took his outstretched hand. "I understand. I have no contact with my parents for very similar reasons. I almost feel like it would be more of a burden in my life if they were to want a relationship."

"Relationships require emotions, sacrifice, and pain."

"Yeah, I've learned that the hard way. It's why I've become a workaholic."

His hand was warm. She liked the way hers felt in it. Their fingers laced, and he pulled her along and out into the cold night air. The town had quieted. The events of the day had left an uncomfortable pall. "Is it always this quiet?"

"No."

After several minutes, Ricco asked, "Why did you get divorced?"

Kim stiffened. No longer wanting contact, she tried to pull her hand from his. No one had ever asked her that question. He tugged her hand back.

"Don't be a chicken. Tell me, I want to know."

"Why?" she said, barely able to speak.

"Call me curious."

She shot him a hard glare. She resented his question, and she also resented his infringement into what had been, for her, a most enjoyable stroll.

"I found out my first husband married me for my money. Or, more precisely, my parents' money. He decided after two months that I wasn't worth the wait. My second husband was a babe magnet, like you. My jealousy was too much for him to live with. I found out after our divorce that I hadn't been jealous enough."

"So they soured you on all relationships?"

"They had some help. I had two serious relationships afterward, and as you have proven repeatedly, men have the irresistible urge to share their seed with more than one woman. I used to be a one-man woman and expected my man to be a one-woman man. As that did not happen, I choose now to do as I have with you: No messy emotional involvements, just feel-good sex. My rules, my terms, my life. Simple." She looked up at him. "Why haven't you married?"

He grinned and felt a little bit like a cad when he answered, "I'm not a one-woman man." But it was the truth.

Kim nodded. "Of course. Silly me to forget that one small fact."

After that, they walked in silence back to the inn. They entered through the back door to the kitchen, and Ricco stopped dead in his tracks. Mr. Maza sat at the kitchen table with a steaming cup of something in his hands. Ezzy bustled about and smiled at her brother as if it were every day he walked in to find their father at the table.

Anger gathered into a storm cloud on Ricco's dark face. He glared at his sister, then at Kim. She shook her head. "I—"

He began to stalk past the old man when he said to Ricco, "Son, can you spare your father just a minute?"

Ricco stopped, rooted to the wooden floor. He turned on his heels and stared at his father, a murderous rage twisting his handsome features. "Don't you mean can't I spare you a few bucks to buy a forty?"

Ezzy gasped.

He turned on her, his dark eyes blazing. "Don't," he

said, low and menacing. "Do not chastise me for what I say"—he pointed to Mr. Maza—"to that person."

He turned back to the man. "I have nothing to say to you, old man." He faced his sister and put it to her. "Him or me?"

"Wha—what do you mean?"

"I won't stay under the same roof as him. Not even for five minutes."

"Ricco! That isn't fair!" Esmeralda pleaded, coming toward him with her arms outstretched.

Ricco was having none of it. "I'm going up to take a shower. You have that long to decide."

He stalked off. Swiping back tears, Esmeralda moved to sit next to her father. "Papa, we told you it would not be easy. Ricco is still very angry. You cannot force him to listen. He must come to you in his time."

Mr. Maza looked up to his daughter, his old eyes glistening with unshed tears. "I have wasted a lifetime. I may not be here in Ricco's time."

Kim felt an inkling of compassion for the man, but the vision of Leticia raped and beaten sickened her. It was this man's fault. Her sense of self-preservation swelled for Ricco. She understood all too well his pain. And while it wasn't her place to have any say in this family's schism, she couldn't help wanting to come to Ricco's defense, especially considering what he had told her about his father. "Mr. Maza, with all due respect,

I don't think Rico will change his mind." She took a deep breath before she continued. "You have wounded him beyond repair. If you love him as you said tonight at dinner, then leave him alone."

Ez sucked back a sob and nodded. She stood wringing her hands and looking as if she wanted to comfort the old man but knowing that if she did so she betrayed her brother. "Papa, she's right. Leave Ricco alone."

The old man made as if to stand. Though he could have used assistance, he waved both Kim and Ez away. He grabbed his cane and slowly came to his feet. "I will respect his wishes. It's past time that I put his feelings before my own." He kissed his daughter on the cheek, smiled at Kim, then disappeared out the back door.

Kim and Ez looked at each other and let out a long breath. Ez closed her eyes, then slowly opened them. "Thank you for that."

"You're welcome."

Ez plunked down into the chair her father had vacated. She dropped her head into her hands and slowly shook her head. "I love my brother. I love him more than any man on this planet except my husband, but sometimes I just want to slap him silly."

She choked back a sob and looked up at Kim. Her eyes were filled with tears. "I don't know what to do."

Kim stood for a long minute, wrestling with the

decision of getting more involved than she should. In the end she decided a little advice couldn't hurt.

"Frankly, I don't really see where the choice is here."

Esmeralda sniffed and wiped her sleeve across her damp eyes. "What do you mean?"

Kim put her hands out, palms up, as if she was weighing something. "Ricco, Enrique. No comparison."

"But—"

"No buts."

Esmeralda sat forward as if to defend her position, but Kim gave her two more cents. "Esmeralda, I understand you want everything perfect, but in so doing you hurt your brother. In his eyes he's been here for you and you've picked your father—the man who wasn't—over him. You need to accept the fact that the gap between father and son will never be bridged. Ricco doesn't want it, no matter how much you, your mom, and your sisters do."

Ez choked back a sob. "I just want everyone to get along."

"Forcing your father on Ricco is only making him dig in deeper. If there is to be any hope, you need to let nature take its course—otherwise you will lose your brother forever."

"We've always been able to cajole Ricco into anything. I guess I thought I could do it this time."

"In the real world that isn't feasible."

Esmeralda laughed, the sound caustic. "But this is Christmas town. Everything is possible here. You just have to believe."

"Sorry, Ez, no matter how much I believed in Santa Claus, there wasn't."

Suddenly Kim was tired. It had been a busy three days. She was ready for bed. "Look, things will work out the way they're supposed to. It just might not be what you want."

Esmeralda stared into space, tuning Kim—and the truth—out. "Good night," Kim said, then made her way up to her room. She drew a hot bubble bath; just as she was about to get in, she remembered she'd promised Nick a phone call. Not wanting to talk to him, she waited until her bath was ready, then forced herself to make the call. She dialed his number on the inn phone.

He answered on the first ring. "I've been waiting all day!"

"I've been just a little busy."

"Give me an update."

She let out a long breath. Since the phone was cordless, she sunk into the hot, soapy tub. Closing her eyes, she luxuriated for a long minute. "Oh, God, that feels so good."

"Who's there with you?" Nick demanded.

Kim's eyes flew open, and she couldn't help a laugh.

"Me, myself, and I. I just sunk into the most decadent bath ever."

There was a long silence; all she could hear were quick, jerky breaths. "How big is the tub?"

"Big."

"Enough for two?"

"Uh-huh." She closed her eyes and let the hot, sudsy water infiltrate her skin and muscles.

"Tell me about the rest of your day," Nick softly said. She didn't care that his mood went from rabid to seductive. She was too tired to gauge his moods and guess at the reason for the swings.

"Not much. I met a few more of the old guard here in town and took a tour of the lake." No way was she telling him about the dead reindeer.

"I bet that was interesting," he said, sarcasm lacing each word.

"Interesting enough."

"How did your meeting with the mayor go?"

She stifled another yawn and said, "It went really well. That new offer of yours has really pissed them off. The council as a whole isn't interested in considering, but there are two members, they own the mistletoe nursery, who are ready to capitulate. They want out big-time. The four other council members are in a holdout pattern."

"Can you get close to the other members?"

She smiled. "I already have. I had dinner at the controller's house tonight, and another council member was there as well. Right now, they're impregnable. If this weather holds, we might have a problem."

"What do you suggest?"

Kim sighed. "I don't know. I'm so tired right now. I do know *Town & Country* is coming in tomorrow for a week. They're shooting now for next year's holiday edition. They're featuring California's best. And at dinner tonight, Leticia, the controller, told me there is a real good chance Kelly Ripa is bringing her family out next week and wants to shoot a segment for *Live with Regis and Kelly*. But that's supposed to be a secret. She doesn't want the kids to be compromised."

"Interesting. I've had the top IT guys dig for info on the internet. Whoever holds the note to those mortgaged properties is buried. Get me that information."

Kim nodded. "I'm working on that. It could take a little time. I do know it's a private consortium. It's not like they're going to give that information just because I ask. In fact, I did, and they clammed up." She yawned again. "Nick, I'm beat as hell."

"Are you sure you don't want me to come up there for a few days?"

She stiffened. "Ask me in a couple of days. Right now I want to focus on what I have to do here."

"Okay, but don't make me beg."

Nick Gold didn't beg for anything. He just bought it. And she shivered; he was, in a sense, buying her. She didn't like the way that felt.

For a long time after she hung up, Kim wondered if marrying Nick was the right thing to do. When she had agreed, it had seemed like the perfect match. The perfect merger. The perfect solution. Now she wasn't so sure.

She toweled off and slipped into a cute little burgundy two-piece cammie and short pajama set. The soft silk felt good on her warm skin. She took her silk-and-velour robe from the armoire and decided she should at least let Ricco know his father would stand back. Maybe he would rest easier.

She wasn't sure why she decided to tell him. He would find out in the morning from his sister, but something drew her across the hall to the Dasher suite. Softly, she knocked on the door. A long moment later, the door opened. She swallowed hard. He was bare-chested, dressed only in long flannel sweats. He glowered down at her. She put her hands up and said, "Don't kill the messenger."

He stood back from the door and she entered the cozy room. The fire crackled in the fireplace, and she smiled at the careless way his clothes flopped out of his duffel bag like limp dolls. "How long before you put your things away?"

"Not everyone on this earth is as compulsive as you."

"There is nothing wrong with being tidy."

"You're anal."

She set her hands on her hips and squarely faced him. "So what?"

He shrugged. "So nothing. Why are you here?"

She wanted to punch him. He wouldn't look at her, as if she no longer held any appeal to him. The thought crushed her. And she chastised herself for it. She'd known it would happen. It always did. She let out a long breath. Nick was not a mistake. Nick was the right choice. No more of this emotional roller-coaster bullshit.

"Your father." He shot her a glare, and she put her hands up again. "I mean your sperm donor has agreed to leave you alone and make no further attempts to contact you. I don't mean as in he's leaving your mother's house, but he won't be back here."

"Oh, so *he* decided not to come back, not Ez?"

"What do you mean?"

"My sister! Was it her choice or his, damn it?"

"What the hell does it matter? He's not coming back here."

"It matters to me that my sister didn't stick up for me, *that's* what's the matter."

Ah. It made sense. His pride was damaged. And she could understand his heart. He had been there for his sister, the father had not, and in his eyes she'd picked the father. "Ez would have told him. He just beat her to it."

"Right." Ricco began to pace the floor. "I love my family, but damn if I'm going to stand by and watch them all get caught up with that drunk, then crash and burn when he milks them for everything they have or leaves in the middle of the night with the silverware, like he's done in the past."

"He can't walk without the aid of a cane, Ricco. I doubt he'll go sneaking off into the night with your mother's silver."

He turned fierce eyes on her. "I can't believe I'm hearing this from Miss Hard-Ass Don't-Fuck-With-Me Michaels."

Kim turned toward the door and put her hand on the knob, but before she said good night she held out her other hand. "I'd like my locket."

He stood scowling at her, but then he turned and opened the drawer to his nightstand. He pulled out a small envelope—the Legacy stationery—and handed it to her.

She opened it, and the locket slid into her hand. A hard jolt of emotion hit her, and she felt the hot sting of tears. She looked up at Ricco, who had lost some of his anger. "I don't know what I would have done if I'd lost this forever. Thank you."

He stood hard and unmoving. "You're welcome."

Before she turned into a blubbering ninny, Kim rushed from the room to hers.

RICCO STOOD STARING AT THE DOOR FOR SEVERAL MIN utes, wondering why he felt so empty at that moment. What the hell was wrong with him? What the hell was wrong with his family, and what the hell was wrong with Evergreen? In three short days, his life was shot to hell. And he didn't like it one bit. It was one thing to be undercover or working an investigation, where you could keep your emotions in a tiny little compartment and not worry about feelings. Police work was cut and dry. No warm, fuzzy bullshit involved. But this! This—family, Kim, and Evergreen stuff—was too much. He didn't want to be the savior of the world.

He paced the room like a caged tiger. Everything and everyone was closing in around him. His flight instinct crouched, poised, and waited for the final trigger. For the second night in a row, Ricco pulled on his running gear and hit the streets of Evergreen. His hot breath curled around his head as he rounded the north end of town for the third time. The streets, while well-lighted, were barren. No strollers, no couples walking hand in hand admiring the stunning array of Christmas lights and decorations. The place was dead. And with a sudden twist in his gut, Ricco knew they were all doomed.

Money couldn't buy happiness, but it could buy towns, and if Land's Edge—a Fortune 500 company flush with cash, he'd learned today—had their eyes set on his hometown, it was going to take an act of Congress or an act of God to prevent it. He didn't hold much hope either one would come through.

As Ricco came down his mother's side of the street he smelled the aromatic smell of a cigar before he saw the red glow of the tip. And latched onto it and walking as spry as a teenager was his dear old dad. Son of a bitch—Ricco had known he was scamming them.

"I'll give you until tomorrow, old man, to pack your bags and head out of town. If you come back, you'll wish you hadn't."

"*Mi*—"

"Save your bullshit lines for my mother and sisters. I want you out of here."

"I'll ask your mother for a divorce then."

Ricco stopped in his tracks. A divorce would devastate his mother.

"No you won't."

The old man smiled, and Ricco's stomach turned. It was that same smile he turned on when he was about to go for your jugular. "Maybe for a price I won't."

Almost thirty years of pent-up anger and frustration unfurled inside Ricco's gut and came out in his fist. He smashed it into his old man's face, sending him backward into the snow.

It took every ounce of control Ricco had not to grab him up by his coat and finish him. Instead he spat on the sidewalk next to him. "You're going to rot in hell, and that's too good for you. I want you gone tomorrow. And if you leave with anything you didn't come with? Consider yourself under arrest for grand theft." He turned then, and the tension that had driven him to run had returned. But this time, it went deeper. Running it out was not going to ease it.

Fourteen

SHE ACHED. LITERALLY. EVERY INCH OF HER. AS IF SHE'D been consumed with fever.

Kim tossed and turned. Several times she woke with a start, her body hot, her breath forced, her heart racing. Each time she crumpled back into the bed she saw Ricco's fiery gaze, and she could almost feel his scathing lips on her throat, her breasts, her belly . . . and lower. Finally, unable to stand the heat in her bed, she threw the covers from her. Even the air was warm. The fire glowed in the corner, and the cool air slipping in from the window did little to ease her discomfort. Frustrated, and knowing she would find no sleep the way she was feeling, she slid from the bed and grabbed her robe. Maybe some of those gingersnaps and a glass of warm milk would help her sleep.

As she turned to softly close the door behind her, a small sound alerted her that someone was near. Her heart pounded; she could feel the pulse of it in her veins and the percussion of it in her ears. The heat in her body, which had just begun to subside, warmed. Her shaky hand slipped from the brass knob, and slowly she turned.

Her eyes clashed and held with the penetrating ones across the hall.

Ricco stood perfectly still save for the heavy rise and fall of his chest. His bronzed skin glistened under the lowlight of the hallway, a fine sheen of perspiration highlighting every ripple and ridge. He was dressed in running shoes, sweats, and a white wife beater. A black hoodie hung from his right hand.

His dark eyes dipped to her lips. Slowly his fingers opened and the hoodie fell soundlessly to the hardwood floor. His eyes rose to hers, and Kim caught her breath high in her chest. Heat, anger, frustration, and pure craving burned bright in the dark depths. Her entire body trembled, and she feared for her balance. "I—," she croaked.

He was across the hall in one long step, his solid arms locked around her waist, yanking her hard against his chest. "Shut up," he growled, then kissed her like there was no tomorrow.

Kim lost her balance, she lost her will to fight what

was between them, but mostly she lost all control at that precise moment. And she didn't care.

Ricco pushed the door to her room open and thrust her inside, his lips never even close to breaking from hers. Her nerve endings tingled, her body filled, responding, wanting to meld more tightly into him. He pushed her against the bed, then onto it. He climbed up after her, his long body pressing against hers. His spicy scent was more pronounced from his run; it added fuel to her primal flame. He smelled completely male, and she wanted all of him, then and there, down and dirty.

He tore her garments from her. He kicked his shoes off and shoved his sweats down his legs, then kicked them off. She ripped his T-shirt down the front of his chest in one reddening tear. Ricco flashed a hard devilish grin that undid any lingering vestiges of her inhibition. Free of all encumbrances, his fingers dug deep into her hair. He brought her mouth to his but did not kiss her. Instead his lips hovered just above hers, his hot breath singeing her face. There was no soft petting, no building foreplay, no sweet words to ready her for him. None was needed. In one deep thrust he entered her, and Kim nearly died on the spot. Her hips rose, her back arched, she squeezed her eyes shut and bit her bottom lip. The sublime feel of his filling her to capacity, his hot, sweaty body above her, his mad passionate taking of her, shook her to her core. Never had anyone responded to her as ardently as this man inside of her. And at that precise, perfect moment, his need for her softened her hardened heart enough that she thought she might wake up a little bit in love with this man.

He pulled her up to him, his hot breath mingling with hers. He thrust again and her eyes flew open. Her body stilled. His eyes were black in his passion. His anger and frustration still lingered deep in their depths. Was he as angry at himself for his need as she was at herself? Did he feel it too? This uncontrollable thing between them that seemed only to quiet when their bodies forged into one?

Kim let herself go in his arms, surrendering her body to his. Ricco seized the opportunity. In another violent thrust he slammed into her, again, and then again. He twisted her hair in his fists, his jaw rigid, his eyes fierce, thrusting again and again, and she'd never been so wet for a man as she was for him.

He kissed her. A hard, ruthless kiss. Then he pressed his forehead to hers and forced her to look at him. "This is only sex, Kim, don't ask me to stay."

Her heart squeezed tight for the briefest of seconds. Emotion welled up in her chest with the velocity of a tsunami. But she understood. Each had their paths to follow, and neither one included the other. She nodded and breathlessly said, "It goes both ways, Ricco."

"Good," he said and closed his eyes. "Good," he said again, this time barely audible.

Gathering her into his arms, he thrust deeply and she screamed with pleasure. He covered her cries with his lips, milking her of her fluids as she in turn milked him of his. And that was how she came, held tightly in his arms, her body driving against his as he filled her to overflowing. Perfectly, their mad rush, their mad need, and finally their mad release, hurdled them both off a steep precipice, where they crashed into a thousand tiny pieces at the bottom. Broken, but sated. For the moment.

It took Ricco more time to recover from Kim than it did for him to recover from his two-hour run. He lay on his back, spent. Kim lay draped across his chest, a limp, wet rag. Her long blond hair clung to his skin like damp mop strings. He could feel the swell of her tits against him and the soft indentation of the cradle of her hips along his thighs. The air crackled with warmth, their musky sex scent hung over them like a summer storm cloud. His nostrils twitched, and he licked his dry lips.

His dick stirred the minute Kim laved his right nipple with her tongue. "Mmm, you taste salty," she murmured.

He slid his hand down the slick curve of her back,

stopping just at the rise of her ass. She had a great ass. Her lips nipped at him, her tongue swirled around his nipple. His body stiffened. He pressed the palm of his hand more firmly against her. It occurred to him at that very moment that he hadn't used a condom. A first. While he had no fear of impregnating Kim, he was surprised she hadn't insisted. Not that he could have stopped his trajectory. He'd lost all control; the only thing that had been important to him had been getting inside of her and letting go.

"We didn't use a condom," Kim said as her fingers traced down his belly to his rising erection.

"I'm snipped and I'm clean." And he'd liked the way he'd felt unencumbered inside her. The act, while one of pure lust, had also held a level of sensuality he had never experienced.

She pressed her lips to his belly. "I just started the pill this month and you're the first man I've been with in two years. I liked the way you felt in me. Raw. Real."

He grabbed her hand as it wrapped around him. He closed his eyes and gritted his teeth. "Cinderella . . ."

She rose up on her elbows and peered at him. "What, Prince Charming?"

He opened his eyes and caught his breath. Two sapphire-colored eyes stared back in quiet question. No sarcasm, no anger, no ulterior motive except sincerely wanting to know why she should stop. "If you keep touching me that way, I'm not going to let you out of this bed," he replied.

She smiled, and he felt the warmth of the sun touch him. It was a genuine smile, one that said she was happy, and feeling a bit full of herself. He bet she didn't smile like that too often. "I can think of worse things." She grinned.

"Why haven't you been with a man in two years?"

"Because I hadn't found one I wanted." She squeezed him. "Until now."

He forced himself to go slow, to find out more about this woman who intrigued him so. "Where do you live?"

"L.A." She licked him. Just beneath his navel. His dick swelled in her hand. He wanted her lips on him. "Where do you live?" she asked.

"San Jose."

"Hmm, maybe the next time I'm in your neighborhood on a business trip, I'll look you up."

Ricco smiled, deciding he liked that idea a lot. "Next time I'm down south, maybe I'll look you up."

Kim's lips trailed down the dark hair that directed her to the root of him. He squeezed his eyes shut, feeling the hot rush of desire fill him. The air pressure seemed to thicken around them, the temperature of the room rose, and her hot, musky scent, as if someone had turned it up, intensified around him. Her essence filled his pores.

When the hot wetness of her mouth closed around the thick head of his dick, Ricco moaned and pressed his hips against her. His fingers slid deep into her damp hair, and he thrust up into her wet cavern. Ricco closed his eyes and let himself go, savoring the erotic charge of her tongue, lips, and hands.

"God, that feels good," he said, his voice low and husky. When she cupped his balls and rubbed her tits against him, he nearly came. "Jesus—," he hissed. Ricco looked down his belly. The erotic vision of Kim's luscious lips locked around his dick and her full tits bobbing against his thighs pushed him over the edge. The tightness in his balls uncoiled in a quick unfettering; he fisted his hands in her hair and set his jaw. The wild, hot release and her refusal to do anything less than take all of him into her prolonged the sweet agony of his orgasm. She rode him out, her hands, mouth, tongue, and tits taking him where he had never gone. If he made it out of the bed before the end of the week it would only be because he'd need to find other sustenance than Kim's body and the incredible things she did to him.

She crawled up his body and kissed him long and deep, her tongue swirling against his, her hands digging deep into his hair, claiming him. When she pulled away, she smiled that little secret smile of hers and said, "We're even. Now you know what you taste like."

He grinned and licked his lips. "Not bad."

She grinned back, but her body stiffened, and slowly her brows furrowed. She looked past him to the window. He turned to see. "What's—" He froze, then immediately rolled from the bed to the window. "Holy shit! The house next to my mother's is on fire."

He grabbed his sweats and jerked on his shoes. "Call nine-one-one!"

Fifteen

AFTER KIM CALLED 911, SHE DRESSED HURRIEDLY AND ran down the street to the house next to Leticia's. It was lit up like a Roman candle. Frantically Kim looked for Ricco, and she nearly died when he came running out the front door covered in soot.

"Empty," he breathlessly said.

"Where are the fire engines?"

"We have one, and it'll be here as soon as Cal gets it started."

"Oh my God, Ricco!" Kim pointed to the woodpile on the side of his mother's house. "Fire!"

"Shit!" He rushed past her to the front door and yanked at the doorknob. "Damn it!" It didn't open.

She thought everyone slept with their doors unlocked.

Ricco banged on the door. "Mom! Jasmine! Open up!" Not waiting for them to get out of bed, Ricco picked up a small redwood planter and hurled it through the nearest window. He kicked out the jagged shards and hopped through the window. Several minutes later, Leticia, Jasmine, Mari, and little Donny, who was wrapped in heavy blankets and fuzzy slippers, came rushing from the house, ushered by Ricco. Kim grabbed Mari's hand and helped Jasmine, who clutched a terrified Donny, to the sidewalk. Finally the distant shrill of a fire engine pierced the crisp, frigid air.

"Ricco, your father! He's in the back bedroom!" Leticia screamed.

Kim looked up at Ricco, who scowled but turned and rushed back into his mother's house. The fire had spread farther. Now it licked at the roofline. Many of the surrounding residents and guests from two of the smaller lodges on either side of Esmeralda's flooded the sidewalk. When the engine rolled up, several men in pajamas helped Cal and Jeff pull out the hose and hook it up to the hydrant right in front of the burning house. The kids fussed, and, try as she might to calm Mari in her arms, Kim could not quiet the child. Her nerves were strung taut. Along with Jasmine and Leticia, Kim watched the front door of the house, waiting anxiously for Ricco to emerge with his father.

The flames hungrily licked the cedarwood along

the copper roofline and now were almost to the front of the house. Just as the hose let loose with a blast of water, Ricco emerged from the house with his father in his arms. Violent coughs racked the old man, and his face was swollen as if he had fallen face-first into a Mack truck. He clung to his son's neck like Mari did to Kim's. Then, for the second time in the wee hours of the morning, Kim found herself falling a little more for the man who strode toward her with his father in his arms, a man he could not even speak to but had not hesitated to save. The sight of Ricco, proud, stubborn, and angry, yet performing such a heroic act, tugged at her heartstrings.

The hot sting of tears suddenly threatened to erupt. Kim swiped at them with the back of her hand, telling herself it was from the acrid smoke blowing in her face. She moved with Mari and the rest of Ricco's family into the street. She noticed Esmeralda, as well as half of her guests, hugging themselves against the chill as they poured from the B&B.

Ricco set his father down on the curb, then turned to help Cal and Jeff save his mother's house. From the looks of it, they were doing a good job. The house next door hissed and sizzled under the melting snow. Once the flames were quelled on Leticia's house, the men turned back to the house next door. Despite the melting snow on the roof, which helped the process along, it took considerably longer to gain control of. The contents of the house were hot fodder. Another group of men took a second hose from the engine and hooked it up to another hydrant across the street, and soon the flames were doused. The two-story log cabin was nothing but a pile of smoking rubble.

"You sure no one was in there?" Cal called to Ricco, who was covered in ash.

"Mom said the Rodgers weren't due up for another week. I cleared it."

Cal nodded and moved to stand at the head of the sidewalk to what was once a cozy little getaway. "Once the embers cool, I'll take a look," Cal said. "Seems mighty strange this should happen on top of all of the other mishaps in town today."

As Kim handed off Mari, she overheard Cal's comment. A little prickle of suspicion jabbed at her gut. She walked up behind Ricco; in an action that surprised her, she reached out her hand to his. He turned, startled, at her touch, but when he saw her, he smiled and drew her close. "Everyone okay over there?" he asked.

A sudden unexpected ball lodged in her throat, and instead of saying yes, Kim nodded, not trusting her voice. He hugged her against his side and turned back to Cal. "I hear exactly what you're saying. I think we need a town hall meeting ASAP. Otherwise we're going to see our cash crop head for the hills."

"Talk with your mom and Jasmine, I'll talk to the other council members, and we'll let the permanent residents know about it. The sooner the better," Cal replied.

Ricco nodded. "You got it. When are you coming back to take a look here? If you need some help, I've worked with a few FDs on arson cases."

Cal's lined face tightened. "I sure hope it wasn't arson, son. If it was, we're in big trouble."

Kim swallowed hard. If she'd been a betting kind of girl, she'd have laid odds the fire had not been an accident. A hard chill frosted her insides, and her anger began to erupt as her suspicions ignited. If Nick was remotely responsible for any of what had happened in Evergreen since her arrival, he would live to regret it.

"Now, Ricco, even though it looks like your mom's place is sound, I don't want to take any chances. I'd rather she and everyone else find somewhere else to spend the night. I want to do a thorough inspection at first light," Cal instructed.

"I'll let them know. I'll see you first thing."

When there was nothing left to do and the crowd had dispersed, Kim found herself walking with Ricco, two of his sisters, his father, his mother, and a niece and a nephew back to the B&B.

"Mama, you can have my bed, I'll sleep on the trundle bed in Krista's room. Donny can have the crib for the new baby. Papa, you can have the sofa," Esmeralda offered.

"I'll go down to Elle's," Jasmine said.

"No, Mama!" Mari cried. "Stay with me."

"You and Mari can have my room, Jaz," Ricco quietly said. "I'll go down to Elle's."

At his offer something in Kim dried up. She wanted to cry out like Mari and say, "No, stay with me." And when the words actually left her mouth, five pair of adult eyes stared in shock at her. The most shocked were Ricco's.

"I, ah, I mean, no need to pack up and go to the other end of town. We-um-you . . . shit! Just stay with me."

Ricco grinned, and even though he was covered in ash, he laughed and pulled her toward him. He pressed his lips to her ear and whispered, "You promise not to take off on me, Cinderella?"

She swatted him and felt like a complete teenager. "I promise."

"Then I'll stay."

And so that was how the night ended. Ricco moved his bag and toiletries into her room. In no time it looked as if a tornado had hit it. While he was in the shower, Kim took his clothes from his bag and divided the armoire in half, then the dresser, and then the cabinet in the bathroom. When he stepped out of the tub wrapping a towel around his waist, Kim stood grinning at the doorway to the bathroom. "You looked really hot with that hose between your legs."

He grinned like the bad boy he was, whipped the towel from around his hips, and snapped it at her. She squeaked and jumped back. Still wet, he stalked her into the bedroom, then onto the bed. He licked her neck and grinned wider. "You taste like a salt lick and look like a soot-smudged waif."

She shoved him off of her and took a quick shower. As she sauntered back into the bedroom, the fireplace roared and the flames illuminated the room in a soft, sexy glow. As she rounded the bed, anticipating Ricco's hard body sliding into her, she stopped instead at the soft sound of his snores.

Her tense body loosened. Her gaze scanned the big man who lay sprawled in all his naked glory on her bed, not a modest bone in his body. She closed the glass doors on the fireplace and slipped into the bed, snuggling up against his smooth, hard warmth. In seconds she was asleep.

RICCO WOKE WITH A RAGING HARD-ON AND A WARM, naked body next to him. He stretched, and in so doing, he swept the length of the pliant body curled up against him. She moaned and stiffened, her tits dug into the side of his chest, and he felt like he was going to explode on the spot. He rolled her over onto her back and spread her thighs with his knee. In one slow, slick slide he was buried deep inside of her liquid tightness. She was wet, she was hot. She was Nirvana. "Cinderella," he whispered against her lips, "were you dreaming of me?"

She arched into him. "Yesss," she sighed and gave herself up to him. And he sunk deeper still into her body and lost all sense of time, of place, of who or what he was. All he knew was he could not get enough of her and if he didn't stop soon he would lose more than his head.

Her legs slid up and wrapped around his thighs, her hands dug into his hair, her lips clung as desperately to his as his did to hers. Slow and unhurried, yet with an underlying sense of urgency, their bodies undulated, moving together, then parting only to reunite again. The fire in the hearth had died but the fire in each of them sparked to greater heights. They came together, rising up, their bodies truly one, with a hard body shudder, only to fall back into the pillows, straining for breath.

And in the aftermath of what had been for him not only a moving physical connection but an emotional one as well, Ricco felt the uncontrollable urge to bolt. To grab his clothes and run as far and as fast as he could away from the woman beside him. She was becoming an addiction he could not afford to have. His time in Evergreen would end on New Year's Day, hers sooner. He didn't want to mope around when she left. He didn't want to feel as if a part of him was missing. He cursed, rolled over to the edge of the bed, and sat up. He raked his fingers through his hair and turned to look down at the root of his problem.

Heavy lids hovered over deep blue eyes, and slightly parted, full, pouty lips begged for more attention. The small, deep sigh of a sated woman escaped her lips, and she closed her eyes. Kim reached up and traced a fingertip around his right nipple. Instantly it hardened, and he felt his blood stir. He grabbed her hand and bent down to it. He bit her fingertip. She smiled a dreamy smile but kept her eyes closed. If she saw the fury on his face she might back down. Maybe that's what he needed to do. Separate. Completely. Now, before it became impossible.

He released her and moved from the bed. "Where are you going?" her soft, sexy voice asked.

"I have to meet with Cal." He hurried into her bathroom and took a quick cold shower. When he couldn't find his travel kit, he cursed.

"I put your things in the vanity. Where they belong!" Kim called to him. He brushed his teeth and decided not to shave but to get dressed and get out of the torture chamber as soon as humanly possible. When he strode back into the bedroom, he deliberately didn't look at the bed.

He held the towel firmly around his waist. When he couldn't locate his bag, he had no option but to look at his bedmate. He froze. She lay on her side, her blond hair wildly flowing around her shoulders and that I've-just-been-fucked-proper look on her face and her rosy body. "Your clothes are in the armoire and your tees and underwear are in the nightstand there."

He grabbed a pair of shorts from the nightstand, then quickly dressed. He moved to the door. With his hand on the knob, he stopped his flight, looked back at her, and opened his mouth to say something, but words failed him. "I'll see you later," was all he could manage. Then he closed the door a bit too hard and ran down the hall and out the front door. The cold air hit him like a sheet of glass, and he was glad for it. He inhaled deeply and let the icy air chill his lungs. Feelings he couldn't seem to control started in on him again, and he felt like if he didn't go for a two-hour run or beat the shit out of a heavy bag, he was going to explode.

He glanced across the street, glad to see Cal's city Jeep parked out front of the burned-out house. As Ricco walked up, he saw Cal walking out of the charred remains of the log home with a burned-up gasoline can in his gloved hand.

"No shit!" Ricco said, and he jogged the rest of the way to the fire chief.

"In the downstairs bedroom. Looks like a bunch of towels were soaked in gasoline, then lit."

"No shit," Ricco softly said again, and as the implication of it all dawned on him, he became angry. The Rodgers could have been in residence. Worse, had Kim not seen the flames from her window, they would have slept through it, and he could very well have been churning through the rubble of his mother's house looking for remains instead of knowing she was safely at his sister's. "I'd check into the Rodgers' finances ASAP and see what their insurance company has to say. Mom said in passing that they had been struggling with filling up the rental schedule. I sure hope they didn't use a fire as a means to snatch up some cash."

Cal shook his head. "They don't seem like the type."

Ricco nodded. "I know. But in my line of work, I've learned the hard way not to trust anyone but to go with your gut and follow the trail to see where it leads you."

Ricco stepped over to his mother's house. He and Cal inspected it together. Thankfully, the greatest damage had been caused by the water pressure from the fire hose. The window near the woodpile was busted, and his mother's office was water damaged. When they finished, Ricco waited for Cal's official opinion. "Looks sound to me. With the exception of the water damage, it looks like just the trim along the roofline got it."

Ricco looked at the barely scorched cedar siding.

"Your mama was smart to spend the extra money for the flame seal. Worked like a charm."

"I'll let Mom know."

Cal nodded. "I called the Rodgers this morning. They're coming up tomorrow. I want to get this mess cleared as soon as we can. It looks bad for business." As he finished the sentence, Ricco noticed several SUVs loaded with people head south out of town. He frowned and looked to Cal.

"That's the second group of cash cows to leave this morning."

Ricco couldn't blame them. Overnight, Christmas had turned into Halloween. "I'll let Mom know she can come home."

Ricco took off at a slow jog across the street to the B&B. As he turned up the sidewalk, the front door opened and two guests emerged with suitcases in hand. Ricco smiled and said, "Y'all heading out for the day?"

The male half of the older couple scowled. "Not the day, the month."

"What changed your mind?"

"You saw the fire, and you saw the shooting. It doesn't take a rocket scientist to figure it out."

"I understand, but let me assure you this isn't—"

The man held up his hand. "Not going to work. We got our money back and we're headed to Incline."

And that was the end of that. Ricco stepped into the

house to see several more guests standing with their suitcases in hand at the rolltop desk in the salon Esmeralda used to check guests in and out.

She looked up at him, and he saw the glitter of tears in her eyes. Her stricken face tugged at his heart, yet he knew there were no guarantees he or anyone else could offer these people. They were panicked. The fire and shooting had been too close to home. They wanted peace and tranquility; as it stood, that was the last thing they were getting in Evergreen.

All Ricco could do was help them out and assure them they were safe in the B&B, but even as the words left his mouth he knew them to be false. He couldn't guarantee his own family's safety—how could he guarantee theirs?

As he made his way back into the house, he came face-to-face with his father. Ricco curbed a smirk. The old man's nose looked like he had gone a few rounds in the ring with a heavyweight. Ricco's gut clenched, and so did his jaw and hands. He would have loved to take another shot, but for the sake of his mother he refrained.

"Thank you for last night, son," the old man said, his voice low and shaky.

"I would have done it for anyone," Ricco said and walked past him. He entered the kitchen to find his other two sisters, his mother, nieces, and nephews crowding around the big butcher block table. His eyes scanned the room for Kim.

"She went outside to make a phone call," Jasmine said.

Ricco shrugged. "Who?"

Elle grinned and wagged her finger under his nose. "You can't pretend around us, Riccito. We know that look in your eyes. But—" She tapped her finger to her cheek. "I have to say, I've never seen you so moody over a woman. Is this the one?"

"One of many more to come." And he tried to say it with conviction, but he fell short, because, quite frankly, he wasn't sure. Kimberly Michaels did something to him no other woman did, and she was going to be gone in less than a week. He would not ask her to stay. She'd made her position clear, as had he.

"I hope you wait until the end of the week to continue your run, Ricco," Kim said from the doorway.

He had the decency to blush. He opened his mouth to defend his callous remark but decided he'd look like a bigger ass if he tried. Instead, he said, "Sorry, that was pretty crude."

She strutted in and looked at the kids, his mom, and sisters before looking him straight in the eye. "Yeah, it was," she said, then stalked past him.

"Ricco!" Leticia said as Kim exited the room. "You were raised better than that!"

His temper flared and he curbed it. He would not take his frustration out on his mother. "I said I was sorry."

He turned back to the salon and nearly flattened Esmeralda. Tears streamed down her face. "I have two guests left. Kim and a single guy who isn't sure if he wants to stay. I have *Town & Country* scheduled to come by for photos later today. How can they take pictures with no guests? How can I pay my bills without guests?" she demanded, on the verge of hysteria.

Ricco hugged her to him and said, "It'll work out, Ez, it always does." He drew her into the kitchen. When they were all together, he asked his sister, "What time exactly is *Town & Country* scheduled to be here?"

She sniffed and stood comforted by his arms around her. "By two."

Ricco nodded and hugged her closer, then he turned to look at his family. He scowled when he noticed that Enrique hadn't left. He'd see to that later. "Okay, family, between the shooting and the fire, Ez has lost all but two of her guests. We all need to play happy guest later today when *Town & Country* comes by for photos. I suggest we look our photo op best." He turned to his mother, then glanced at Jasmine. "Cal agrees with me that we need a town hall meeting ASAP." He looked at his watch. "It's almost nine. Do you think we could have a quorum by eleven? Then come back here and give *Town & Country* the shoot of all shoots?"

Leticia set her jaw and nodded. "I'll make it happen." Then she moved to her daughter and took her from Ricco's embrace into hers. *"Mija,"* she soothed, brushing Esmeralda's hair from her cheeks, "it will all work out. I promise."

Once it was settled and Ricco was about to head into town, he remembered why he was there. "Cal says you can go back into the house. Some of the trim and the woodpile burned. He apologizes for the water damage to your office. He offered to come by later and help you clean up."

"That's sweet of him, but Kim is going to help me."

Ricco frowned. "Why?"

Leti cocked her head at her son. "Not that I have to clear such things with you, but she offered, and I accepted. I thought it was nice of her."

Ricco stood for a long minute trying to find a justifiable reason for Kim not to help his mother. He realized he didn't want her ingratiating herself into his family. And he wasn't exactly sure why. Part of it, he knew, was selfishness. He wanted her all to himself for the rest of the week. If that occurred, however, one of two things would happen—he'd be glad to see her go, having gone to the well too many times and become bored, or he'd fall into the well and be unable to climb out of it. As much as he wanted to keep the separation between her and his family, he couldn't stop it now. Not without good reason. It would make him look like the ass he was becoming. Maybe the best thing to do was just play it all out and see what happened, then deal with the fallout. Inwardly he cringed at the idea. He wasn't up for more turmoil. Not this kind. The kind that you carried with you, under your skin, in your heart, and soul.

Give him cops and robbers any day.

"Sorry. I'll let her know to come on over."

As Ricco turned to leave the kitchen, he caught his father's contemplative gaze. Ricco set his jaw and moved past the old man. No one—least of all the man who called himself his father—had room to chastise Ricco for how he conducted his love life. Never had he led any woman to believe there was anything more than that night. Most, but not all, of the women he encountered received the same precoital disclosure: "I don't do mornings. So if you're good to go with that, let's play." He was always amazed at the women who tried to get him to stay with the promise of more sexcapades followed by breakfast in bed. What was it with women wanting to make more out of a one-night stand? Were they all out to find a husband? A hard shiver shook him from head to toe. The thought of settling down made him queasy. There was too much to give up. The loss of his freedom and philandering did not outweigh the minimal gain of the same woman for eternity.

He found himself standing at Kim's door, battling his urge to flee. He was not a coward. He'd never run from a challenge in his life. But the woman on the other side of the door made him afraid. Afraid he would not be able to make a clean break and walk away, as he had done hundreds of times before with as many women.

He knocked.

"Come in," Kim called.

He wasn't surprised to see his duffel bag packed and sitting next to the door. He pointed to it. "Is that your way of telling me I'm no longer welcome in your room?"

She stood at the window, her arms crossed over her chest, her jaw set, her eyes flashing. He'd really pissed her off. Part of him wanted to beg her forgiveness and carry on the way they had, the other part wanted to drive the wedge wider.

"Ya think?" She unwound her limbs and came around the end of the bed. "It was nice while it lasted, but I won't be spoken of that way in public. Take your bag and hit the road."

She moved past him, but he grabbed her arm and whirled her around to face him. "What if I don't want to?"

Kim stiffened in his grasp. "Take your bag or hit the road?"

"Maybe both." His declaration shocked them both. Kim's eyes went from narrowed slits to saucer wide. She yanked her arm from his grasp but didn't move away from him.

"Look, Ricco, sex with you is great. The best. Hell, the best ever. But your moods are so damn hot and cold. I'm not a damn doormat!" She began to pace the carpet. "I mean, if it were just about the sex, that would be one thing. But it's—" She stopped and slapped her hand over her mouth.

Holy crap, she couldn't believe what she'd just been about to say. She watched Ricco's eyes go from guarded to curious. "What's it about, Kim?" he softly asked.

Shit shit shit! "It . . . ah . . . it's about your family!" Whew, great save.

He cocked one of his dark eyebrows, and a slow smile crept across his full I-can-put-Brad-Pitt-to-shame lips. He wasn't buying it. "Oh? What does my family have to do with us and sex?"

"Well, I've gotten to know your family, and it isn't all about us, or the sex."

He pushed off the door and moved toward her. "Again, I don't see how that applies to us."

"I like your family. I like you too, so if we break up—I mean if we stop sleeping together—it could get weird when you bring your new girlfriend, or fuck buddy, or whatever I am or she will be around while I'm hanging out with your mom or sisters." Her rambling made no sense to her, and she doubted it made sense to Ricco. She felt like she was grasping for straws, because the real issue was her desire to be with Ricco for more than the sex. And that realization terrified her. If she felt this strongly now, how would she feel later when he moved on? Her body seemed to have suddenly lost the energy necessary to support it. She fought off the unnerving sensation. Taking a big, deep breath, Kim told herself she was a big enough girl with enough defenses to thwart a hostile takeover of her heart.

"But you're leaving at the end of the week. I doubt I'd dump you and find a new fuck buddy in that time."

His words had a double impact. He was committing—if you could call it that—for the rest of the week, and that elated her, but he was also letting her know what she didn't want to hear: He was walking as soon as their time was up. She punched his arm. "I was going to tell Ez I'd like to extend my stay for a few days. I haven't been able to do what I need to do for my client. So can you now see my dilemma?"

Ricco grinned. "Let's make a deal. For as long as you're here in Evergreen, we can be—" She watched his face redden as he struggled to say the word, "an *item*" or some semblance of the concept, but he couldn't say the words.

Kim smiled, suddenly wanting to hold him to her breast and soothe his hurts as a mother would a child. "Have you ever been half of an item, a couple, a pair?"

He jerked his head up and down. "Once or twice."

"And how did it feel?"

"Smothering."

Kim frowned and stepped away. She began to twirl her hair, and for a long time she tried to think of a response. Maybe it wasn't a good idea for her to stay longer. Admittedly, though she tried to convince herself that staying was for the sake of the buyout, she knew that wasn't completely true. At the rate things were happening in Evergreen, it would be like taking a sucker from a two-year-old. No, it was because she wanted to be with Ricco, and if she was really honest with herself, it went beyond that. She liked the uncomplicated lifestyle of the people in Evergreen. There was, for her anyway, absolutely no performance pressure.

Her gaze rose to Ricco's. Gone was his boyish grin; in its stead was the face of a man very serious about committing, or, in their case, not committing. She inhaled a deep breath and let it out. "Smothering is not a good verb when it comes to relationships. No matter how casual." She continued to twirl her hair, then said, "Look, I'm not the kind of girl who can have sex with a guy one day, and watch him hit on another woman the next and not have feelings about it. I'd liked to think I was that uncaring, but I have my limits. And since you appear to have commitment issues on just about every level, let's not waste our time." And though she meant every word of it, the room was suddenly colder at her admission and what would follow in its wake.

"I'm not a damn dog, Kim!" Ricco said. "You act like I hump anything that turns her ass my way."

"Well, excuse me for noticing how every bitch in this town is in heat over you!"

It was Ricco's turn to pace. "So what?"

"So *what?* So, it's annoying to have your man be groped and drooled over at every turn." Heat flooded her cheeks. That was it. No more conversation. She strode to the door, opened it, and said, "Just take your bag and leave me alone for the rest of the time I'm here."

He stood for a long time, staring down at her. He moved beside her and bent to pick up his bag. As he did so, his gaze traversed her face, and try as she might, she could not read him. His face was completely passive. Of course it was—she'd just called him "her" man. Bad Kim. She was no doubt playing out a scenario he was all too familiar with. Unfortunately, it was one she was all too familiar with as well. History, it seemed, was destined in her case to repeat itself. Relentlessly.

When he walked out of her room and slowly shut the door behind him, a swell of emotions she wasn't prepared for encompassed her heart. She took a big deep breath and told herself it was just sex. It was the lust phase. It was hormones and pheromones, and she was at that time in her life where she was sexually peaking. That was all it was. Like anything that felt good, you wanted to rinse and repeat. She'd get over it soon enough. Besides, she had work to do, and being free of any form of sexual haze made it that much easier.

She nodded and walked toward the window. She stood back and watched Ricco's tall form stride down the sidewalk. A lump formed in her throat. She'd promised herself many years ago that she would not get sucked in by a guy who was out of her league. Once again she'd failed, but at least now she had a man to fall back on. Someone who respected her and her brain, who was steady, solid, and lived for the same things she did—power and wealth. Kim smiled, but it took an effort. Right now all the power and wealth in the world could not make the queasy feeling in her stomach go away.

But in time, it would. And knowing that, she moved away from the window and hurried from the room down to Leticia and the girls. She had loan docs to find, and what better way to do it than under the pretense of helping clean out a waterlogged office?

It was a mess but not unfixable. "Mama," Jasmine said, "I can come back after school and help. But I can't go to the council meeting if you call it at eleven. Can you schedule it for after three?"

Leticia picked up a stack of gooey, sodden papers and nodded. "I'll shoot for four, that way we can help Ez out with her photo shoot and then get down to business. It will also give everyone else time to make arrangements." She looked up at Kim and smiled a slow, sad smile. "I must apologize again for my son's deplorable behavior. I don't know what has gotten into that boy. He was raised with better manners than that."

Kim smiled in return, feeling as sad. "I don't let it bother me. I know he's under a lot of pressure right now, and I think he's feeling a little claustrophobic."

Leticia's smile brightened, as if the excuses made up for his behavior and somehow also let her off the hook. "You're right. But he usually doesn't get antsy until after his second week here. By New Year's Day you can't tie him down."

Jasmine picked up a soaked box of copy paper and tossed it out of the broken window, onto the charred deck. "He's like his father that way."

"Jasmine!" Leticia hissed.

Jasmine looked at her mother and shrugged as she picked up another soggy box. "It's the truth. Stop glossing over the fact your little *papi* is his father's son. Only difference is, Ricco doesn't leave a wife and kids behind to the wolves of society every time he gets an itch."

"Jasmine!"

The second oldest daughter dropped the box in her hands. When it hit the sodden floor it came apart at the seams. She turned to fully face her mother. "No, Mama, I'm tired of pretending. Papa screwed *all of us*, you most especially. So is it any wonder his son should mimic the behavior? I don't think less of my brother. I love him. For crying out loud, stupid me, I married a man like my father!" Her dark eyes were fierce, but Leticia's flashed as hotly. Still, Jasmine continued, "So let's not sugarcoat what is our reality, Mother."

"How dare you be so disrespectful!"

"Sorry you find the truth so hard to swallow. You gave up your life pining away for a good-for-nothing drunk, and when a good man like Cal came around, a man who would treat you with the dignity you deserve, you blow him off, then take back the man who deserted us repeatedly. What kind of lesson did that teach? And you wonder why his son, who took up the slack at six years old, doesn't want a thing to do with him?"

Leticia stepped closer to her daughter, her face a murderous shade of red. "No, Mommy," Jasmine said, standing her ground. "Hear me out. Because of my father, my brother can't even commit to a damn houseplant!"

Leticia's face suddenly lost all gravity. In the space of

the time it took for Jasmine to unload the truth, her face had sagged as if she'd been one hundred years old instead of fifty something. Her big hazel eyes, so much like her son's, glistened with unshed tears. Kimberly felt the overwhelming urge to put her arms around the woman who had sacrificed so much in the name of her children but in so doing had taught them the wrong lesson.

Jasmine stood rigid, unmoving, a steel rod. "I'm sorry for upsetting you, Mommy, but not for what I said. I love you and will defend you to my last breath, but it's time for you to once in your life live for yourself and give Ricco some room. Stop bombarding him with requests to come home and to do this and to do that. We all need to. We've allowed him to lug us around as if he were the father. He's not. He's my baby brother and your son. It's time we stood up for ourselves and took responsibility for our lives."

Kim swallowed hard as many of the puzzle pieces that were the man Ricco Maza fell into place. And once again a little piece of her heart thawed for the proud man.

Leticia looked from her daughter to Kim. She swiped the tears from her eyes and bowed her head. "My apologies for dragging our skeletons out of the closet."

Kim smiled, reached out to the woman's shoulder, and lightly touched it. "I feel honored."

Jasmine snorted. "Girl, you are crazy! Watch! Now that the lid has been blown off, the fireworks will begin in earnest. You'd better take cover."

Kim continued to smile. "I've never had anyone in my family stand up for me for good or bad reasons. I was a simple means to an end. I think it's great you can hash out your feelings this way. Hell, it's amazing to see feelings like this."

Leticia slipped an arm around Kim's waist and drew her near. She repeated the gesture with Jasmine. She kissed her daughter's cheeks. "I love you, *precia*. And I am so sorry for letting you down."

Jasmine's dark eyes watered, and she nodded. "Mommy, you did what you did out of love. There is no forgiveness for that. But I realized that I am in charge of my choices, not you. I need to grow up a little myself."

Leticia kissed her again, then turned to Kim, hugging her close and placing a kiss on her forehead. "Your mama must be blind. You are a precious daughter."

Kim smiled and ignored the hot sting of moisture in her eyes.

Leticia laughed and released both girls. She stepped back. "Okay, okay, no more time for emotions. Jasmine, go to your students. Kimberly, I appreciate any help you can give me here, but I must go muster the council for a meeting. We have a town to save!"

And as simply as that, the two Maza women disappeared, leaving Kimberly feeling oddly disconnected. For a long moment she stood in the water-soaked room and looked around, not knowing where to begin. When she thought of her ulterior motives for helping out, that baby pang of guilt grew some. Now it was big and ugly, clawing at her insides. She stood unmoving for a long time before she turned to the file cabinets and pushed warm fuzzy images of the Maza family from her brain.

When, after pulling several soggy files from the cabinet under Leti's desk, she hit the mother lode, all thoughts of family, love, and heartwarming dinners evaporated.

Marcus Rand Consortium. A private group out of Lodi, of all places. She never would have guessed. Just as she'd scribbled the information down, a soft cough from the doorway startled her.

She gasped and dropped the pen in her hand. Then she shot to her feet.

"Did you find what you were looking for, young lady?" Enrique Maza asked from the doorway. Gone was the frail voice, gone was the woe-is-me look; in their place was the angled look of a fox. A very wily fox.

"Yes, as a matter of fact I did."

"Care to share?" he said, walking into the room. It occurred to Kim that he was walking quite easily without the aid of his cane, and though his face was beginning to bruise around what was obviously a broken nose, she could easily read the face of a grifter. Ricco had been right all along. And for that she was so very sorry. She had hoped that somehow father and son would mend the broken fences between them.

"You're not dying."

"In one form or another we all are, are we not? But me? Now? Of cancer?" He grinned, flashing her the killer smile his son had perfected. "No, not today or any other day. Like you, I am here under false pretenses."

Kimberly gasped. "I'm not here under—"

He put his hand up and shooshed her. "Don't even try to sheist a master."

He moved in closer and looked around the room in disgust. "Did you happen to find my wife's safe while you were stealing her personal information?" He grabbed the paper she had written the lender's information on. "Marcus Rand Consortium? Who are they and how are they connected to my wife?"

"I don't know."

He smiled again, and the look was anything but warm and friendly. "Is this the group who holds this town by the financial hairs?"

Kim kept her breath, as well as her urge to give the man another broken nose, under control. "I'm not sure," she lied.

"But you have ways to find out." It was not a question.

She nodded. "I do."

Enrique moved deeper into the room. "What benefit would one have with this information?"

She shrugged and played along, deciding that while he was looking to pump her, she would in turn pump him. The more information one had on an adversary, the better prepared one was for the inevitable conflict, and Enrique Maza was most definitely a conflict in the making. The primal mama bear every woman possessed when it came to those she loved began to quickly take form as a category five hurricane in her heart. If she could spare Ricco and his family from this man, she would do everything in her power to see it done.

"Not that it's any of your business"—she snatched the paper from his hand and smiled when his eyes narrowed—"if there is a way with my experience to help Evergreen out of its jam, I will do what I can."

"Liar."

Kim folded the paper and slid it into her back jean pocket. "No, not like you."

He laughed softly, the sound low and throaty; it gave her the willies. "With one phone call I can let this consortium know that Evergreen is tied down and naked, waiting to be raped."

"No you won't!"

"How can you be so sure?"

"Because you won't make a dime off of it, and that's what drives you."

He smiled then, showing his perfectly straight, villainous looking teeth. "How much are you willing to pay me not to make the call?"

Kim threw her head back and laughed. "I don't know what you're smoking, old man, but you need to quit." She moved in closer and said, "Keep making your demands and I'll let your family in on what a skunk you are."

"I'll deny it. And my wife will stand by me. Give me a hundred grand and I'm gone. Forever."

Kim shook her head. "I have no loyalty to anyone here, so go get screwed."

He grinned and turned to the mess. In a quick role reversal, he grabbed his cane and acted the poor dying father. "Here, my dear, allow me to help you. My wife will appreciate my efforts."

Kim folded her arms across her chest and scowled at the man. "Why don't you do something noble for once in your miserable life and crawl back into the hole you crawled out of and leave these people alone."

He coughed, feigning the sickly elder to a tee. "So tell me, Miss Michaels, what are your intentions toward my son?"

She shot him a glare and turned to get to work on the sodden mess. "You're mistaken. I have none."

"Who's the liar now?"

Kim fixed him with a stare, then started stacking soaked files on the desk. "Maybe you need to mind your own business."

"My son is like me, you know? He will never stay in one place with one woman for long. It's part of his DNA. Like his dark eyes, he can't help it."

Kim ignored the man and continued to clean out the file cabinet. Enrique Senior was wrong!

Ricco's eyes might be brown like his father's; but there was enough of his mother's green to make the difference.

Kim stood and slammed down the stack of squishy files. "You're wrong about Ricco. He might have your DNA, but he is ten times the man you could ever hope to be. Don't drag him down to your subterranean level."

"You do the same thing my son does, and I continue to do."

"You don't know anything about me." Kim shook her head at the old man, disgust filling her so thoroughly she could barely look at him. She completely understood how Ricco felt. Enrique was the scum of the earth and would never change. As she strode past him, she stiffened at his parting shot: "You run away when the pressure gets too much. You're a coward!"

She resisted the urge to turn and tell the man she didn't run from pressure, she thrived on it! And to prove it to herself, as soon as she stepped out of Leti's house, she took her cell phone out of her pocket and punched Nick's speed-dial number.

Sixteen

"Gold."

Kim scowled. So they were back to that, were they? "It's Kimberly Michaels."

"I know that."

"Then act like it!"

"Jesus Christ, Kimberly, what the hell is going on up there? From the minute you landed in Reno you've been acting like a hormonal teenager."

Kim paced the sidewalk, wanting to tell him that maybe she'd like a little emotion from her almost fiancé. Yanno, a "Hey babe, how are you?" Or "I can't wait to see you." Or at the very least, acknowledge her importance by not saying his last name when he answered the phone!

"Maybe, Nicholas, I'm having a bit of a midlife crisis up here. Did it ever occur to you that I might be a little bit more than a giant money generator? That I might just have a few feelings?"

"Okay," he slowly said.

"Forget it. Look, this town is on the fringe of self-imploding. Tourists are leaving in droves, and the townsfolk are sick of worrying about money. Later today there is an open town hall meeting. The council is going to discuss a course of action to save freakin' Christmas!"

"Sounds to me like Christmas is going to be a thing of the past for them."

"Yeah, no shit. Give them a few more days of this crime wave and they'll be paying us to take their property off their hands."

"How do you explain what's happening? I thought crime was nil there."

Kim took a deep breath and slowed her headlong descent into running away from Evergreen and the people in it. "I wanted to talk to you about that, Nick. It seems too coincidental, this so-called crime wave."

"What are you implying?"

"I'm implying that if there is any behind-the-scenes nudging going on, it had better stop before someone gets hurt."

"I'm getting a little offended here, Kimberly."

"Good. Let's keep everything honest and win the old-fashioned way, by outmaneuvering our opponent."

The silence was so pronounced that she thought they had lost their connection. "Nick?"

"Look," he started, "what is done is done and it's worked out to our benefit. What we need is the name of the consortium. Do you have it?"

Now it was her turn to pause. That little voice she always listened to scratched madly at her belly. "I think I have an idea."

"Do you have a name?"

"A consortium out of Lodi. I'm working on it."

She could hear Nick tapping his pen on the edge of his inlaid mahogany desk, which he had had hand-crafted by a Venetian artist. He only did that when he was perturbed. "Time is money, Kimberly."

She sighed and looked back toward Leti's house. Enrique stood at the unbroken window, next to the one that was boarded up, his dark gaze locked on her. "I know. I know."

Kim hung up and turned back toward the center of town. Her body stiffened more. Ricco was walking straight toward her. She turned and crossed the street, then walked toward him on the other side. She'd grab a bite to eat at the teahouse, then come back for the shoot, and hopefully after that be a fly on the wall at the town hall meeting.

By the time she got to the teahouse, there was a flurry of chatter about the crime spree in Evergreen. Kim felt bad for Maddy; it was obvious she didn't want to hear about it. Talking about it kept it alive.

"Are y'all going to come down to the ice rink tonight for the skate with Santa-thon?" she asked a group of ladies sitting by the front door, their hands tightly grasped around their purses. Kim couldn't help a smile. It wasn't like lightning would strike twice.

"I don't know how to ice-skate," one of them said.

Maddy grinned and said, "Well, sugarplum, that's the beauty of it. We have some really hunky Santas and you *want* them to hold you close and teach you a few moves." She winked and looked at Kim, then said, "Just ask her about how hunky our Santas are. She has firsthand knowledge."

Kim felt the heat rise in her cheeks, and just as she was going to agree, the bell to the shop tinkled and all eyes turned to see who was coming through the door. A collective gasp rose from every woman in the small shop. A tall man dressed in casual clothes with a ski mask pulled over his face entered, wagging a semiautomatic pistol in front of him.

"Good morning, ladies. Don't make a scene, or my buddy outside will have to come in and help me shut you up."

All eyes darted to the lone man standing guard at the

door, casually sipping a cup of coffee. He was dressed like the man inside—tourist casual—except the man out front didn't have his ski mask pulled down, covering his face. But all Kim could see was the back of his dark head.

"Give me your wallets and your jewelry. Do it now, do it quick, and do it quiet."

Just as Kim handed over the cash in her pocket, the masked man shook his head. He pointed the barrel of his gun at her throat. "Necklace goes too."

She grasped it. "No!" He grabbed her hand and yanked it from her neck. Kim seethed; she didn't fight for her locket only because she didn't want to get anyone hurt. As the bad guy made his last sweep, she saw, out of the corner of her eye, Ricco walking toward the shop. Her heart rate accelerated. She wanted him to come in and save the day, but she was also afraid for him. Holding her breath, she watched him glance at the guy out front, then into the shop. Then he kept going. And she knew then that he knew.

The guy out front poked his head in and locked eyes with Kim. She, along with every other woman in the place, had a picture-perfect look at his face. Caucasian male, midtwenties, brown hair, brown eyes, and a nose that looked as if it had been broken a few times. When his thin lips pulled back from his teeth, she noticed that his bottom front teeth were chipped. "We just got made," he said in a flat, unaccented voice.

In a twinkle they were gone, and just as fast Ricco was after them.

Kim ran to the edge of the boardwalk and watched the two men split. Ricco went after the guy with the gun. When he turned and started shooting, she screamed. Ricco, along with every other person in proximity, hit the ground. But what Ricco did next amazed her. On his belly, he returned fire! When had he started carrying a gun? To her horror and amazement, the thug went down with a thud, just like the reindeer had the day before. Her body began to shake uncontrollably; suddenly the stakes had gone too high. Something insidious had taken over this sleepy little town, and it was now just a matter of time before one of its residents was seriously injured or killed. Tentatively Kim ventured off the boardwalk, not knowing what to do. But she did what her gut told her, and that was to go to Ricco. He was kneeling down beside the bad guy, feeling for a pulse. But she knew the minute she looked at the hardening, muddy eyes that he was dead.

"Are you all right?" she softly asked Ricco.

He looked up at her and squinted against the glare of the morning sun. "I'm fine. Did he hurt you or anyone else in there?"

She shook her head. "No, he just took our wallets and jewelry." She pointed to the satchel a few yards from where the body lay. Several wallets and pieces of jewelry littered the ground near it.

"Okay. I want you to go back to the shop and wait for Jeff and Peyton. You don't need to see this." His voice was deep and unusually calm. Kim knelt down next to him and looked into his face to find not a man who had a problem with what he did but a man attending to his business. But how did you kill someone—even a bad guy—and not have it affect you?

"Are you sure you're okay?"

Ricco smiled. "I've been down this road before. I have no problem going to bed after a righteous shoot."

She stood and looked down at the dead man again. "Okay, but if you need anything . . ."

"I'll be fine. Now go tell the guys what happened."

Carefully, as if she'd been barefoot and treading on broken glass, Kim made her way back to the gathered crowd. Assumptions, recantations, and speculation abounded, but one common thread was clear. The tourists were done with Christmas in Evergreen. And Kim couldn't blame them. She wanted to leave too. And she would have, except . . . her gaze roamed across the crime scene to the tall, dark-haired, dark-eyed man who stared back. Except for him.

Several hours later, after the body was put in the coroner's van and everyone was questioned, Kim waited for Ricco. The sun had begun its set in the western sky. While life had seemed to stand still for Kim those few hours, it had not for Esmeralda. Her world had darkened. Right after the shooting, *Town & Country* had pulled up stakes and left town. Kim was now Esmeralda's only guest, and the town's seasonal population was reduced to a small percentage of what it had only been three days before. The town hall meeting was scheduled for eight that night. It had been scheduled for that time so the merchants could keep their doors open for every sale, then meet when they closed for the night. But Evergreen was now a ghost town. It didn't matter.

Kimberly felt an incredible sense of loss for these people. As she walked with Leticia and her daughters, she felt as if she'd been walking to the gallows. As she entered the courtroom in city hall, she watched as the townsfolk filed in. She saw resignation, anger, and pure depression scribbled across the many faces.

As she sat down, her cell phone vibrated. She looked at the number. Nick. Quickly she answered and excused herself from the room.

"Hey, they're just getting the meeting started," Kim said out of earshot of any lingering townsfolk.

"I just made another offer. The Tomlinsons will have it. Make sure when those folks bust a vein you convince them that in your business experience it's their best recourse."

Kim's mouth went dry. "I thought we agreed no more backroom offers?"

Nick laughed. "Baby, you are losing your objectivity."

She set her jaw. "What's the offer?"

Nick laughed, the sound diabolic. She could just see him rubbing his hands together, then twisting his Snidely Whiplash mustache as he gloated over his good fortune and their loss. "Forty cents on the dollar."

"Nick! That's unethical!"

"Unethical? Are you kidding me? What the hell, Kimberly? Last week you would have been giving me gold stars for the maneuver, now you tell me I'm unethical?"

She shook her head. "I've gotten to know these people. It's their lives."

"Well, their lives just went on sale. And I'm buying."

"I know, but—"

"No buts. Are you in this with me or not?"

She shook her head, not wanting to continue. She wanted out, she wanted to pack up and drive fast and far. But if she did, what was the alternative? Failure? To miss out on the opportunity of a lifetime? "I'm in," she slowly said.

"Good girl. Now, I want details when it's over."

She hung up. And looked up to see Ricco standing in the doorway, staring at her. She couldn't meet his gaze. Instead she moved past him and into the courtroom. The debate was hot and heated. "It's easy for you to say sit it out, Leticia, you have equity. You haven't mortgaged your house," challenged Ben, the owner of Santa's Workshop.

"It's been six years since this town has been in the black. My loan is due the end of the year. I can't pay it," a merchant said.

"Even if I could," another person said, "it would clean me out for next year. I can barely pay my utility bills as it is. And forget about my taxes."

Leticia put her hands up and called for quiet. "Please, please, I hear what everyone is saying. We're all in this together. Let's find a way to pool our resources to help our neighbors."

"So we all go down?"

"No, so we can all stay afloat."

"For how long? Did you see the line out of this place today?"

"Ricco, Jeff, what the hell?"

Ricco stepped forward. "I have information that might change your minds. It appears the thug who I killed, Joseph Watters, was a gun for hire out of L.A. The tags on the Suburban that used the pedestrians as target practice the other day were found ditched in Sparks. Watters's fingerprints were all over it. The purse snatcher, out of L.A."

"What's the L.A. connection?" Cal asked.

"Where is Land's Edge out of?" Ricco countered.

"L.A.," Kim whispered. Cold infiltrated her bones, and her breath wheezed out of her chest.

And it all made perfect sense to her. Nick had lied to her! And, by association, she was an accomplice! Her shock quickly subsided as anger took hold of her. She hadn't signed up for terrorism tactics. Not wanting to call attention to herself, Kim took a deep breath and steadied her shaking hands.

The crowd became a swarming mass of fury. And despite her efforts to keep calm, Kim felt her blood pressure rise as well.

"How do we prove it?" Jasmine demanded.

Ricco shrugged. "It's speculation right now. If the purse snatcher talks, which seems unlikely, since he's lawyered up and has a shark of an attorney, we don't have much to go on unless we strike a deal." He glanced at Kim. "Have you heard of this company in your business dealings?"

She swallowed hard and nodded. "They play hardball."

"No-rules hardball?"

"No-rules hardball." All seemed lost for the tiny Christmas town. She was about to recommend that the town capitulate when she looked up into Ricco's dark eyes. Then she looked around the room, at his family and the townsfolk, and something deep inside her shifted. There was the right way to dismantle a property for acquisition and there was the wrong way, and what Nick was doing was wrong. "What's the current offer on the table?" she asked instead.

Donna Tomlinson stepped up. "I just got a call from the Land's Edge representative. Now that I think about it, the timing is kind of interesting. It seems like each time there is criminal activity and we lose tourists, we get a call."

"What is it?" Kim asked again.

"Forty cents for every dollar owed."

"That's ridiculous!"

"Robbery!"

"Isn't that against the law?"

Kim shook her head. "No, but coercion and extortion are."

"So is murder," Ricco said. He turned to Kim. In front of the entire town, he asked her, "Will you help us save Evergreen?"

Fear, doubt, and the knowledge that if she agreed she would lose everything she had worked so hard for grabbed her hard by the throat. And for what? To keep a few Stepford folks out of the mouth of the big bad wolf? If the Evergreen deal fell through for Land's Edge, there would be no marriage to Nick. That she could live with, but could she live with that man's death on her conscience? Because of the information she had given Nick, he'd taken it upon himself to hike up the ante.

She thought back to the most recent acquisition, the Sierra Resort in Laughlin. The place had been run down, but it had been operating in the black until the Banshee motorcycle gang had taken up residence and all hell had broken loose. Just like here. Had Nick resorted to terrorism to get what he'd wanted? In her gut she knew the answer.

One way or another, she'd find out.

"I need all of the numbers, the loan docs, everything financially attached to this town. Give me twenty-four hours and we'll meet again," Kim said softly, then added, "but I can't promise you I can fix this."

Ricco smiled. "I know you can find a way."

"What do we tell the Land's Edge rep?" Donna asked.

Kim caught her worried gaze. "Tell them to shove it up their ass," she replied.

The crowd erupted, but she saw more than a few doubting Thomases amongst the crowd. She wasn't so sure either, but she knew how to bring a town down and take it apart; now she would have to find a way to do the opposite.

With no guests to disturb her, Kim set up shop in Esmeralda's kitchen. Booting up her laptop, she got to it with an adding machine and a mountain of paperwork. In short order she had each loan labeled and categorized, every one of them neatly stacked for easy reference. The more she dug, the deeper shit she found Evergreen in. At first she was angry at Leticia for allowing the town to get into such bad loans, but as she dug deeper she saw that Leticia had thought they would be able, with time and money to spare, to get out of debt. But the longer they took to repay and defer the interest, the more it accumulated. They needed over three million cash to just keep afloat for another month. And Nick knew it. She knew she shouldn't have given him the consortium information. As a CPA, didn't Leticia know that rule number one was always have an airtight contingency plan?

Even if the town could come up with the cash at the end of the month, they would need the consortium to allow them to refinance the loans, no doubt at a desperation interest rate. The winds of recession were blowing fiercely across the country. Foreclosure was no longer a hush word; in California, it was as common as a housefly.

Several times Esmeralda came in and asked if Kim needed anything. Ricco stayed away. But several times she looked up, feeling his gaze on her, to find the doorway empty.

At midnight her cell phone rang. It was Nick. She ignored him. After he called back every minute for fifteen minutes straight, Kim answered. "What is it?"

"What the hell is going on? My rep was told to take the offer and shove it up his ass!"

Kim smiled. "I don't doubt it. Evergreen is on to you, Nick."

"What's that supposed to mean?"

"Your hired thugs. Even for you that's scraping the bottom of the barrel."

"What are you talking about?"

"Oh, stop it! One of your guys was shot in the back today. He's dead! By the cop he was shooting at. Is that what you wanted? I was the victim of a mugging by the same creep right before he got his. He took my grand-mother's locket! When we searched the bag of loot it was gone. Who knows where it is!"

"I don't know what the hell you're talking about, Kimberly!"

"That's bullshit." She took a long breath and ex-haled. "Look, Nick, I didn't sign up for terrorism."

"Kimberly, I swear to you, I did not hire anyone to strong-arm Evergreen into submission. It's not my style. You know that."

"Did you hire that motorcycle gang in Laughlin?"

"I swear to God, Kimberly, that was an ugly fluke that worked in our favor."

She wanted to believe him. Really she did. But something nagged at her intuition. Nick was not an in-nocent. To that end it was better for Evergreen and for herself to keep Nick's confidence in her.

"I want you to come home, Kimberly. There's nothing

left for you to do there. We have them by the short hairs. Let nature take its course now."

She'd let him think so. "You're probably right."

His voice was low and soothing. She rubbed her temples, a sudden migraine erupting behind her eyeballs. "Do you want me to come get you?" he softly asked her.

That was the last thing she wanted. "No. Actually, I'm going to head out of here tomorrow and go down to the La Playa in Carmel for a few days and regenerate."

"How about if I meet you there? We can get to know each other better."

A week ago she would have leapt at the opportunity. Now? She just wanted to be alone. "Nick, I think we need to talk when I get back to L.A."

"Are you having second thoughts about our marriage?"

"I'm having second thoughts about a lot of things. I'll call you when I get settled in Carmel. Give me a day or two?"

She hung up the phone, laid her head down on the table, and closed her eyes.

"Who's Nick?" Ricco asked from the doorway.

Her body stiffened, and her heart rate jumped.

She turned her head on her hands. "You have no right to ask me anything."

He strode into the kitchen, his face contorted in fury. She sat up straight. What had he heard?

"You're right, I don't—not about you personally, but I want to know how he fits in with the town I call home."

"Really? You call a place you hit and run for less than three weeks out of the year home?"

"Who are you? Why are you here? What do you want?"

Kim stood and arched her back, suddenly exhausted. Her sudden trip to Carmel had been a ruse to keep Nick away from Evergreen. Now she thought it wasn't a bad idea. "The answers to your questions are irrelevant."

"What are you hiding? Why are you really here?"

"You're a cop, you figure it out."

Ricco smirked. "You're a cold one, Misses Grinch."

"And you're a commitmentphobe, Mister Playboy." He scowled. She smiled. "Truth hurts, huh?"

"You make not wanting to commit sound like a disease. What's wrong with not making promises you won't keep? What's so wrong with being honest about not wanting a committed relationship?"

She shrugged. "Nothing—if you have ice for a heart."

"Me? *Ice* for a heart? Are you kidding me? I'm a furnace inside!"

"You're lukewarm at best. You can't stand the heat, so you run far and you run fast."

"You don't even engage."

She raked her fingers through her hair. "Fine, turn it around and beat me up. Bottom line is, your old man couldn't commit and somehow you think if you make a commitment and break it you're him. Get a clue, Ricco, promises are made to be broken. It's life."

"And just because your parents and every guy you've slept with disappointed you, you expect it from every other man."

"Duh."

"Not all men are pieces of shit."

"Maybe you're right, but I don't care enough to find out."

"You're a liar."

Her head snapped back. He walked into her space. "You want what every other female in this world wants."

"I suppose you're going to tell me what that is."

"You already know what it is, you just won't admit it."

"Really? If you know so much, tell me exactly what my heart's desire is."

Ricco swept her hair from her shoulders and pressed his hand to her chest. Her heart leapt against his palm. "You want a man to put you up on a pedestal. You want him to love and cherish you. You want him to never lie to you or ever cheat on you. You want to know that you above all other women are the one he chose to spend the rest of his life with, and nothing or no one can change that."

Her chest fluttered beneath his touch and his words. Every word he'd said was the truth. "Cinderella, if I were man enough for you, I'd sweep you away right this minute and set you up on that pedestal."

"Why can't you?"

"Because I'll screw it up somehow. And I care too much about you to see you fall and get your heart broken."

She leaned into his hand, feeling more fatigued than she could remember. "I don't think you're afraid to commit, Ricco, I think that's an excuse."

"For what?"

"You're just as afraid as I am of being abandoned by someone you love." He stiffened, and she knew she'd hit home. "It doesn't make you a coward, Ricco, it just makes you human."

He smiled sadly and nodded his head. "Maybe there is truth in that." He drew her into his arms and kissed the top of her head. "It's been quite a roller-coaster ride since we met."

She drew back and smiled. "You can say that again."

He pulled her along with him and up the stairs to her bedroom door. "Get some sleep. You have a town to save in the morning."

* * *

When Ricco came downstairs several minutes later, dressed for a run, he stopped short just outside the kitchen doorway. A small noise alerted him to someone's presence. He went for his gun but frowned. Jimmy had had to take it after the shooting. He didn't have a backup weapon.

He peeked around the corner to see his father scrolling through Kim's cell phone.

"Find what you need?" Ricco asked, striding into the room.

Enrique had the grace to blush.

"I told you last night to hit the road. Why are you still here, and why are you going through Kim's phone?"

The old man sighed heavily. Leaning on the cane he didn't need, he sat down in Kim's vacated chair. "I have a suspicion about your friend."

"Really? Are you going to ask me to pay for that information?"

"No, son. Believe it or not, I do have affection for you and don't want to see you hurt."

Ricco threw his head back and laughed long and hard. His cheeks strained and his eyes actually teared. When he calmed down he looked his old man in the eye and said, "You don't care about anyone except yourself. Get out of here before I call the cops."

Enrique stood and faced his son. "I'll go, but before I do, be warned, I have a hunch your friend Miss Michaels has ties to the people who have been terrorizing Evergreen."

"That's it." Ricco grabbed him up none too gently by the elbow, thrust the cane into his hand, then shoved him toward the back door. "Get out!"

Once the image of his father was gone, Ricco locked up after himself for the first time since he could remember. Then he did what he always did to clear his mind. He ran. And ran. He pushed the visions of his father, his mother, and his sisters out of his mind. For a few miles he even managed to push from his mind Kim's last words to him and her smiling blue eyes. Replacing it was the still body of the man he'd killed that day, and while he was never one to feel sorry for a criminal, he did have regrets for taking a life. But they were short-lived. It was the old law of the West—kill or be killed. He'd do it again one hundred times over.

And once he reminded himself that it could have been Kim or himself in the black body bag, he didn't give it another thought. But he gave Kim more thought. His father's accusation niggled at his brain. And every time he thought of Kim tied in with Land's Edge he felt like he was going to puke. So he pushed it away and took the accusation with a huge grain of salt. It was just his father's way of fucking with his head some more. The man didn't care who he hurt in the process.

Ricco bellowed in rage, and his fists punched the air.

He was sick and damned tired of his peace being destroyed by his father's past, present, and future. Ricco came to the abrupt conclusion that most of his frustration wasn't what his old man had done to them; it was the fact that he continued to do it. He wanted the man to stop. To come clean. Not that he longed for father-son fishing trips, but he wanted to be rid of the emotional burden of knowing he could never trust the man with himself or his family. He was afraid it would never happen.

He ran until his brain could not formulate another thought if his life depended upon it. Nevertheless, he came to a decision, one that terrified him as much as it thrilled him. Kim was right. He wasn't afraid to commit; he was afraid of being abandoned. And that realization brought him to another one: For the first time in his adult life, he was willing to stick his emotional neck out and take a chance, despite the record amount of turmoil in his life at the moment.

He headed back home, where he showered and slipped on a pair of flannel sweats, then dug around in his duffel bag, looking for something special.

Kim woke from a deep slumber to light knocking on her door. Sleep swirled around her muggy brain. There it was again. "Who is it?" she called.

The sound of a key slipping into the lock alarmed her. Was it an intruder? No, she reasoned, they wouldn't knock first. But still . . . Looking around, she jumped from the bed and grabbed the iron fire poker.

When Ricco emerged from behind the door she let out a long breath of relief. Until she saw his dark gaze. He leaned up against the jamb, clad only in black flannel sweats. "I've come to a decision, Cinderella."

She lowered the poker, but her blood quickened. "And it couldn't wait until morning?"

He shook his head. "No, it couldn't. And once I tell you, I think you might agree."

"I'm all ears."

He sucked in a long breath and released it. "I am willing to try this commitment thing, at least while we're both here, if you are."

You could have knocked her over with a breeze. "What?"

"You and me, an item, a couple, a pair. Stay until the New Year at least."

Kim was stunned, flabbergasted. In shock. "I—"

Ricco grinned. "I feel your pain. Believe me, this is uncharted territory for me as well." His grin widened, and he opened the hand he held over his head against the jamb. A pair of handcuffs clanked together. "I want to tie you up and have my way with you all night long."

She thought she would melt into the floor right then and there. "I—"

He sauntered into her room and shut the door behind him, soundly turning the lock. "C'mon, princess. What is the ultimate fantasy of a control freak like you?"

"I—"

He moved her back against the bed. Taking her right hand, he slipped one of the cuffs around her. The soft click of it locking around her wrist sent shivers rushing up and down her spine and to all points in between. He pushed her back onto the bed and pulled her left arm over her head. Then he slipped the chain through the bedpost and slid the other cuff around her left wrist. The soft click of the clasp had her wet, shivering, and wanting him more than she had ever wanted a man.

"Ricco," she whispered, "take me there."

"I'm going to do more than that, sweetheart." He brushed his lips across her cheek. "I'm going to love you all night long and into the morning. I'm going to love you until you cry out for me to stop."

"We'll be here for eternity."

His lips lowered to hers. "I'm all for that."

Seventeen

KIMBERLY LAY BACK INTO THE PILLOWS AND CLOSED HER eyes. For the first time in her adult life, she allowed another human to take her control away. As his lips trailed from hers to her neck then to the high mound of her breasts, she wanted more. But she could not force him to do more. His hands were on either side of her head, his body raised above hers. Only his lips, that soft warm flesh of his, touched her scalding skin.

He nibbled at her collarbone; he took her nipple into his mouth through the fabric of her cami and suckled her. She arched into him, her back coming off the bed. Her fingers reached for him as her arms strained to touch him to press him more firmly against her. Her thighs parted, her hips undulated. Yet he only touched her with his lips.

"Ricco," she gasped, "please stop. Touch me harder. Touch me everywhere."

With his teeth he pulled down her panties. Twisting, she tried to press her hips into his face, but he continued the slow slide of her panties down her legs until he slid them off of her. He tossed them to the floor. His hot breath flushed her already sizzling nether region. When he came so close to her core that she could feel his hot breath move across her damp curls, she cried out. When his hands ran up her thighs, she almost came on the spot. He pressed her hips back into the sheets and nibbled the inside of her thigh. "Ricco," she begged, "touch me with your mouth. Put your finger in me."

In a slow, light slide he licked her creamy lips. She cried out, this time not caring who heard. Lucky for her they were the only guests. His tongue swirled across her, his lips suckled, his big, thick finger slid feather soft back and forth across her clitoris. Her body shuddered. When he slid his finger into her hot, wet cavern, she screamed. Slowly he moved in and out of her, his finger swirling inside of her as his lips blazed a trail up her belly to her quivering breasts. When he latched onto a nipple, she lost it. In a slow, wet wave she came all over him.

Delirious, she pulled at the handcuffs and twisted beneath him, her hips quivering as spasms wracked through her. "Unlock me," she demanded.

"No," he answered. "Not until you can't move."

He slid off his sweats, and his long, warm body pressed against hers. The hard, thick length of his penis rubbed against her thigh. She wanted to touch him. Feel the heat and passion of him in her hand. But he kept himself from her. He teased her by turning around to face her feet, his jutting erection just out of reach of her mouth. When his lips descended between her thighs and his fingers slid along her wet cleft, they moaned together. He did wicked things to her body, teasing, taunting, giving her just enough to drive her up the steep ledge only to take away from her and leave her hanging, begging for completion. His erection pressed against her side, the full head of him weeping with anticipation. She tried to reach for him, wanting desperately to touch him to take him into her mouth, to tease him as he teased her, but he kept himself from her.

She begged him. She pleaded with him. She promised him anything and cajoled him to let her go, to give her control. But he ignored her. His hands, his lips, and his teeth tormented every inch of her. When she could no longer stand it, he entered her, filling her inch by sweet savage inch until he filled her to capacity. And when he did, she turned liquid. The sublimity of him made her weep, it made her catch her breath and it made her terrified, knowing she would never again be taken to the heights this man took her.

He was her drug. Her fix, her desperate need for fulfillment. Her orgasm came so hard and so fast and with such a velocity that Ricco moaned. "Jesus, Kim, I can feel that."

She gasped for breath, her hips pressed against his, her body spasming. And then she sank into the linens and let him take her on his flight. His body was like a well-oiled machine, a slick, hot engine. He powered into her, his hips thrusting, hers answering. He gathered her up into his arms, his body bent over hers, and in one long, hard thrust he exploded deep inside of her. *"Dios míos,"* he gritted out as his body convulsed against hers. Like an out-of-control engine, his body took time to come to rest against hers. His chest heaved, his slick body slid off hers. He pressed his forehead against hers, and his breath, in slow bursts, pummeled her cheeks. He dug his long fingers into her hair and pulled her up to meet his lips. Her body, still attached to his, twitched.

She wanted to cry. She wanted to touch this man and tell him he made her feel like Cinderella. Like she was truly special to him.

"I don't have the key," he softly said against her lips.

Kim laughed and tried to touch him. "I think it'll be pretty funny when the maid comes in in the morning to make the bed and she finds me half naked, hanging off the headboard."

Ricco relaxed against her, pressing his head to her belly. His fingers trailed across her wet curls. He pressed his palm against her sultry heat. "You're still hot."

She pressed her mons to his hand. "Ricco, that was amazing. Right now my entire body feels like one exposed conduit."

He kissed her belly. "Give me a minute and I'll light you up again."

"I want these cuffs off so I can return the favor."

He turned his head and looked up at her. Kim melted. His face was flushed, his lips full, and his eyes so sexy and dark that she thought she'd come again just looking at his postcoital glow. "No way."

She smiled lazily. "Oh, really?"

"I'd go crazy in handcuffs."

"Really?"

"Yes, really." He reached down, grabbed his sweats from the floor, and dipped into the back pocket, where he pulled out the small key. Deftly he uncuffed her.

Ricco woke to warm, wet moistness around his hard-on. A towel, warm water. He smiled, keeping his eyes closed. A sponge bath. He moved his hands to touch her but found them caught up by . . . His eyes flew open. Kim laughed and continued to wash him.

"You little minx. Unlock me."

She smiled at him, her blond hair swirling around her full, perky tits. He loved her tits. His fingers ached to touch them. But she had done to him what he had done to her. And for a man who had thought he would go ballistic in handcuffs, he found the opposite to be true. His cock filled with more blood. In some weird way he was okay with being the victim of Cinderella's lascivious ministrations.

Kim set the towels aside and climbed up alongside him in the bed. She smoothed her palm across the underside of his dick, and he surged. His arms pulled at the constraints. "Let me make sure those are secure," she softly said. She rose up against him, her sweet, musky pussy brushing up against his shoulder. The wild scent of her sent more of his blood south. He turned his head and strained his neck toward her, wanting to press his lips to the fiery spot. But she pulled back just far enough away that he could see her moist pink lips hiding behind the soft blond curls, her heady scent swirling temptingly around him but not close enough to taste. His fingers reached out to her, and he managed to grab a hank of her hair.

"Let go!" she cried out.

"No." He pulled her toward him, and her neck bowed. "Press into me." Her body stiffened. He pulled her hair harder. "Now."

Grabbing the headboard for balance, she pressed her hips closer to his mouth. But not close enough for him to taste her. "Closer," he commanded.

When she hesitated, he pulled her hair tighter. She cried out and moved close enough so that his tongue could just catch the tip of her straining clitoris. She gasped, and he knew he had her.

In a slow undulation, she pressed full into him. He wanted to dig his fingers into her ass, but he couldn't reach her. "Straddle me," he commanded, and this time there was no hesitation.

She grabbed the headboard and, steadying herself, moved hotly against his mouth. He felt her orgasm, the way her body shifted in momentum. And when she came, he sucked her as deeply as he could. She gyrated and shuddered against him, and he thought his cock was going to explode. When she slid her hot box down around him, fitting him like a snug glove, he nearly spilled at that moment.

As much as she tried to set the pace, he did—even handcuffed—and she was at his mercy. In a wild, combustive explosion, they erupted inside each other, and it was a long time before she could move her noodle-limp body from his.

When she released him, he took her into his arms and smoothed back her damp hair, kissing her cheeks, whispering to her how precious she was to him. He meant it. And while that should have terrified him, it didn't.

KIM SNUGGLED INTO THE CROOK OF HIS ARM AND smiled. "Did you like that?"

"Which part?"

"All of it!"

Ricco laughed and drew her back to him, the heady scent of their sex enshrouding them like a warm blanket. Their scents meshed well, creating an entirely unique scent unto them. It smelled good, strong, and potent. She would remember it always. That thought triggered another one. What would happen after the New Year? They lived at opposite ends of the state. Her body stiffened. Nick! She'd forgotten about Nick.

"What's wrong?" Ricco asked, his voice low and sleepy.

She traced her fingertips across his chest, trying to memorize every detail of every inch of him. "I was just thinking about Christmas."

He rolled over onto her, his hooded eyes searching her face. "What do you want for Christmas?"

She smiled. "World peace."

"Something realistic."

What she wanted she couldn't have, so she would settle for what she could have. "I just want every day leading up to New Year's Day to be as perfect as this right now."

He dropped a kiss on her nose. "I know this guy in a red suit. I'll see what he can do."

The vision of Ricco as the hunky Santa made her smile. "I think I have a way to help Evergreen. But it's going to take everyone pooling resources."

He frowned. "That may be difficult. Especially with the residents who aren't drowning."

"Then there is no chance, unless a benefactor comes forward. The balloon payment is large, and it's due at the end of the year. If it's met, there are still the mortgages, which are pretty hefty, but they can be refinanced to lower rates and payments, but not until the balloon payments are made."

"I thought a balloon payment was the balance of the loan."

"Not in this case. The loan was structured to infuse cash back into Evergreen, and the payments were deferred. For three years. Three years is up December thirty-first. There is still the principal and interest balance of the original mortgage. If the combined total of the deferred payments plus the interest they accrued—because it was, in a sense, a loan in a loan—are not met, the entire loan goes into default."

He frowned. "So let me get this straight. For the last three years those merchants who mortgaged their properties deferred their monthly payments. For that break they have to not only pay back those payments with the interest of the original loan but more as well, for the mortgage holder fronting them the money?"

"Exactly."

"How the hell did that happen? Who the hell okayed that?"

Kim took a deep breath and slowly exhaled. "Your mother."

"What?"

"I can see why she took the risk. It was a good bet. If you played the odds, the weather had to break. But she didn't count on five straight years of bad weather, then a recession the last two of those years. No one saw it coming. And when she mortgaged the city properties, she did so at a higher rate and higher appraised value than what the properties are worth now. The foreclosure rate in California is among the highest in the country. You can be sure the consortium that holds the notes will not be in the mood to restructure. I checked out the company. They are cash flush. This is the perfect scenario for them. And then you have Land's Edge wanting to buy up everything for a fraction of what it's worth. It's a win-win for everyone except Evergreen."

Ricco rolled over onto his back and slapped his hand across his forehead. "Son of a bitch."

"Yeah. No bueno. We need to come up with three and a half million dollars in cash by December thirty-first."

"Christ."

"Yeah." She pressed her body against his. "Let's get a shower and get some sleep. We have a lot of convincing to do."

"Yeah, and my lieutenant is coming up from Montrose to boot."

"Why?"

"I killed a bad guy, remember?"

"Oh, yeah." Her gaze searched his face for fear or anxiety. "How are you feeling about that?"

He shrugged. "The guy was trying to kill me, he could have killed you. I did what I had to do."

"It doesn't bother you, that you took a life?"

"It was him or me. I'm glad to be the one here."

"I've heard stories about cops who end up killing themselves because they couldn't bear the guilt."

"Lots of guys nut up over a shoot. Sometimes it was a bad deal for everyone involved. This is my seventh officer-involved shooting and my second kill. Every time, I was justified."

"I couldn't do what you do."

"I couldn't do what you do."

"Well, if you ever want to talk about it, I'm a good listener."

Ricco smiled, rolled off the bed, and grabbed her up to his chest. "I just did. Thanks. Now let's get in the shower so we can get all sweaty again."

KIMBERLY WOKE TO SUNLIGHT STREAMING THROUGH her window and the aroma of fresh brewed coffee. She stretched and reached over to where Ricco had passed out after another round of really good sex. She sprang up in the empty bed. She knew he wasn't in the bathroom.

Wild thoughts ran through her head, different scenarios of his having had his fill and sneaking off to his own room, not man enough to tell her he was done and thanks a bunch, the sex was great. She washed her face, brushed her hair, and threw on a pair of jeans and a sweater. She couldn't pull her boots on fast enough. She was halfway down the stairs when she heard his deep, robust laughter. "Jase, I never would have pegged you for the marrying type. Congratulations."

As her pace slowed, she heard an equally deep male voice. "You and me both, brother. You and me both."

"Are you sure you want to stick around with this guy, Jade? He has a habit of taking off like a tomcat and only coming back when he's hungry."

A deep, sultry, extremely sensual voice ruffled the

downy hair on Kim's neck. "He can go as long as he wants. Just so long as he doesn't tomcat around."

Kim walked into the parlor and stopped dead in her tracks. The black-haired goddess sitting on the love seat next to a dark-haired Adonis struck her dumb. Now that was the kind of woman she saw Ricco with. Not her, a plain-Jane blonde.

"So Cinderella joins us," Ricco said, coming up to Kim and taking her hand. The handsome man on the love seat stood and extended his hand. "Jase Vaughn." He turned beaming eyes down to the beautiful creature beside him. She smiled warmly up at Kim. "My fiancée, Jade Devereaux."

Kim extended her hand to Jase's big warm one. Wow. "Kimberly Michaels." She shook the big hand, then the soft, finely boned one of Jade. "I'm pleased to meet you."

Jade's smile widened. "Ricco has been telling us about the dilemma Evergreen finds itself in and what a whiz you are with the numbers. I wish you the best of luck."

"Thank you," Kim said, feeling a wee bit out of her class at the moment.

"Ty and Phil are on their way up for a few days, but he says Phil has to puke every other mile, so he's not sure when they'll be here."

Ricco grinned. "Pregnant?"

"Yep, due in May."

"How about Reese and Frankie? He said they were going to try and make it out for a few days before heading to Sedona."

"Snowed in on the ranch right now."

Ricco nodded. "I'm glad those two managed to work things out."

Jase nodded and sat back down next to Jade. "I wasn't sure there for a while, but they seem to be okay with six months in the city and six months on the ranch."

Ricco poured Kim a cup of coffee from the urn on the sideboard and pulled her to the other love seat, then down next to him. He sat back and stretched out a long arm behind her on the backrest of the sofa.

"Is Ricco in trouble?" she asked Jase.

His ocean blue eyes widened in surprise. Then he smiled. "If I know my man there, it was one hundred percent justifiable, and that being the case, he's not in any trouble."

"How do you determine that?"

"An IA. I'll start by interviewing witnesses, including yourself. When I'm done with witness contacts, I'll write a report. In the meantime, Ricco will be interviewed by one of the DA's investigators. It's arduous but necessary."

Kim sipped her coffee and nodded, feeling stressed out for Ricco. She glanced up at him; sensing her anxiety, he smiled and squeezed her shoulder. "It'll all work out. It always does."

"Ricco tells us you're into real estate. Are you into commercial or residential?" Jade asked.

Kim's hand shook as she set the coffee cup down on the end table. "Both, mostly corporate buyouts, but I dabble in an occasional residential property here and there."

"Is that why you're here in Evergreen, or are you just vacationing?"

"A little of both," she said quietly. Suddenly lying seemed really dirty. "I have a client who's interested in property here. I'm trying to get the lay of the land."

Jade sipped her coffee. "Ricco told us what's been happening. How terrible for everyone here."

Kim nodded, feeling very uncomfortable in the hot seat. Jade must have sensed her unease, because she smiled softly and sat back, leaning into Jase's arms. Kim looked up at Ricco, and he smiled down at her. Not caring his friends were just across the room, he put his hand beneath her chin and raised it up to his lips. He smiled and said, "I didn't get to say good morning." His lips brushed across hers and heat swelled in her body. The sound of the front door of the B&B opening and then closing didn't stop her from melting into Ricco's arms and lingering there.

"I can see why you didn't want me to come up," a familiar male voice said much too close. Kim stiffened and broke away from Ricco. She thought she was going to throw up.

Nick!

She moved away from Ricco, but he caught her hand. She yanked it away and stood, feeling very guilty. She didn't look at Ricco's friends; she stared at Nick instead, and her anger erupted. "Why are you here?"

"Why are you kissing that man?"

Ricco came to stand behind her. She wanted to just melt into him and let him take her out of the room, but she couldn't. She would have to face her fiancé sooner or later, and it looked like sooner was here. Kim took a deep breath. Not wanting to make a scene, she stepped toward Nick. "I can explain."

"Explain what, Kim?" Ricco asked.

She stiffened and turned to face him. Very discreetly Jase and Jade moved from the sofa to the kitchen. Kim stood between both men and closed her eyes. She took a big, deep breath, but before she could utter a word, Nick stepped past her and extended his hand to Ricco. "I'm Nick Gold, Kimberly's fiancé, and if you touch her again, I'm going to kick your ass."

Kim cringed. She could barely glance at Ricco, who looked as if he had just been kicked in the gut. The color drained from his face and his eyes looked shocked. Slowly, anger replaced his shocked expression. Kim shook her head. "No he's not, not yet, not until—" She almost let her reason for being there slip. She swallowed hard, suddenly unable to get air into her lungs.

"You can tell him now, sweetheart. He served his purpose."

Kim whirled around to Nick. "What are you talking about?"

"Pumping him and his family for all of the juicy information. I trust you documented everything."

"What the hell is he talking about, Kim?" Ricco demanded.

She whirled back around to face Ricco. "Nothing! I—"

"Kimberly is Land's Edge's number one shark, and her job was to exploit Evergreen's weaknesses so I could capitalize on them." He grinned at Kim. "And she delivered, as she always does. That's what I love so much about her," Nick threw at Ricco.

Kim froze where she stood and felt her blood drop to her feet. Suddenly she was very cold and very afraid. But not for herself.

Ricco nodded and stepped back from her. His face clouded over so quickly that she could not read him. But she knew what he was thinking, and it broke her heart. "You almost had me, Cinderella, you almost had me," he softly said, and with his words she crumbled inside.

He turned and stalked off to the kitchen. She turned

to go after him but stopped after three steps. Would it matter? Their time was up in just a matter of days anyway. Yet she took two more steps toward the kitchen when she heard the back door slam shut. She stepped through the threshold to see Jase and Jade looking at her, shock clearly written across their faces as well. "I-I didn't mean to fall in love with him," she whispered, then turned and ran back to the parlor, where Nick stood holding his Gucci bag.

"It's been a long trip here. Where's your room?"

She felt like she was outside of her body, watching a play. She saw herself point up the stairway and say, "Vixen suite." She watched him go up the stairway and heard Esmeralda asking Jase and Jade why her brother had stomped past her. Kim stood alone in the parlor, not knowing what to do. She wanted to go upstairs and calmly tell Nick to fuck off, then run after Ricco and tell him—what? That she wanted to keep seeing him even after Christmas? That she loved him? The thought struck her numb.

She wanted to be angry with Nick for barging in on her time here and telling the ugly truth to Ricco, but could she blame him? For the first time since they'd made their agreement to marry, he'd acted like he was remotely invested in her as a woman. She started to laugh. How ironic was that? After all this time, her fiancé actually showed he cared.

Her laughed turned sour, then to a strangled sob.

It didn't matter. Not now. Not anymore. She'd lost something more precious than her marriage to Nick. She'd lost the trust and respect of the only man who had put her on the pedestal she had so desperately wanted, only to take herself off because of her own duplicity.

Eighteen

Several minutes later Esmeralda came into the salon and stopped short when she saw Kim. Their gazes locked. "I'd like you to leave," Esmeralda said tersely.

Kim's heart fell to her feet. "I—"

"Just go," Esmeralda said and swept past her and out the front door.

Slowly Kim walked up the stairs. For a long time she stood at the door, not wanting to go inside. She turned the knob and pushed open the door to find Nick sprawled out on the comforter, the sheets in a heap on the floor beside the bed. The scent of sex swirled in the warm room.

"This room smells like a cathouse."

Kim closed the door and pressed her back against it.

She closed her eyes and envisioned Ricco laying on the bed, a damp towel draped around his narrow waist. When she opened her eyes, she saw Nick. "I want you to leave."

"Not on your life. I'm too close to clinching this deal. I'm going to call Evergreen's hand. I'm going to personally make the next offer. *Personally*. I've already contacted the council." He looked at his watch. "In one hour at city hall." He lay back into the striped pillows, put his hands behind his head, and closed his eyes. "I didn't peg you for the sex kitten type, Kimberly, but I have to say it's a pleasant surprise."

She moved to the armoire and pulled her bag out from the bottom drawer. She began to pack. She needed separation.

"What are you doing?" Nick asked from the bed, his gaze locked on her.

"I was asked to leave."

Nick laughed. "It will only be temporary; you'll own this dump by the end of the week."

"I don't want to own this dump. I just want to go home."

He sat up and hopped off the bed. Slowly, as if weighing her acceptance of him, he came closer to her. He reached out a hand and touched her cheek. "I can make you feel like he did." He moved in closer. While he smelled really good, he didn't smell like Ricco, and his touch did nothing for her. No, it did—it made her want to pull away. He raised her chin up to look at him. His clear blue eyes quietly questioned her. When his lips lowered to hers, she expected to feel repulsed. She only felt nothing.

And after what Ricco had done to her she would not be satisfied with nothing the rest of her life.

Slowly she pulled away from him. "I don't want to marry you, Nick."

He stiffened and backed away. "Because that guy gets you off?"

She gasped at his crudity. "No, because when you touch me I feel nothing."

"Fine! Fuck him all you want, just be discreet about it."

She shook her head and felt the hot rush of tears. Nick would never cherish her over all other women. He cherished what she could bring him. Money. And the status her last name would bring. And with perfect clarity, she understood. He was like all of the rest. He'd never wanted her.

She moved past him, packed her overnight case, then opened her drawer. A small wrapped box was tucked into the fold of her sweaters. A small note written in Ricco's handwriting attached to it read Do Not Open Until Christmas. Her heart rate accelerated, and she put it along with the sweaters into her suitcase. She was done in less than fifteen minutes. Nick watched her the entire time, a nasty scowl twisting his face.

Several minutes later she was in her car and driving south out of Evergreen.

RICCO STORMED DOWN MAIN STREET LOADED FOR BEAR. *Son of a bitch!* How could he have been so blind? He'd been played by a pro. She'd made damn sure she'd snagged him at the Legacy, and it had been easy pickings for her after that. And he had fallen for it! He'd actually— He punched the air with his fists. He'd actually thought there might be some way they could still see each other after the New Year. It was only a forty-five-minute flight from San Jose to L.A.—or a five-hour drive, or four hours the way he drove. They could meet up on the weekends and see where things went.

Son of a bitch! He'd trusted her! He'd actually thought she could help the town. Holy hell! When his mother found out she'd played right into the Wicked Witch's hand, she would be beside herself and blame the fall of Evergreen on herself. *Shit.*

He needed to tell his mother what was going on. She'd be down at the city office this time of day.

When he walked through the door, he knew by the tight expression on her face that she knew something was up. "Ez called. Apparently Kim's fiancé is the CEO of the company trying to buy us out."

Ricco scowled. "Apparently."

"Where are all of the documents?"

"Locked up in Ez's safe."

Leti sat back in her chair and let out a long breath. "We meet with Mr. Gold in half an hour. He's making another offer. I don't know what we can do."

"Kim said something about those in town who had liquid assets pooling them to the tune of three and a half million to cover the balloon payments to buy time."

Leti shook her head. "We don't have that kind of money."

"She seemed to think we did."

"Then, *mijo,* she knows something I don't."

RICCO STOOD BEHIND HIS MOTHER AT THE COUNCIL meeting. He scowled when his father walked in assisted by Esmeralda, who pushed a stroller with Krista sleeping soundly inside. The room swelled with residents. Every person who had a stake in Evergreen was there. Nick walked in like the conquering hero in a town who wanted to be left alone. The tension in the room was palpable. Nick stood smug and alone before them all.

His presence stirred their emotion; realizing he might have made a mistake coming in alone, Nick lost some of his bravado. Ricco seriously doubted that if the mob let loose on the prick, he'd lift a finger to stop them. Anger and jealousy swirled inside him. The guy was as tall as Ricco, blond and dressed in what was obviously threads straight from Italy. Not that Ricco didn't appreciate fine clothes: He did, but this guy's shoes cost more than what most people made in a month. And he was Cinderella's fiancé. Ricco shook his head in disgust.

He had not seen that coming. Not. At. All.

"My name is Nicholas Gold, and I am CEO of Land's Edge Development Corp." Boos and hisses erupted. Nick stood quietly and let it die down. "I'm going to cut straight to the heart of the matter. Evergreen is in trouble. My solution is paying each one of you twenty-five cents on each dollar of your current property value."

The assembly erupted into a fearsome rebuttal. Once again Nick waited. Ricco watched the faces of the people who had taken him and his family in so long ago. Never once had they asked anything of him. All they had done over the years was give, and more than anything he wanted to come through for them. He had a decent nest egg put away. Maybe there were others who would make the same sacrifice. He swallowed hard and strode out toward Gold.

"We have until the end of the year to pay the deferred payment and interest and, by so doing, keep what we have. Until then we will not entertain any offer from you. Leave before your safety cannot be guaranteed."

"On the thirty-first my offer will be half of what it

is now." Nick turned to the assembly. "Can this town come up with three point six million in ten days?"

A collective gasp rose. Nick drove the last nail in deeper. "Then make good on the monthly payments after that? Because if the loan that's tied to each and every one of you in one way or another goes into default, then you lose everything." He turned to the council. "Cut your losses now. And when I rebuild here, you will all have jobs. Secure jobs. Jobs with benefits."

"You'll have jobs, all right," Kim said as she strode into the room. "Nonunion minimum-wage jobs and benefits with enormous deductibles. This place will turn into Potter's Field."

Nick smiled despite her eruption. "For those who don't know her, my soon-to-be vice president of acquisitions, Kimberly Michaels."

She turned on him. "Ex-fiancée and never-to-be vice president." She turned to Evergreen. "You have time, precious little time, to pool your resources together and pay off the balloon payment." Smugly she turned to Nick. "I read the fine print. Technically there is a ten-day grace period after the payment date." She turned to the town. "So in effect you have until January ninth."

Nick's deep laughter rang throughout the room. Kim knew that laugh, and it terrified her. It was the laugh of a man who had hedged his bets and had the final ace in the hole. "Did you read the deed, Kimberly? It clearly states the loan can be called at any time with no grace period. I'm calling the loan."

"You can't. Only the consortium can call it."

Nick reached into the breast pocket of his jacket. "I just bought out the controlling share of Marcus Rand."

Kim had her own ace in the hole. "I'm sure when the cops catch up with your terrorists, they'll have a lot to say."

"Tahoe PD nabbed the guy who got away the other day," Ricco said, striding toward Nick. "How do you feel about doing time in Quentin for second-degree murder?"

"I don't know what the hell you're talking about."

"You hired those thugs to terrorize the town. One was killed in the commission of a felony. That makes you as accountable as if you'd taken part."

"Prove it."

"I intend to."

The energy in the room turned dangerous. The crowd had galvanized, and they drew closer together, moving toward Land's Edge's CEO. "Nick, you had better leave here before you get hurt," Kim said, keeping a wary eye on the progressing mob.

He shook his head and looked at her with utter contempt. "I can't believe you fell for the crack. What happened to my shark?"

"She got a conscience. Now go."

He turned to face the assembly. "On the thirty-first my offer will be ten cents on the dollar." He stalked out of the room and bedlam ensued.

Once Kim had everyone quieted down, she said, "Two things have to happen for this to work. One, we need almost four million cash in ten days. Secondly, Evergreen cannot continue to live and die by the weather and economy. There has to be something to come before and after Christmas."

"We don't want any big corporation coming into town!" Jerry, the florist, said. "It'll ruin everything."

"And no big box store either!" Maddy said.

Kim smiled. "Miss Maddy, you don't have to worry about a box store in Evergreen. There isn't enough population to support it."

"That's another thing, we don't want a bunch of strangers coming in and messing up the ecology," someone else said.

For almost an hour Kim listened to the town debate and voice what they didn't want. When they were done, she asked them, "Do you want to stay here?"

A resounding yes erupted. "Then you will have to make some sacrifices on your end," she replied.

A collective groan followed. Ricco stepped up. "Listen to her, all of you! *Our lives, our livelihoods* are at stake here, and all you can think about is your own selfish needs? Have we all been living a lie all of these years? What happened to the caring people who took my family in? We need to come together as one unit and trust that the man or woman standing next to us has our back. Getting pissed off and laying down or walking away isn't an option. Fight, damn it! Make some concessions and let's get this town back on its feet!"

"Easy for you to say, Ricco, you come and go, your life isn't tied here. Stay a year, then tell me I have to make concessions," Peyton challenged.

Ricco turned on Peyton. "Life, my friend, is about making concessions. The status quo is killing us. I'm willing to do whatever is necessary to make things work here. I have money I'll gladly give, but I won't do it if there isn't a plan, as Kim said, to go forward. It's the twenty-first century, for Christ's sake. Let's move with the times."

But try as they might, once the tallies were counted, they were not only two million dollars shy of the goal but they also had no viable means—not even an idea—for a future of financial security. It seemed that the small town of Evergreen would have nothing to celebrate on Christmas Day.

Nineteen

KIM FOUND HERSELF TAKING THE FULL BRUNT OF EVER-green's demise on her shoulders. While in her head she knew it was poor financial planning and bad loans that had them on the verge of bankruptcy, she still felt respon-sible. Several times she had attempted to speak with Ricco, but he'd avoided her. There had been no warm reception from his mother or sisters either. Only Enrique hobbled over to her as she was about to exit the town hall.

He grinned and said, "How guilty are you feeling right about now?"

She scowled. "Guilty enough. What do you want?"

"I just went on sale. Fifty thousand and I disappear."

Kim laughed, and because she did feel so guilty, she pulled out her checkbook and wrote out a check for fifty thousand dollars. She tore it off and handed it to the crook. "The check is my receipt. Come back here after you leave tonight, I show them the canceled check, and you can kiss their pity party good-bye."

He grinned up at her and kissed the check. "Merry Christmas, Miss Michaels, Merry Christmas." He hobbled off, and as he met up with his daughters, Kim caught Ricco's dark frown across the way. She started toward him, determined to say what she had to say, then leave.

He moved toward the front of the building and she followed him.

"Ricco!" she called to his retreating back. He kept walking. "Fine, walk away like you always do. Be the coward!" He hesitated in his step but kept going. Kim ran after him.

"Stop for once in your life and let someone who made a mistake apologize!"

He did stop then. Slowly he turned around. A storm waged on his face. "The next thing you'll be telling me is I'm a coward for not playing nice with my father."

"No, I understand how you feel. I don't know that I could ever forgive him. And I think you're right, anyway. He hasn't changed."

"Why do you say that?"

She shrugged, not wanting to add to this man's misery. "A hunch."

He stood glowering down at her.

She opened her mouth several times to say what she felt, to lay it all on the line, but the fear of complete rejection paralyzed her. "I-I just wanted to tell you I'm sorry."

"Glad you have a conscience."

"I have more than that. I have feelings. I hurt too, you know!"

"Cry me a river, Kimberly. You've lied, cheated, and lied some more. You're as bad as that piece of crap you call your fiancé."

"My *ex*-fiancé. Hell, he never was officially!" Ricco's anger was so absolute that he could not see through the haze of it. Any attempts to convince him how bad she felt would go unheard. He needed time, she decided. And so did she.

"Good-bye, Prince Charming," she softly said, then walked past him to her car and drove out of town.

Instead of wallowing in heartbreak and self-pity as the miles mounted between them, Kim's brain went on high alert. She was not a quitter and never a loser when it came to the art of the deal. She'd be damned if she'd lose this deal and her man in the same day! Her brain churned, it plotted, it connived. There *had* to be a way to save Evergreen. She pulled up in Auburn and took a room at a local hotel, where she pulled out the laptop and started making phone calls.

Long after midnight she crashed, still clothed, on the bed. She was up at first light and back on the computer, making calls and calling in favors for phone numbers to CEOs who were getting ready to celebrate Christmas halfway around the world. But it paid off. Two days later she had an investor. And better than that, she had one who was willing to give Evergreen the resources to remain fiscally solvent, even if, like this year, Christmas was canceled. She was as excited as a little kid on Christmas morning!

Kim jumped into the shower. After she dried off, she pulled out a sweater from her case. As she did so, the small box Ricco had put in her drawer plopped out. For a long moment she didn't reach for it, but she couldn't help herself. She wanted to be a part of anything that was a part of him. With a shaky hand she reached for it and slowly lifted the lid. Hot tears erupted and she gently touched the gold heart locket. It wasn't the one her grandmother had given her, but it was close. He knew how precious the locket had been to her, and he must have moved hell and earth to find one so similar in what must have been only a matter of hours. She opened it up and caught her breath. Engraved inside were the words *To new beginnings*.

She clutched the locket to her heart and closed her eyes. For long moments she didn't move. She barely breathed. He got her. He understood her fears because they were his fears. They were so much alike it was scary. But in that, she knew what she had to do to convince Ricco she was worth taking another chance on. A new determination filled her. No man had ever fought for her, and when she thought about it, she hadn't fought for any one of them either. But she was going to fight for Ricco. After all, it was Christmas Eve, and everyone knew miracles happened! And she would not stop until she bagged him. She smiled and quickly packed the rest of her things.

As she drove toward Evergreen a light snow began to fall. When she hit town Kim expected the lights to be dim, the cheer and happiness to be gone. She truly expected to find a wasteland. Instead she found the entire population of Evergreen in the street with candles in hand held before them. She parked the car in front of Esmeralda's B&B and listened. Like angels from above, she heard the song "Silent Night" being sung. Slowly, mesmerized she followed the procession of carolers toward the gazebo. As the people of Evergreen formed a circle around the stable that had been erected for the reenactment of the birth of Christ, Kim caught her breath as a sudden rush of emotion choked her.

Sweet little Mari, in a white robe and blue veil, held a baby doll in her little arms and looked lovingly down at it. She kissed it and placed it in the manger. Kim's eyes filled with tears as she watched and listened.

Despite the town being in the throes of complete financial disaster, they'd come together as one to celebrate the true reason for the season. Her gaze caught that of Leticia, who smiled at her, then Elle's and Jasmine's who also smiled. Esmeralda stood with a handsome man in uniform, who she looked adoringly at, and Kim almost lost it. But what caused her more emotion was the sight of Ricco standing beside his father. While there was no great affection coming from Ricco, there wasn't that perpetual scowl that always showed up when Enrique was present.

Kim flinched at the sight and grappled with the reality that she would have to be the one to tell the man she loved his father was a fraud. How she would tell him she had not the slightest clue. He'd been through enough hurt already, and the last thing she wanted to do was crush his heart more.

When Ricco looked across the gathered crowd and locked eyes with her, she saw a spark of something. Hope? Happiness? Whatever it was quickly vanished and was replaced with shaded anger.

She stood back and waited. And watched. His friend Jade and Jase were standing nearby with another striking couple, who seemed to be quite enthralled with each other. Kim felt a stab of jealousy. She watched the easy, loving way they touched each other and smiled. The man pressed his hand to the woman's belly and leaned into her for a long kiss. Jase and Jade grinned up at Ricco, who, in response, turned to stare at her. His eyes were blank, but she could see the tightness of his jaw and knew he was still angry with her—but more, she could guess, hurt.

When the vigil was over and the crowd broke up, she moved toward Ricco. He stood and waited for her, and for that small token she was eternally grateful. He couldn't hate her that much if he was willing to speak to her.

She smiled, feeling suddenly shy and vulnerable. "Merry Christmas, Ricco," she said.

He nodded. "Merry Christmas."

"That was beautiful. I can't believe after everything that's happened everyone is so . . . so . . ."

He cocked a dark brow. "Into the reason for the season?"

"Yes."

"There's more to life, Kimberly, than money."

"Don't call me Kimberly."

"Fine, Kim. So what brings you back here?"

"A couple of things, actually, but you mostly."

"Then you've wasted time and gas."

She stiffened and moved in closer to him. "I don't think so. I think the proposal I'm about to make is worthy of a listen."

He stood as rigid and as cold as an icicle. "Go on."

She pulled the locket out of her pocket and opened her palm. "First of all, I wanted to thank you for this.

Aside from the locket my grandmother gave me, this is the only gift anyone has ever given me. It means more to me than you know. Thank you."

"You're welcome," he said through clenched teeth.

She opened it up and read, "To new beginnings." Then looked up to him. "It's what I want. With you. And the only thing I can promise you, Ricco, is I will never lie to you."

"It's too late for that now."

"Why?"

"Because in the time you've been gone, I've decided I liked the way my life was. Uncluttered, uncomplicated, and"—he looked down at her, an earnest expression lighting his handsome face—"unemotional. I'm man enough to admit I don't like the hurt that goes with emotions, Kim."

It felt as if a ten-ton boulder had just landed in her belly. "I can't believe I'm hearing this from you. You go out and catch bad guys, get into gunfights, and kill people, but you can't find the courage to open your heart just a little?"

He opened his mouth to speak, but she halted him. "I'm in love with you, Ricco. I want to be with you more than I want money or a big house. I want to be where you are. I want a second chance. I want you to be as brave as I'm being right now."

He reached up and took the locket from her hand.

"When I bought this, I felt brave. Like I was king of the world, but I was scared shitless too. These last few days have been the worst days of my life, and not because this town is going under, but because you left me."

"I—," she started, but he halted her this time.

"In my heart your betrayal was abandonment. It terrified me. It still does. I'm afraid to give you my heart and find out one day you've tossed it away."

She reached up and touched his cheek. "I'm afraid too, Ricco, but if we don't try, then we lose even more. What happens if it works? Look at what we'd miss."

He took a big, deep breath and slowly exhaled, handing her back the locket. "I . . . can't."

"You're a big pussy, Maza," Jase said from behind him. As he came to stand next to Kim, he winked at her. She almost smiled. Another man, the one who'd kissed the beautiful dark-haired woman and rubbed her belly, came around to stand on Ricco's other side.

"I told Jase you didn't have the balls for this love stuff," he said and turned to Kim, extending his hand. "Ty Jamerson, embarrassed friend of this wimp who calls himself a man."

This time Kim did grin.

"So this is how I see it, Ricky," Jase began. "You fall for Kim here, she falls for you, she screws up, you get your widdle pussy-ass heart cracked, and now you want to take all of your toys and go home?"

Ricco scowled at his friends. "It's not that simple."

"The hell it isn't!" Ty said. "Man up, Ricco, give the woman another chance, for crying out loud. I'll be damned if I'm going to watch you mope around San Jose for the next two years crying about how you got your heart broken."

"It's now or never, buddy," Jase said.

"You should listen to your friends, Ricco," Kim softly said.

His scowl deepened. "I can't."

"You won't."

He nodded. This time, to her utter shock, Enrique stepped in. The swelling in his face had subsided, and now sparks of anger flashed in his dark eyes. "Son, if I can change, and your saint of a mother can give me another chance after giving me one hundred and then some, then by God you can give this girl and yourself a chance at real happiness." As his words trailed off, Enrique dug into his back pocket, pulled out his wallet, and extracted the check Kim had written him. He handed it to her. "I don't need this after all."

Ricco's eyes narrowed. "What's that?"

"The fifty grand your girlfriend gave me to leave you all alone." He grinned up at his son. "As you know, I decided to come clean with you and to put the old ways behind me. I have no need for that money now."

Ricco turned dark eyes on Kim. "You did that? For me and my family?"

"I knew he was rotten to the core," she said, and her cheeks reddened. But at the time, it had been true. "I didn't want to see you all get hurt again."

He pulled her away from the small group to a secluded corner. "Cinderella—"

She stood up on her toes and pressed her lips to his. "Shhh, just give us a chance, Prince Charming."

His arms slid around her waist and he brought her hard against him. Then it was as if all his doubts were let go; his kiss deepened, and she felt the rush of his body against hers. "I'll . . . try," he said against her lips.

Her heart swelled and she grabbed his face more firmly against hers as she molded her body as tightly against his as humanly possible. "You'll do more than try."

He grinned against her lips. "I thought I wore the pants in this family."

"We both will." She pulled away from him and said, "Call the town back. I have news."

Ricco didn't hesitate to put his fingers in his mouth. He whistled several times and called to his mother to gather the residents.

Once they had assembled, Kim stood up on a bench with Ricco beside her. Disgruntled murmurs rippled through the gathered crowd. "Everyone, I have good news," she called out. They stood silent, yet hope flashed across many faces. She drew a piece of paper from her jacket and held it up. "This is a conditional agreement from GoSunGoGreen.org—a private company that is the recipient of some serious federal funds for research for yet more ways to develop earth-safe energy. Solar energy specifically. They want a refuge where they can set up shop in an ecofriendly mountainous environment. They need wind, snow, water, and heat. Evergreen has the wind, snow, water, and heat in the summertime. It's not only a perfect venue for GoSunGoGreen's corporate headquarters but it's also the perfect town to transform into the perfect prototype for nature-powered energy. For the privilege of being amongst Evergreenoians they are happy to shell out serious cash, serious enough to more than cover the deferred payments of everyone who is due at the end of the week. In return they ask for property on which to build an ecofriendly headquarters that will fit in with the current town architecture, and for the entire town to convert within the next two years—at GoSun's expense—to total solar-, wind-, and water-powered energy."

"What's the catch?" Peyton asked.

"I just told you. They want to use Evergreen as part of their marketing strategy for any USA town to go totally solar. It's a great opportunity."

"I'm all for it!" someone from the crowd shouted.

"Just like that the company is willing to bail us out?" Peyton asked.

Kim nodded. "They had just begun a location search in the Sierras last month. I have eyes and ears everywhere. I contacted them when I heard the whisper on the street they were looking to settle up here. The internet is a beautiful thing, Pey. With what I know first-hand they were able to amass from several other sources and the internet on the geography of the area they realized what a gem Evergreen was. The deal is a solid one, and it's on the table."

Peyton rubbed his jaw. "We'll have to take a vote—"

"We vote yes!" a group shouted. It was echoed by everyone else in earshot, which was pretty much the entire town.

"Then let's talk to them," Peyton said, his voice high and excited.

Kim smiled. While she knew there would have to be an official city council vote, she knew it was but a formality. Ricco pulled her down from the bench and into his arms, and she felt like she had come home. And home would be wherever Ricco was. Either here, San Jose, or Timbuktu.

Kim smiled and hugged him close. She turned in his arms and smiled at his friends Jase and Jade, Ty and his wife, and the familiar faces of Evergreen, a town that had taken her in not once, but twice.

All at once Leticia, Enrique, the sisters, and the kids swarmed Ricco and Kim, and as she laughed and hugged her new family, Kim looked up into the black sky. Far off into the distance, one star in the north sparkled with a brightness that outshined all the rest, and with it she felt a peace in her heart she had never felt before. And with that peace, a love deep and profound in her swelled to ten times its normal size. She feared she might not be able to handle it all, but when Ricco drew her away from his family and whispered, "I love you," in her ear, her heart swelled again, and she knew she would always have the magic of Christmas and the love of a family to keep it filled to capacity.

Pocket Books
proudly presents

MASTER
OF
TORMENT

*The next book in the passionate
new historical series by*

Karin Tabke

Coming in December 2008
from Pocket Books

Turn the page for a preview of the latest book
in the Blood Sword Legacy series . . .

May 12th 1067
Draceadon, Mercia

ORNATE SCONCES BURNED BRIGHTLY ALONG THE STONE walls of the opulent chamber, illuminating it and all of its vivid colors like a gem-encrusted crown. Velvet-appointed furniture a king would envy graced the thick wool rugs, but what caught one's eye when they walked into the chamber was the enormous bed. Though the heavy curtains of the elaborately carved four poster were drawn, deep snores from the occupant permeated the lavish chamber alerting anyone near to a presence.

'Twas her runaway groom, the earl of Dunloc.

The bile in Lady Tarian's belly rose. She breathed in slowly and exhaled slower, listening intently to be sure his breaths were of a man in the deep throes of slumber. Her fingers fondled the leather hilt of her broadsword, anxious to see the deed done.

Once her circumspect inventory of the room showed there to be no other escape route but the thick oak portal she had just come through and that her men were in place, Tarian glanced over to Gareth, her captain of the guard, who held the lord's squeamish manservant. His honed sword blade leveled snugly against the servant's throat. She nodded to her captain before turning back to the shrouded bed.

Despite the encumbrance of her mail Tarian glided a step closer to the bed. She pressed the tip of her sword into the slitted fabric and slowly pushed it aside. Only the orange blush of a tallow candle and the pale skin of a man's back glowed within the darkened space.

A knot formed in her belly, not of fear but of revulsion. 'Twas whispered her betrothed preferred to spend his time with squires, not maids. 'Twas also rumored he had commissioned a dungeon to be built in the bowels of the fortress where he "entertained."

"Malcor, did you think I would not come for you?" Tarian demanded, her husky voice ringing clear in the room.

Most men would have risen in stark surprise and fear. Not so her intended. Without the barest hint of surprise or concern for his well-being, Malcor rolled over and speared her with a malicious glare. The linen sheet rode low on his thighs and for all that he was a well-muscled man, knowing what she knew of him, the view repulsed her. Tarian set her jaw and stood fast, her motive for her appearance unwavering despite the lewdness of the man who had run like the coward he was.

He stretched and answered lazily, "Did you think, Lady Tarian, that I would care?"

Tarian forced a blithe smile. She did not feel so

carefree as her gesture indicated, but this man would only see her for the true warrior she was. To show him weakness on any front would find her a victim of the earl's sadistic nature. Carefully, her gaze held the glittering angry one of her betrothed. She felt no anger with her guardian for his choice. It was either marriage to Malcor, the perverted Earl of Dunloc, or the convent. For no other mortal man would have her to wife.

The cloister did not want her, nor she them. Her Godwinson blood, while a curse, was also her salvation. She was bred to fight, bred to lead, and, despite the sins of her father, bred to breed with the finest blood of Europe, not spend endless days and nights on her knees praying for forgiveness she seriously doubted any god, even one so forgiving as hers, would grant.

So, marriage to the earl it would be. And with God's blessing a child would be born of their union. Her smile tightened. She required only one thing from this man, and despite his preference for squires she would extract it from him—at sword point if necessary.

"How remiss of me, Malcor, to think a noble such as yourself would hold sacred a betrothal contract. 'Tis well I know beforehand the character of the man I will marry."

"There will be no marriage," he ground out.

Barely perceptibly, she inclined her head toward her betrothed. From behind her a score of armed soldiers fanned out, their swords at the ready. Tarian pressed the honed tip of her own sword, Thyra, to Malcor's chest. Pale lips pulled back from long yellow teeth.

She could not honestly begrudge him his anger. She

was, in effect, forcing a marriage on him he did not desire, and she would if necessary force him to perform his husbandly duty. How ironic would it be, then, that she conceive a child of a man who despised women? And she, the daughter of a royal rapist. Was she not following in her illicit sire's footsteps? "The sins of the father will be repeated in the sins of the daughter." She had heard the words all her life; now she would breathe truth into the curse.

"We will wed this night, milord, or you will not wake to see the morn." She looked up to her right just past her shoulder and smiled at Gareth, who had handed off the servant to another of her guard. "See that Earl Malcor is a properly dressed groom."

She turned back to her intended. He may not fear her, which was foolish, for she was well schooled in the art of war, but her guard was a force all of his own to be reckoned with. He would not stand back should Malcor decide to get heavy-handed with her. Tarian grinned up at the enormous man and shrugged, suddenly not caring a whit for what Malcor desired. "Or not, if he doth protest too much."

"You will regret your action, Lady Tarian. Your guard cannot always be within reach," Malcor softly threatened.

The edge of steel in his words alerted her. A small ripple of apprehension skittered down her rigid spine. Her gaze fell to his. Stark contempt filled Malcor's pale blue eyes. His pallid face blanched whiter beneath his flame-colored hair. She would find no succor from this man, soon to become her husband. She would find only hardship. But with a child and the title of Lady of Dunloc much could be forgiven. For life in a convent that cringed at the mere mention of her name would drive her mad. She nodded ever so slightly to her intended. "Your own priest awaits us, milord, pray do not dally."

As she swept regally from the chamber she said to Gareth over her shoulder, "And, Sir Captain? Be sure he washes all traces of squires from him. I would see my husband clean in my wedding bed this night."

"Thou art the devil's spawn! I will not wed with thee," Malcor screamed.

"Aye, you will," Gareth said as he pressed his point with his sword.

"Nay! 'Tis said she is cursed!"

Tarian turned at the door, her sword raised. "Are we not both cursed?"

He stared at her in mute horror.

Stepping back into the chamber she leveled it at her reluctant groom. "Make no mistake, Malcor. This eve will find us both in that bed as man and wife. And should you continue to resist me?" She glanced at Gareth and smiled. "I am not above forcing myself upon you." She stepped closer. She could see the wild dilation of his pale eyes. "Try now for once to be a man of your word. Honor your vow to me."

Malcor moved back into the furs. "Nay! *Never.* I will not have the mark of a witch upon me!"

Tarian smiled tolerantly and nodded. "So be it then. You will not be the first reluctant bridegroom in England."

* * *

A fortnight later Tarian knelt beside the sapphire- and gold-embroidered pall that covered her dearly departed husband. The priest's low voice droned one prayer after another. The dull ache in her back throbbed. But 'twas not from the endless hours of kneeling, then standing, only to kneel again. It was from the force of her dead husband's foot on her back when he kicked her from their bed three days past. For him it was the last time for all things earthly. Where his soul traveled at this moment she could only guess. And she did not care. There would be no alms to the churls of Dunloc, and there would be no alms to Hailfox Abby just down the way for the priests to pray. Nay, Earl Malcor deserved where he was going, and she held no guilt in watching his speedy decent to hell.

Finally Father Dudley's voice came to an abrupt end. Silently he signaled to the gathered few that prayers were at an end. The body would be taken to a prepared place just outside of the chapel doors. As was the custom, neither Tarian nor any others would witness the internment.

She was helped to her knees by her stalwart guard, Gareth. "Milady?" he said softly, awaiting her direction. She smiled up into his concerned eyes. His unwavering devotion to her was her only salvation in these dark days. Had he not been the mouse under the bed since her arrival at Draceadon, *she* would be the one being buried, not Malcor. Her gaze darted across the pew to Lord Rangor, Malcor's ambitious uncle. His arrival the day before Malcor's death had been a blessing in disguise. When questioned on the state of their marriage, Malcor had unbelievably confirmed not only were they wed, but the relationship was *in facto consume.*

Only she, her dead husband, Gareth, and her nurse knew the truth.

Rangor, dressed in rich scarlet and saffron-colored velvet, with the requisite black arm band, gesticulated toward the altar and the dearly departed, then presented his arm to his niece-in-law. "Lady Tarian, do me the honor of accompanying me back to the hall." It was not a request but a command. And since she was curious as to what he was about, Tarian nodded her head to Gareth and took Rangor's professed arm.

As he swept her down the long aisle and out into the warm May breeze, her black hair whipped around her head. She had not bound it as a wedded woman, nor as a widow, should. Indeed, she left it down and be-ribboned. Nor did she wear a widow's black. She could never be accused of false emotions. The relationship she had with Malcor was not veiled for the sake of propriety. They had despised each other. That he was dead was of his own making.

Wordlessly they approached the stone and wooden fortress known far and wide as Draceadon. Dragon Hill. It was a worthy structure and one she would call home for many years to come. She chewed her bottom lip and wondered just how she would orchestrate such a maneuver. Whilst she had no chance to produce an heir, the law, as it was, was on her side. But England was a swirling cesspool of intrigue and anarchy. The old ways may not hold sway.

At the threshold of the great hall Rangor stopped and took her hand into both of his. "My Lady, I would have a most private word with you if I may," he entreated.

Once again Tarian acquiesced to him. Not because he demanded it, but because she did. He looked past her to where Gareth, along with half of his garrison, stood. A most formidable sight to any man or woman. As always, she was grateful for their presence. "Completely private," Rangor insisted.

"My man will stand back."

Rangor's manservant appeared from inside the hall as well as Ruin, Malcor's sniveling manservant. Her bile rose; the two were a matched pair. She'd see Ruin gone from Draceadon immediately. Easily, Rangor led her across the wide threshold of Draceadon. No sooner had she stepped into the coolness of the great hall than the heavy doors clanged shut behind her and the bolts were thrown. She whirled around to find a half score of Rangor's men blocking her retreat. She turned to Rangor who stood too full of himself beside her.

Gareth's loud voice called to her from the other side. He was pounding on the door, demanding entrance.

"What is the meaning of this!" she demanded.

Rangor smiled. It held no warmth. "I have a proposition for you, Lady Tarian, one I wish you to think about with no council from your man Gareth—or anyone else, for that matter. And I would have your answer now."

Dread churned in her belly like the crashing waves of the ocean on the jagged rocks of the Welsh coast.

She cast a subtle glance around her. Rangor's men surrounded her on all sides. "Ask me what you will."

Rangor bowed, then stood erect and faced her. "I propose we visit the priest after my nephew is secured in the ground."

Tarian frowned. "For what purpose?"

"To wed."

Tarian gasped. The continued pounding on the door coupled with his shocking proposal rattled her every nerve. Marry Rangor? Never! Inconspicuously her eyes darted around her for the closest weapon. While her jeweled dagger hung from her woven girdle, a sword would better suit what she had in mind. She could wield the weapon as well as any man, yet none was in her reach, and Rangor's men were many and fully armed.

Her best defense, then, was her shrewd mind. Her initial reaction was to tell the man under no circumstance would she wed him, and she would not, but the game they played must be played with a level head. She was well aware she trod on very thin ice. "I am honored, milord, but I am a widow of only three days. 'Tis not decent to wed so soon."

Rangor's smile widened. He bore the same long yellow teeth as his nephew. Involuntarily, Tarian shivered as she relived the pain of Malcor's teeth in her back. And though the family resemblance was strong, where Malcor's skin had been smooth with the barest hint of a beard for a man of four-and-twenty, Rangor, twice his nephew's age, had the rough freckled skin of one afflicted with the pox. Nor did he have the tall muscular shape of his nephew. Nay, Rangor reminded her of a spineless eel, and any contact with him on any level was out of the question.

"I promise you, milady, I do not covet boys in my bed. I am a man on every level and would prove a lusty groom."

Tarian kept her composure and quickly formed a lie to bide her more time. "Be that as it may, sir, your nephew had no problems in the marriage bed. Indeed, for as virile as he was, I should be heavy with child by the New Year."

Rangor's smile faded, but he pressed further. "I do not believe you. I know my nephew, and I know he could not stand the sight of a woman."

"The bloodied linens were produced."

"Sheep's blood."

"Nay!" she denied, shaking her head. "My virgin blood!"

He waved her off. "'Tis of no consequence. I would have us wed by sunset on the morrow."

"Nay, I cannot."

"You will," Rangor pressed.

She stiffened with resolve. "Nay, I *will* not. You cannot force me."

"You forced Malcor."

Tarian forced a smile. "I but reminded him of his public and private oath to wed with me."

"Would you give up title here?" Rangor asked, sweeping his arm out toward the vast hall.

Tarian stood her ground. "My title here is not contingent upon my wedding with you, Rangor."

"It will be when I inform the king you murdered my nephew."

Tarian's defiance cooled. There was that. "Malcor's death was of his own making."

Rangor inclined his head toward Ruin. "He says different."

Tarian narrowed her eyes at the simpering fop. "He lies." She turned back to the noble, and despite the continued pounding on the door, she spoke calmly and played her hand. "But it matters not. I anticipated your intervention here. I have sent word to Normandy. I would have William decree me Lady here over you. The messenger left the day of Malcor's death."

Rangor's pale face flushed crimson, his cheeks puffed and his fists opened and closed at his sides. "You will rue the day, Lady Tarian! Draceadon and all that belong to it are mine by rite of blood. I will not have a murderess sit upon the dais while my nephew molds in the earth by her hand!" He turned to his guard. "Take her to the dungeon!"

Tarian drew the jeweled dagger from her girdle. Whirling around, she stabbed the closest man to her, then backpedaled to the door that quaked under Gareth's wrath. The guards pressed close upon her, but she would not go down without a fight. She whirled around again to attack the next nearest man, when her hand was caught from behind. A fist squeezed her fingers until the dagger dropped clattering to the stone floor. Unceremoniously she was hoisted onto a set of wide shoulders. "I will kill you for this, Rangor!" she screamed.

The ignoble stalked toward her. It took three men to subdue her sufficiently. He pressed close to her face but was smart enough to keep away from her teeth. "You have time to change your mind. A fortnight I will give you. Either we wed by the time William's messenger arrives, or I will inform him you are dead, executed for the murder of my nephew and earl!"

"Be prepared to present my body, Rangor, for I have Malcor's will. He leaves all to his lawful wife!" She laughed in his face. "And I leave it all to the Abby at Leominster!"

Rangor blanched white. "Where is it?" he whispered.

She spat at him. "You will never find it!"

In a slow swipe, he wiped the spittle from his face. "Enjoy your stay with the rats, milady. I hear they have a taste for human flesh."

24346855R00189

Made in the USA
Lexington, KY
16 July 2013